BLUE APES

blue apes

phyllis gotlieb

TESSERACT BOOKS
an imprint of
The Books Collective
Edmonton
1995

Published by Tesseract Books
an imprint of The Books Collective
214-21 10405 Jasper Avenue,
Edmonton, Alberta, Canada T5J 3S2.

The publisher gratefully acknowledges The Canada Council
for financial support. Also, thanks to Wayne Fitness and
Screaming Colour Inc., a division of Quality Color Press,
Edmonton.

This edition was edited, designed and typeset (in Baskerville
10/12) by Gerry Truscott.
Cover art by Robert Pasternak.
Cover design by Gerry Dotto.
Printed in Canada by Priority Printing, Edmonton.
Production assistance by Timothy Anderson, Sally Sproule,
Tara Steigenberger and Christina Truscott.

Canadian Cataloguing in Publication Data

Gotlieb, Phyllis, 1926-
  Blue Apes

  ISBN 1-895836-14-X (bound) -- ISBN 1-895836-13-1 (pbk.)

  I. Title.
PS8513.O7B68 1995   C813'.54   C95-911236-7
PR9199.3.G67B68 1995

CONTENTS

To Gerry Truscott
for my first science fiction book
published in Canada

AMONG YOU

Rain wakes in semiform as always, rising out of oceanic twilight and sharpening his senses. Above him is the sky-light, colour of dark water. He stretches his arm, opens his fingers for the keypad, touch, the dome depolarizes and the room fills with blue morning light, like a well.

It is rare now that he lets himself relax into trueform. He has never lived on his own world, and has never known more than three or four of its people, his siblings. He recalls flashes of green in the skies he dreams of, and jagged white, yellow or grey growths that surge upward at sunrise and fall blackened toward night, and he dreams of himself in his true form among them. But there is no way to live in that shape on this world.

Rain gets off the bed and straightens the covers that are barely rippled, then goes to the bath unit where he washes his skin gently with froth and sprays it with a fresh coat of dermfix. So he can bear to put on the shirt and pants and those ugly shoes.

He stands with eyes closed and slowly reshapes the cartilage of his night face, his lax body, into his daily image, but he does not look at himself in the mirror until he has put on the wig and eyelashes. They are both fine-textured and an inconspicuous dark blond. He studies himself there for a moment, decides that his nose is too pointed and broadens it a bit, then colours his lips a very pale pink. He appears much the same as he has done the day before, and the years before that. He snaps a holo of his head and graphs it against the standard in the 3-D plotter. It matches well enough, and is different enough to keep him from freezing into that one shape, let him keep earning his living.

He takes his breakfast, a jug of cloudy liquid, out of the cooler set in the wall beside the bed and drains three mugfuls. "Ambrosia," he says, and snickers, because he seldom jokes, even to himself. A firm called FLUX delivers it three times a week.

The door of his bed-sitter leads to his studio. There are more electronics, holos and screens, a deck with pads, rollers, dials, lightpens. He taps a screen and finds his three appointments listed. Business nowhere as good as those early years. A chime sounds and he flicks the screen again. It flares to show a middle-aged woman coming into his foyer and sitting down, gloved hands folded on the bag in her lap. He feels déjà vu for the thousandth time. She looks as she did on the viewcomm when she called. Debora Pivnick, one more in a long line of Deboras and Pivnicks. She is very plain and has mixed grey hair.

He pushes a button to call up the file she's given him. Husband Albert, another in the line. He is dead seven years; Rain hasn't had to do much ageing on Albert's holo, or work very hard replicating Albert. He presses one more button and the door to the foyer slides open.

He calls, "Come on in, Mrs Pivnick," and she appears in the doorway, gripping her bag with both hands, her mouth pinched so that her smidgen of lipstick becomes a red dot.

"Albert?" she says doubtfully.

"You'll see him in a little while. My name is Rain." He offers his hand.

She touches it without clasping. "I thought it would be Albert."

"No, I can't do a sim-form before I can be assured my client knows it's an assumed identity. It's a safety precaution." *In case Albert's been banging some woman whose husband likes to carry a gun.* He has only narrowly escaped that one. "Would you like to take off your coat?"

"No thanks, I'll keep it on ... it's cool here, you know."

"Yes. I find it more comfortable to work in." He says carefully, "Did you have something in particular you wanted to discuss with Albert, Mrs Pivnick?"

"I want to know why he left me."

"Your husband is dead. I can't tell you why he died."

"He died after he left me. He didn't have to –" She cuts herself off. "Never mind. I want to see him, I just want to see him."

He knows all of it, really. But she's paying. "Are the colours in the hologram accurate?"

"Yes, as far as I can remember."

"His hair would be greyer now, I think."

"No! I want to see him just the way he was in that holo picture ."

"All right. I have to prepare myself and I'll be back with you in just a few minutes."

"I thought you'd just – be him."

"I could do that, Mrs Pivnick, be all of him, if I had to, but it's hard work and I wouldn't be able to do anything else all day. So I use wigs and clothes to help me – and you."

"Uh – I guess I understand."

"You'll see him in a few minutes."

"He used to call me Deb."

"Yes."

He has seen the camcorder film record, he knows how Albert walked and talked, and in his wardrobe for a long time he's had the grey-templed wigs of all the other Alberts, their dark suits with shiny seats, their thick black shoes and the loud ties with the soup spots. He takes a little longer than necessary pushing down the height and thickening the waist. He hates poor Albert.

He reappears from behind the shuttered screen of his work-cubicle, comes up to her and stands there, hands in pants pockets rattling change as Albert had done. "Hullo, Deb. Here I am."

She raises her hand to her mouth. "Oh my God, Albert." Shaking her head in wonder, just a fraction. "You are Albert." She doesn't try to touch him. He stands waiting and she keeps staring at him until something desperate grows in her eyes.

Rain waits. His Albert has no clues. He says finally, "Well, Deb, you must have wanted to say something to me after seven years."

Tears gather on her eyelids. She whimpers once, swallows and says, "I can't! I can't!" She finds a handkerchief and wipes her eyes.

He relaxes just slightly, into a neutral face. "What am I doing wrong, Mrs Pivnick?"

"You aren't doing anything wrong! It's just I –"

"Have you never had sym-therapy before? With Thorbian World practitioners like me?"

"I've had it three times! One was too young and didn't know how, another one didn't care how he did it, and the last one wasn't one of your people, just some old actor who used to do impressions on the TriV." She blew her nose. "They couldn't make me believe at all, but you – you're really Albert, and I can't –" The tears gathered again.

"Too good?" He's never been accused of that before.

"It's not your fault, I don't want my money back or anything, I haven't got any complaints, I just won't ever try it again, that's all. I should never have come. My children think I'm crazy wanting to see him again." She wipes her tears and blows her nose one last time.

"What did you really want to say?" he asks hesitantly, not to open up a can of worms. He's had one in his own history, *Can of worms, definition: ship from Thorb full of Thorbian embryos; message: HELP! Save our children! Last desperate hope! Silence. From seventeen known extrasolar worlds, four or five incoherent signals, no message but one, and nothing ever heard from that world again....* Albert had been silent, had sent no messages, he guesses.

She shakes her head.

Carefully he shifts back into the form. "I know I never got in touch with you, Deb...."

She lifts her hand, palm out, to say no, or nothing.

"And I haven't very much of an excuse for –"

She opens her mouth with a little stuttering sound and slips into the track, almost in spite of herself. "I never wanted to hear all that much from you, Allie." Tasting these first words as she speaks them. She pushes herself. "I got pretty tired of your tricks after all those years, and then Lily and Jake moved away, and Buck got sick and you wouldn't look at him. All that happened when you left was that I got a full-time job so I could get him into a hospice," her eyes flick at and away from him, "but when they found you rammed up a street pole with that hooker in the car – everybody started to laugh at me, you know, people next door and down the street ... or I thought they did, you know, it was like eating away inside me like termites in a wooden timber." The echo of her shrill voice hangs suspended.

She swallows. "I stayed a while in a hospital – Buck

was dead by then – and somehow I got my mind back, and I can see straight, or nearly. But sometimes I think I just want to yell at you, that's all, for all the good it would do."

She looks straight at him and he speaks quietly, "I guess I haven't got much to say to that, Deb." She begins to stiffen and he goes on without missing a beat, "You know I've never been an apologizer, but I wouldn't ever have wished any of that on you."

"That's true enough." She looks away for a moment and licks her lips, and as she glances back at him he is already fading away from Albert into Rain, taking the wig off, rising up into his thin shape so that his clothes hang, to keep her away from the level of anger where she would be trapped.

"You see," he says, holding up the pants to keep them from dropping, letting himself look a little ridiculous to help her down.

But she is already spent. "You must think I'm awful."

"No, no, Mrs Pivnick." *Just human.* But he can't say that or she will start looking at him strangely. "You only wanted him to listen."

"I wanted more than that," she mutters. "But I guess I got to say a few things," she says, and smiles faintly.

"You can come again, you know. Second sessions are cheaper."

"I don't think I want to see Albert again. Not for a long while."

On Tuesdays at noon Rain goes to see an old man named Beveridge, who lives in an upscale Seniors' Home, one of several that pays Thorbians a little money to imitate loved ones lost many years back. For Beveridge, Rain becomes Berenice, the daughter who ran off with a married accountant thirty-five years ago. In this case it is important that Rain appear right away as this remembered daughter, and he does not mind walking down the malls as Berenice, a cheerful red-cheeked girl with bright eyes and mouth, and a smooth helmet of dark brown hair.

Berenice always takes one of the old man's trembling hands while the nurse removes his lunch tray, and says, "Hello, Dad."

"Berenice! You came back! Ohh Berenice, girl, you got to forgive me for cursing you like that, I didn't mean it! Say you forgive me!"

"Of course I forgive you, Dad! I never took it to heart!"

"You always were a good girl, Berenice." And he drifts into his afternoon sleep.

This day the door to the old man's room does not open, and the message plate in its panel flares with a sexless holo face that says, "Report to Secretary 3. Mrs Hustring."

He pushes button 3 on the panel and Mrs Hustring's face flicks on in seven colours.

"Oh Bereni – I mean Mr Rain, didn't we call you? Mr Beveridge passed away last Thursday, poor old man. So we won't be needing you for him any more, though we may call you later. Of course we'll be glad to pay you for your trouble today – unless you'd prefer to donate the money to keep services like yours alive."

"I think Dad would have wanted me to have the money," Berenice says.

He's wearing a trouser suit and turtleneck so it's only a matter of finding a washroom, carefully wiping off the makeup, flipping wigs and doing a quick refinish on his face. He pulls off one earring, and packs Berenice away forever.

Too quick a cure of Mrs Pivnick, and now out of an-

13

PHYLLIS GOTLIEB

other job. But that's how they come, like any kind of acting. He has never believed he could sustain an actor's
part, every word and movement almost the same every
time, again and again, allowed to change only the subtlest of gestures.

He climbs out to the street from the glassed-in places,
for air, and a look at the few people on the sidewalks.
They are walking hands in pockets, blinkered with
shades or plugged into one-eye vids, kicking at piles of
trash as a child will kick leaves in autumn. A dog sniffs at
him and finds no scent.

The wall of the building across the street is a giant
screen bursting with turbulent movement, a commercial
promo for the newest TriV sensation, holos of faces and
bodies morphing in burning colours through all the
numberless characters, human, animal, phantasmagori-
cal combining, bodies twining and thrusting into a thousand orgies at once, wound with serpents, chimeras,
sphinxes and hippogryphs, Rain cannot help himself but
must stop and watch. Arms, legs, heads and hooves leap
out at him, the faces pulsing, bleeding, howling, teeth
become tusks and noses swirl into grotesque trunks, eyes
become mouths, spit stars and embryos, each with its
screaming song, it gapes and engulfs, becomes
Leviathan in a million cascading scales –

He gapes, he is the scaled Leviathan –

Someone who has not been blinded or deafened is
watching him, he sees himself in those eyes and, startled,
catches his reflection in the glass panel of a door: rigid
carp mouth opening into the whale's ribbed cavern,
pearl eyes and opalescent scales scattering down his jaw,
the monster.

He recoils in terror, does not know where to run.

"Rain, is it?" the face says. "Thought I recognized
you, Rain."

14

The voice is kind. The face is Korzybski, his liaison, curly black beard and eyes popping with contacts not quite the right colour. Down the street three transvestite men in Cleopatra wigs are gesturing and grinning at Rain with their blue jaws. He is shaking. *Do I recognize myself? I am Rain.* His face wanes slowly into the old mask.

Korzybski waits with a calm face for him to get settled. "Just taking a break." He is a neurologist and also visits patients at Seniors' Homes. "Join me in a cup of coffee?"

Earthly food will not nourish Rain but it is not poisonous either. He falls into step with Korzybski, regains his sidewalk self. It is almost time for their monthly appointment anyway, Rain's endless reorientation with the alien world.

They begin a mild discussion about Thorbian affairs. Korzybski brings up the possibility of getting funds for Thorbians from various levels of government, to help them meet each other, make more effective job placements, become a real culture among the multicultures of nations.

Rain drinks his coffee iced and says nothing. He is sure that Korzybski knows how many Thorbians there are in the world and he does not know or care. Sometimes in the corridors or on the moving ramps, sometimes even up in the almost empty streets he sees others that he thinks might come from the world Thorb. There are three or four on-line that he plays electronic games with, or even visits at rare times. He and the others call the world "Thorb" because Earth calls it that. He doesn't know what its inhabitants call it because he knows none of its languages. He remembers reading long ago of a parrot that was the only living speaker of its owners' language.

The message was deciphered by military decoders

15

from Earth by methods used over millennia, making use as well of what had been learned about the signals from those other few worlds. Perhaps the desperate battlers on "Thorb" who were aiming their message at Earth had learned their own codes from Earthly communications. But the few adults tending the crèche in the ship were found dead, and could tell the worlds nothing of themselves except their vaguest outlines, had only broadcast their children as seeds out into the void.

Of course Earth was frightened then of the seeds taking root and there were fifteen years of quarantine when the nations stared at the children of Thorb through razor wire, watching how the colours flickered on them, how their shapes trembled and reformed. Rain had seen all of that himself a thousand times on the vid records. Nations had even stopped their warring to meditate on Thorbians. Twenty-three hundred and seventy-four religions have flared and died around them. But there was no money in them, and everyone has seen them and their shape-shifting on TriV. Unavoidably the world has found other marvels, moved away from them. Now it does not even matter if they mate, or reproduce – their bodies, not their dreams have told them how to do that.

But they are afraid.

Rain knows that without asking. And he does not think that the governments that cannot keep the streets clean and the skies clear are likely to find funds for Thorbians or their children.

He pays for his coffee, says goodbye to Korzybski and continues down the street. Perhaps one day holograms will walk down this street, superimposed on the garbage, and even visit old men in the hospital.

Home, Rain lies drowsing, waiting for the last task of the day, an evening one. Toward evening Thorb's sun sinks down its western slope, and the morning growths of white and gold in the green-flash sky burn smokelessly and fall away into blackness and hazy blue. There is no moon on this world of Rain's dreams. Perhaps the world is a moon itself, and the lights in its sky are sun and planet. Rain believes his dreams are racial memories but is afraid to tell them to the others on his network for fear they are nothing but wish-fulfilment's, his World nothing more than a dream. He has never even felt familiarity with the trueform shape the vids have shown him.

At seven o'clock Rain rises from bed, refreshes his form and dresses in a tuxedo to escort a woman – who has asked him, is paying him to "come as you are" – and take her to the opera. Man of a thousand faces, which is he?

He watches her head and shoulders rotating in the 3-D, her laughing brown face, neck scarfed with diamonds, and piled-high black hair with its streak of white lightning. Her earrings hang to her shoulders and glitter as she turns.

As you are, he summons his hopeful morning face, and hides the formal wear under a black waterproof and a fedora. It's not good to look prosperous in the malls.

He doesn't expect Lucilla Farrell to be young or beautiful; none of the employers buying his evening presence ever have been. Some vain customers want him to be a beauty, man or woman, some want a lost love, or perhaps even a double. Some only want not to be alone at dinner, theatre, or gambling casino. Rain pushes the button at her door.

The panel lights up with its holo, her laughing face cries, "Come on right in!" and the door opens.

He steps into the foyer carefully among the acrylics and white leather.

"Just a minute!" A rustle, a flurry and she bursts on

17

him. "Helloo, honey, are you ready for me?"

He stands a little back from this wave of colour and scent. "I hope so!" She is spangled in rainbow colours, an older but accurate version of the holo she'd sent him.

"Hello, Rain! Rain, I like that name." She rattles bracelets and stands back in turn to look at him. No need to explain; she knows Thorbians. "Hand me that coat out of the closet there, sweetheart, and let's go!"

She wraps herself in black velvet, whisks him up to the roof, into a helicab, across the city. He listens and dares relax under the barrage of exclamation points. They are not aimed at him. Her tongue rattles with gossip and he need not answer.

The cab alights on the landing pad of the Opera House along with a hundred others, laying passengers like eggs and rising again like brilliant winged beetles. The elevator shaft is crystal, and the theatre a nest of plush and carpet. He has never been among so many people, his skin prickles slightly at the closeness of all this flesh and fabric, and even the brilliant lights seem smothered by it. But he pushes down the mild terror of guiding Lucilla to her seat while she waves to acquaintances and shows off her escort subtly by giving no sign of his attendance.

Once he has slipped away from his fear he wishes his eyes were cameras to record the features and movements of all these people, the men in heavy black and the women in shimmering dresses. He has never seen any kind of live performance, Earthly music is nothing to him and he does not understand and hardly hears the opera, Montecassini's *Great General in the Gulf of Persia*, with Ishiro Hoshizaki singing the role of Schwartzkopf. He watches the little figure, stamping around in gold braid, to see how his limbs move, and the gestures of his head and hands.

It is intermission, the lights come up again, and there are more people in the lobby. He wonders if there are other Thorbians here, and watches, while Lucilla waves and yoo-hoos. He drinks mineral water with a twist of lime, studies and imitates the attitudes of the men, hand in pocket, elbow on the bar. No one is looking at him. He is perfect.

Or nearly. There is a couple, "Hello, Lucilla dear!" A very thin white-blonde woman in a dress beaded with lilies, and a bulky man with a red face and black hair kiss the air near Lucilla's ears.

"Lee and Jerry Woodson," Lucilla says, "friends of my husband. This is Rain."

This woman, Lee Woodson, really looks at him. "Yes," she says. "How do you do. Do you come to the opera often?"

"No, this is my first time," Rain says.

"Really? Well," she says. "Lucilla is very fond of Thorbians."

Lucilla looks up from her gin sling and says coolly, "Keeping track of me, are you, Lee?"

"Only as a friend, Lucie. Tell me, Mr Rain –"

"I'm getting another drink, back in a minute." Jerry Woodson is searching around the room for another bull-of-the-woods to measure himself against. Lucilla tries to find others to halloo at, but Lee will not be dislodged.

Rain braces himself against the intensity of this vulpine woman.

"Tell me, Mr Rain, I imagine people ask you many questions?"

"Not always, but sometimes they do." He waits for the one she is determined to ask him.

She says in a low steady voice, "Has anyone ever asked you what you've got under all those human clothes?"

19

"Yes," he says, smiling.

"And what do you say?"

He laughs gently, "I say, Give me a kiss and I'll show you!"

Bells ring to end intermission and Lucilla pulls him away quickly. Her hand is very hot on his arm. "I heard all that," she mutters. He can feel rather than see Lee's sharp white face shrinking to a dot behind him. "Your husband needs some new friends." He lets the bitter words slip quickly, his guard overcome for once, and regrets them, but she shakes her head and sets her earrings swinging.

"I went along with them for his sake," she snaps, then with a grin adds, "He was a sweet guy and I gave him his money's worth before he wore out. They just think he married a long way below himself."

In his mind Rain can hear Lee Woodson saying, *Poor Lucie, reduced to buying Thorbs, and she used to think she was really something.* He pushes that away, but there is not much to say after that, and he watches the Great General Schwartzkopf conquering his enemies and winning beribboned medals and golden crowns, and after that the great tenor Hoshizaki being draped with wreaths and garlands.

As they rise to the roof in the crystal elevator they can see the helicabs descending from above, and it is no more than a few minutes until they are standing before her door. In the mirrored hall he catches one flash of his reflection: a blond man in a tuxedo, coat over his arm.

Her door is open and she faces him. He would not go in among all that leather and acrylic if she asked. She is smiling. "Don't be hard on them. I'm a whole other kind, and it was a good evening." *You go along with them.* But she is laughing and alive. "Give me a kiss and I'll show you," she says with a dirty snigger, "I love it!" then takes his face between her hands and kisses his mouth. "Goodnight sweetheart, I love you." She steps back into her world, the door closes, its panel is blank.

He stands there with her kiss on his lips, in that moment, he finds himself burning with a feeling, a passion not for her but for fulfilment and a being who would truly share it with him. No one has ever touched him like this, a real touch in which he feels whole-bodied among the aliens. It's a fearful feeling too, the threatening hope of love. He cannot afford it.

He backs off, waves away the helicab. It cannot take him where he is going. Her money will fall silently into his account, as it fell into the cabman's. He finds the elevator and descends, descends, trying not to think of this as symbolic, because he will sink into self-pity.

There are many deep levels, but he comes out at his own, even with the street. He has nearly an hour's walk through the arcades of shops, restaurants, little gardens that keep the cool air moist and fresh. He passes a holovue theatre featuring something called "A Thorbian Lover," advertised in a fountain of lights promising "Dangerous Satisfactions," without pausing or turning aside, walking in the shadow with his coat buttoned to the neck and his hat pulled down. People are coming out of the theatre and he keeps neatly ahead of them. There are more theatres and restaurants, bars and sex shops, a little park with a lot of hands-on lovers, then an open market selling star-fruit, marijuana plants and dried jimsonweed.

Beside it there is a Beggars' Square, an arrangement of painted squares with a tree planted in the centre, and by city ordinance the beggars must keep inside the squares and not harass the shoppers. Rain keeps coins to give the beggars, it is a kind of rent he pays the world, but coins cannot liven their dead eyes, and he always hurries away after tossing a few into their cups and bowls. "Mister! Mister!" they call and wave, and he stands undecided with his hand in his pocket.

One beggar catches his attention. He is moving, but not like the others who gesture; he is shimmering. This beggar's eyes are not dead but feverish, and as they rest on Rain his body shifts and flows to become Rain, a blond man in a black coat. It seems to Rain that he has poisoned himself with weed or alcohol, toxic for Thorbians. The fever heat is coming off his body. He lifts his hands in imitation of Rain's surprise.

"No, no!" Rain whispers, pulls the handful of silver from his pocket, flings it into the bowl and backs away.

Three young loungers in silk and leather have begun to tease the beggars. Now they glance aside and find this one. He looks up at them hopefully and in turn – rippling and wavering into cloudy and then distinct form – becomes the girl in leather with the blond flat-top, the teenager with slick hair in the silk suit, the man in his twenties with the blue velvet suit and beard dyed to match. As if poison has given him the energy to do endless whole-body modelling without having to think or plan.

"Look at this one!" Bluebeard says. "Let's see!" He kicks the bowl and sets it spinning, flinging arcs of silver.

The other beggars freeze, Rain feels himself shrinking in his clothes and takes an involuntary step back. The Thorbian's impetus halts. He stops in half-gesture with his hands out and his face gone featureless and slack like the canvas face of the Scarecrow in the Wizard of Oz.

The three of them guffaw and kick at him. "What're you gonna be now, blobbo?" The other beggars have scuttled off their squares and run out of the park, no one is left but the four. The Thorbian shimmers, trying to pull away, trying to find a form that will let him.

"Who! Who!" they yell.

"Please!" he cries weakly, "My name, I am Frost." Water begins to seep from his skin, he cannot do more than wave his arms.

"Frost! I think yer melting, Frost! Look, he's peeing!"

Rain recognizes the shrinking-from-danger syndrome that he had spent so much time learning to control in his own youth.

"Look at that! That's disgusting!" They aim more kicks.

Rain wants nothing but to run away and finds himself leaping forward screaming "Stop that! Damn you bastards, stop!"

They turn on him. "What've we got? This's another one!"

Rain can smell them now, they are so close, he is terrified but he cannot stop. He flicks off his hat and crouches screaming, or roaring, his head and neck push thickly out of his collar, his shirt opens, the tie snaps and falls away, his arms reach out of his sleeves, they are fanged and furred, tawny, spotted and savage. He is sinuous in his long and awkward coat, his claws splay out –

The three tormentors freeze.

The girl swallows, licks her lips and says, "Aw, that's nothin'! That isn't real, its just one of his shapes."

Rain roars and takes a step forward, and she backs away.

They breathe hard for a moment and Bluebeard snarls, "I don't give a fuck what he is, there's a cop coming and I'm outa here."

Rain stands stupefied watching them run away while his fangs dig into his lower jaw and his milky blood trickles and drips off his chin. He is frightened at the jolt of creepy pleasure his savagery has given him, does not even know what he has been trying to make of himself, some generic cat, ocelot or lynx he has seen on the vid. His hearts are going *beatbeatbeatbeat*, his neural ganglions are throbbing, He feels the water beginning to run off his own skin, and if he cannot replace it in a few minutes he will be too small for his clothes and look like a clown. The beggar, shrunk somewhat but not badly hurt, is moving weakly to pick up the coins, and Rain wants to help him but does not dare. He's sure someone will yell, "Hey you! Blobbo!" and he is terrified. He also does not want the police near him.

He grabs his hat and ruined tie. Carefully maintaining what form he can he searches out a fountain. There is one just over there in that little park. He drinks, then sits down on a bench. His hearts slow down, his head clears. No one is looking at him, no one will bother him. He's had a panic attack, that's all, rebounding from the anger, but now he is in control. He lifts his hand to loosen his sweaty collar and finds that there are still claws on the ends of the fingers, and stubby hairs around them.

He stuffs his hand in his pocket hastily and lets it re-shape, gets up and walks home. No one notices him.

The beggar haunts him. *I am Frost.*

I could have sheltered Frost. No he can't, not one so sickly and half mad too. Frost needs the kind of care Rain was given that time he had the fungus disease, with a specialist in that little hospital place that Korzybski arranged for him. He will ask Korzybski, something he can do.

He prepares for bed, puts the tuxedo away in his wardrobe with clothes to be cleaned, throws his shoes into the cycler: they were wrecked by the talons that sprang through them. He washes himself, settles carefully into his semi-shape. Once he came home after a hard night, lay down as he was and woke as the same pale blond man. He doesn't want to be imprisoned in that shape.

Tomorrow there will be a live Albert wanting to tell a dead or divorced Debora how he hates her guts and misses her. Albert and Debora, Lucilla and Berenice pay for his life among the aliens.

In his dream the green sky flashes and the grey and yellow growths surge up as the sun rises.

1993

TAUF ALEPH

Samuel Zohar ben Reuven Begelman lived to a great age in the colony Pardes on Tau Ceti IV and in his last years he sent the same message with his annual request for supplies to Galactic Federation Central: *Kindly send one mourner/gravedigger so I can die in peace respectfully.*

And Sol III replied through GalFed Central with the unvarying answer: *Regret cannot find one Jew yours faithfully.*

Because there was not one other identifiable Jew in the known universe, for with the opening of space the people had scattered and intermarried, and though their descendants were as numerous, in the fulfilment of God's promise, as the sands on the shore and the stars in the heavens, there was not one called Jew, nor any other who could speak Hebrew and pray for the dead. The home of the ancestors was emptied: it was now a museum where perfect simulacra performed seventy-five hundred years of history in hundreds of languages for tourists from the breadth of the Galaxy.

In Central, Hrsipliy the Xiploid said to Castro-Ibanez the Solthree, "It is a pity we cannot spare one person to help that poor *juddar*." She meant by this term: body/breath/spirit/sonofabitch, being a woman with three tender hearts.

Castro-Ibanez, who had one kind heart and one hard head, answered, "How can we? He is the last colonist on that world and refuses to be moved; we keep him alive at great expense already." He considered for some time and added, "I think perhaps we might send him a robot. One that can dig and speak recorded prayers. Not one of the new expensive ones. We ought to have some old machine good enough for last rites."

O/G5/842 had been resting in a very dark corner of Stores for 324 years, his four coiled arms retracted and his four hinged ones resting on his four wheeled feet. Two of his arms terminated in huge scoop shovels, for he had been an ore miner, and he was also fitted with treads and sucker-pods. He was very great in size; they made giant machines in those days. New technologies had left him useless; he was not even worthy of being dismantled for parts.

It happened that this machine was wheeled into the light, scoured of rust, and lubricated. His ore-scoops were replaced with small ones retrieved from Stores and suitable for grave digging, but in respect to Sam Begelman he was not given a recording: he was rewired and supplemented with an almost new logic and given orders and permission to go and learn. Once he had done so to the best of his judgement he would travel out with Begelman's supplies and land. This took great expense, but less than an irreplaceable person or a new machine; it fulfilled the Galactic-Colonial contract. O/G would not return, Begelman would rest in peace, no-one would recolonize Tau Ceti IV.

O/G5/842 emerged from his corner. In the Library he caused little more stir than the seven members of the Khagodi embassy (650 kilos apiece) who were searching out a legal point of intra-Galactic law. He was too broad to occupy a cubicle, and let himself be stationed in a basement exhibit room where techs wired him to sensors, sockets, inlets, outlets, screens, and tapes. Current flowed, light came, and he said: LET ME KNOW SAMUEL ZOHAR BEN REUVEN BEGELMAN DOCTOR OF MEDICINE AND WHAT IT MEANS THAT HE IS A JEW.

He recorded the life of Sam Begelman; he absorbed Hebrew, Aramaic, Greek; he learned Torah, which is Law: day one. He learned Writings, Prophets, and then Mishna, which is the first exegesis of Law: day the second. He learned Talmud (Palestinian and Babylonian), which is the completion of Law, and Tosefta, which are ancillary writings and divergent opinions in Law: day the third. He read thirty-five hundred years of Commentary and Responsa: day the fourth. He learned Syriac, Arabic, Latin, Yiddish, French, English, Italian, Spanish, Dutch. At the point of learning Chinese he experienced, for the first time, a synapse. For the sake of reading marginally relevant writings by fewer than ten Sino-Japanese Judaic poets it was not worth learning their vast languages; this gave him pause: two nanoseconds: day the fifth. Then he plunged, day the sixth, into the literatures written in the languages he had absorbed. Like all machines, he did not sleep, but on the seventh day he unhooked himself from Library equipment, gave up his space, and returned to his corner. In this place, he turned down all motor and afferent circuits and indexed, concordanced, cross-referenced. He developed synapses exponentially to complete and fulfil his logic. Then he shut it down and knew nothing.

But Galactic Federation said, O/G5/842, AROUSE YOURSELF AND BOARD THE SHIP *ALEKSANDR NEVSKII* AT LOADING DOCK 377 BOUND FOR TAU CETI IV.

At the loading dock, Flight Admissions said, YOUR

SPACE HAS BEEN PRE-EMPTED FOR SHIPMENT 20 TONS NUTRIVOL POWDERED DRINKS (39 FLAVOURS) TO DESERT WORLDS TAU CETI II AND III.

O/G knew nothing of such matters and said, I HAVE NOT BEEN INSTRUCTED SO. He called Galactic Federation and said, MOD 0885 THE SPACE ASSIGNED FOR ME IS NOT PERMITTED IT HAS BEEN PRE-EMPTED BY A BEING CALLED NUTRIVOL SENDING POWDERED DRINKS TO TAU CETI INNER WORLDS.

Mod 0885 said, I AM CHECKING. YES. THAT COMPANY WENT INTO RECEIVERSHIP ONE STANDARD YEAR AGO. I SUSPECT SMUGGLING AND BRIBERY. I WILL WARN.

THE SHIP WILL BE GONE BY THEN MOD 08 WHAT AM I TO DO?

INVESTIGATE, MOD 842.

HOW AM I TO DO THAT?

USE YOUR LOGIC, said Mod 0885 and signed off.

O/G went to the loading dock and stood in the way. The beings ordering the loading mechs said, "You are blocking this shipment! Get out of the way, you old pile of scrap!"

O/G said in his speaking voice, "I am not in the way. I am to board ship for Pardes and it is against the law for this cargo to take my place." He extruded a limb in gesture toward the stacked cartons; but he had forgotten his strength (for he had been an ore miner) and his new scoop smashed five cartons at one blow; the foam packing parted and white crystals poured from the break. O/G regretted this very greatly for one fraction of a second before he remembered how those beings who managed the mines behaved in the freezing darkness of lonely worlds and moons. He extended his chemical sensor and dipping it into the crystal stream said, "Are fruit drinks for desert worlds now made without fructose but with dextroamphetamine sulfate, diacetylmorphine,

2-acetyl-tetrahydrocannabinol –"

Some of the beings at the loading gate cried out curses and many machines began to push and beat at him. But O/G pulled in his limbs and planted his sucker-pods and did not stir. He had been built to work in many gravities near absolute zero under rains of avalanches. He would not be moved.

Presently, uniformed officials came and took away those beings and their cargo, and said to O/G, "You too must come and answer questions."

But he said, "I was ordered by Galactic Federation to board this ship for Tau Ceti IV, and you may consult the legal department of Colonial Relations, but I will not be moved."

Because they had no power great enough to move him they consulted among themselves and with the legal department and said, "You may pass."

Then O/G took his assigned place in the cargo hold of the *Aleksandr Nevskii* and after the ship lifted for Pardes he turned down his logic because he had been ordered to think for himself for the first time and this confused him very much.

The word *pardes* is "orchard" but the world Pardes was a bog of mud, foul gases, and shifting terrain, where attempts at terraforming failed again and again until colonists left in disgust and many lawsuits plagued the courts of Interworld Colonies at GalFed. O/G landed there in a stripped shuttle which served as a glider. It was not meant to rise again and it broke and sank in the marshes, but O/G ploughed mud, scooping the way before him, and rode on treads, dragging the supplies behind him on a sledge, for 120 kilometres before he came within sight of the colony.

Fierce creatures many times his size, with serpentine

necks and terrible fangs, tried to prey on him. He wished to appease them, and offered greetings in many languages, but they would only break their teeth on him. He stunned one with a blow to the head, killed another by snapping its neck, and they left him alone.

The colony centre was a concrete dome surrounded by a force field that gave out sparks, hissing and crackling. Around it he found many much smaller creatures splashing in pools and scrambling to and fro at the mercy of one of the giants who held a small being writhing in its jaws.

O/G cried in a loud voice, "Go away you savage creature!" and the serpent beast dropped its mouthful, but seeing no great danger dipped its neck to pick it up again. So O/G extended his four hinged limbs to their greatest length and, running behind the monster, seized the pillars of its rear legs, heaving up and out until its spine broke and it fell flattened in mud, thrashing the head on the long neck until it drove it into the ground and smothered.

The small beings surrounded O/G without fear, though he was very great to them, and cried in their thin voices, "Shalom-shalom, Saviour!"

O/G was astonished to hear these strangers speaking clear Hebrew. He had not known a great many kinds of living persons during his experience, but among those displayed in the corridors of the Library basement these most resembled walruses. "I am not a saviour, men of Pardes," he said in the same language. "Are you speaking your native tongue?"

"No, Redeemer. We are Cnidori and we spoke Cnidri before we reached this place in our wanderings, but we learned the language of Rav Zohar because he cared for us when we were lost and starving."

"Now Zohar has put up a barrier and shut you out – and I am not a redeemer – but what has happened to that man?"

"He became very ill and shut himself away because he said he was not fit to look upon. The food he helped us store is eaten and the Unds are ravaging us."

"There are some here that will ravage you no longer. Do you eat the flesh of these ones?"

"No, master. Only what grows from the ground."

He saw that beneath the draggling grey moustaches their teeth were the incisors and molars of herbivores. "I am not your master. See if there is food to gather here and I will try to reach Zohar."

"First we will skin one of these to make tents for shelter. It rains every hour." They rose on their haunches in the bog, and he discovered that though their rear limbs were flippers like those of aquatic animals, their forelimbs bore three webbed fingers apiece and each Cnidor had a small shell knife slung over one shoulder. All, moreover, had what appeared to be one mammalian teat and one male generative organ ranged vertically on their bellies, and they began to seem less and less like walruses to O/G. The prime Cnidor continued, "Tell us what name pleases you if you are offended by the ways we address you."

"I have no name but a designation: O/G5/842. I am only a machine."

"You are a machine of deliverance and so we will call you Golem."

In courtesy O/G accepted the term. "This force field is so noisy it probably has a malfunction. It is not wise to touch it."

"No, we are afraid of it."

Golem scooped mud from the ground and cast it at the force field; great lightnings and hissings issued where it landed. "I doubt even radio would cross that."

"Then how can we reach Zohar, Golem, even if he is still alive?"

"I will cry out, Cnidori. Go to a distance and cover your ears, because my voice can pierce a mountain of lead ore."

They did not know what that was, but they removed themselves, and Golem turned his volume to its highest and called in a mighty voice, *"Samuel Zohar ben Reuven Begelman turn off your force field for I have come from Galactic Federation to help you!!!"*

Even the force field buckled for one second at the sound of his voice.

After a long silence, Golem thought he heard a whimper, from a great distance. "I believe he is alive but cannot reach the control."

A Cnidor said, trembling, "The Unds have surely heard you, because they are coming back again."

And they did indeed come back, bellowing, hooting, and striking with their long necks. Golem tied one great snake neck in a knot and cried again, *"Let us in, Zohar, or the Unds will destroy all of your people!!!"*

The force field vanished, and the Cnidori scuttled over its border beneath the sheltering arms of Golem, who cracked several fanged heads like nutshells with his scoops.

"Now put up your shield!!!" And the people were saved.

When Golem numbered them and they declared that only two were missing among the forty, he said, "Wait here and feed yourselves."

The great outer doorway for working machines was open, but the hangar and storerooms were empty of them; they had been removed by departing colonists. None had been as huge as Golem, and here he removed his scoops and unhinged his outer carapace with its armour, weapons, and storage compartments, for he wished to break no more doorways than necessary. Behind him he pulled the sledge with the supplies.

When his heat sensor identified the locked door behind which Zohar was to be found, he removed the doorway as gently as he could.

"I want to die in peace and you are killing me with noise," said a weak voice out of the darkness.

By infrared Golem saw the old man crumpled on the floor by the bed, filthy and half naked, with the shield control resting near his hand. He turned on the light. The old man was nearly bald, wasted and yellow-skinned, wrinkled, his rough beard tangled and clotted with blood.

"Zohar?"

Sam Begelman opened his eyes and saw a tremendous machine, multi-armed with wheels and tread, wound with coiling tubes and wires, studded with dials. At its top was a dome banded with sensor lenses, and it turned this way and that to survey the room. "What are you?" he whispered in terror. "Where is my kaddish?"

He spoke in *lingua*, but O/G replied in Hebrew, "You know you are the last Jew in the known universe, Rav Zohar. There is no one but me to say prayers for you."

"Then let me die without peace," said Begelman, and he closed his eyes.

But Golem knew the plan of the station, and within five minutes he reordered the bed in cleanliness, placed the old man on it, set up an i.v., cleansed him, and injected him with the drugs prepared for him. The old man's hands pushed at him and pushed at him, uselessly. "You are only a machine," he croaked. "Can't you understand that a machine can't pray?"

"Yes, master. I would have told that to Galactic Federation, but I knew they would not believe me, not being Jews."

"I am not your master. Why truly did you come?"

"I was made new again and given orders. My growth in logic now allows me to understand that I cannot be of use to you in exactly the way Galactic Federation wished, but I can still make you more comfortable."

"I don't care!" Begelman snarled. "Who needs a machine?"

"The Cnidori needed me to save them from the Unds when you shut them out, and they tried to call me Saviour, Redeemer, master; I refused because I *am* a machine, but I let them call me Golem because I am a machine of deliverance."

Begelman sniffed. But the sick yellow of his skin was gone; his face was faintly pink and already younger by a few years.

"Shmuel Zohar ben Reuven Begelman, why do you allow those helpless ones to call you Rav Zohar and speak in your language?"

"You nudnik of a machine, my name is not Samuel and certainly not Shmuel! It is Zohar, and I let myself be called Sam because *zohar* is 'splendour' and you can't go through life as Splendour Begelman! I taught those Cnidori the Law and the Prophets to hear my own language spoken because my children are gone and my wife is dead. That is why they call me Teacher. And I shut them out so that they would be forced to make their own way in life before they began to call *me* Redeemer! What do you call yourself, Golem?"

"My designation is O/G5/842."

"Ah. Og the giant King of Bashan. That seems suitable."

"Yes, Zohar. That one your Rabbi Moshe killed in the

land of Kana'an with all his people for no great provocation. But O is the height of my oxygen tolerance in Solthree terms; I cannot work at gravities of less than five newtons, and eight four two is my model number. Now Zohar, if you demand it I will turn myself off and be no more. But the people are within your gate; some of them have been killed and they must still be cared for."

Zohar sighed, but he smiled a little as well. Yet he spoke slowly because he was very ill. "Og ha-Golem, before you learn how to tune an argument too fine remember that Master of the Word is one of the names of Satan. Moshe Rabbenu was a bad-tempered man but he did very greatly, and I am no kind of warrior. Take care of the people, and me too if your ... logic demands it – and I will consider how to conduct myself off the world properly."

"I am sure your spirit will free itself in peace, Zohar. As for me, my shuttle is broken, I am wanted nowhere else, and I will rest in Pardes."

Og ha-Golem went out of the presence of the old man but it seemed to him as if there were some mild dysfunction in his circuits, for he was mindful – if that is the term – of Begelman's contempt of the Satan, Baal Davar, and he did not know for certain if what he had done by the prompting of his logic was right action. How can I know? he asked himself. By what harms and what saves, he answered. By what seems to harm and what seems to save, says the Master of the Word.

Yet he continued by the letter of his instructions from Galactic Federation, and these were to give the old man comfort. For the Cnidori he helped construct tents, because they liked water under their bellies but not pouring on their heads. With his own implements he flensed the bodies of the dead Unds, cleaned their skins, and burned their flesh; it was not kosher for Begelman and attracted bothersome scavengers. He did this while Rav Zohar was sleeping and spoke to the people in his language; they had missed it when he was ill. "Zohar believes you must learn to take care of yourselves, against the Unds and on your world, because you cannot now depend on him."

"We would do that, Golem, but we would also like to give comfort to our Teacher."

Og ha-Golem was disturbed once again by the ideas that pieced themselves together in his logic and said to Begelman, "Zohar, you have taught the Cnidori so well that now they are capable of saying the prayers you long for so greatly. Is there a way in which that can be made permissible?"

The old man folded his hands and looked about the bare and cracking walls of the room, as Golem had first done, and then back at him. "In this place?" he whispered. "Do you know what you are saying?"

"Yes, Zohar."

"How they may be made *Jews*?"

"They are sentient beings. What is there to prevent it?"

Begelman's face became red and Og checked his blood-pressure monitor. "Prevent it! What is there to them that would make Jews? Everything they eat is neutral, neither kosher nor tref, so what use is the law of Kashrut? They live in mud – where are the rules of bathing and cleanliness? They had never had any kind of god or any thought of one, as far as they tell me – what does prayer mean? Do you know how they procreate? Could you imagine? They are so completely hermaphroditic the word is meaningless. They pair long enough to raise children together, but only until the children grow teeth and can forage. What you see that looks like a penis is really an ovipositor: each Cnidor who is ready deposits eggs in the pouch of another, and an enzyme of the eggs stimulates the semen glands inside, and when one or two eggs become fertilized the pouch seals until the foetus is of a size to make the fluid pressure around it break the seal, and the young crawls up the belly of the parent to suckle on the teat. Even if one or two among twenty are born incomplete, not one is anything you might call male or female! So tell me, what do you do with all the laws of marriage and divorce, sexual behaviour, the duties of the man at prayer and the woman with the child?"

He was becoming out of breath and Og checked oxygen and heart monitors. "I am not a man or woman either and though I know the Law I am ignorant in experience. I was thinking merely of prayers that God might listen to in charity or appreciation. I did not mean to upset you. I am not fulfilling my duties."

"Leave me."

Og turned an eye-cell to the dripping of the i.v. and removed catheter and urine bag. "You are nearly ready to rise from your bed and feed yourself, Zohar. Perhaps when you feel more of a man you may reconsider."

"Just go away." He added, snarling, "God doesn't need any more Jews!"

"Yes, they would look ridiculous in skullcaps and prayer shawls with all those fringes dripping in mud ..."

Zohar, was that why you drove them out into the wild?

Og gathered brushwood and made a great fire. He cut woody vines and burnt them into heaps of charcoal. He gathered and baked clay into blocks and built a kiln. Then he pulled his sledge for 120 kilometres, and dug until he found enough pieces of the glider for his uses.

He fired the kiln to a great heat, softened the fragments, and reshaped them into the huge scoops he had been deprived of. They were not as fine and strong as the originals, but very nearly as exact.

He consulted maps of Pardes, which lay near the sea. He began digging channels and heaping breakwaters to divert a number of streams and drain some of the marshes of Pardes, and to keep the sea from washing over it during storms, and this left pools of fresher water for the Cnidori.

Sometimes the sun shone. On a day that was brighter and dryer than usual Begelman came outside the station, supporting himself on canes, and watched the great Golem at work. He had never seen Og in full armour with his scoops. During its renewal his exterior had been bonded with a coating that retarded rust; this was dull grey and the machine had no beauty in the eyes of a Solthree, but he worked with an economy of movement that leant him grace. He was surrounded by Cnidori with shovels of a size they could use, and they seemed to Begelman like little children playing in mud piles, getting in the way while the towering machine worked in silence without harming the small creatures or allowing them to annoy him.

Og, swivelling the beam of his eye-cell, saw an old white-bearded Solthree with a homely face of some dignity; he looked weak but not ill. His hair was neatly trimmed, he wore a blue velvet skullcap worked with silver threads, black trousers, and zippered jacket, below which showed the fringes of his *tallith katan.* He matched approximately the thousands of drawings, paintings and photographs of dignified old Jews stored in Og's memory: Og had dressed him to match.

Begelman said, "What are you doing?"

"I am stabilizing the land in order to grow crops of

oilseed, lugwort, and greenpleat, which are nourishing both to you and the Cnidori. I doubt Galactic Federation is going to give us anything more, and I also wish to store supplies. If other wandering tribes of Cnidori cross this territory it is better to share our plenty than fight over scarcity."

"You're too good to be true," Begelman muttered.

Og had learned something of both wit and sarcasm from Begelman but did not give himself the right to use them on the old man. His logic told him that he, the machine, had nothing to fear from a Satan who was not even a concept in the mainstream of Jewish belief, but that Zohar was doing battle with the common human evil in his own spirit. He said, "Zohar, these Cnidori have decided to take Hebrew names, and they are calling themselves by letters: Aleph, Bet, Gimmel, and when those end at Tauf, by numbers: Echod, Shtaim, Sholosh. This does not seem correct to me but they will not take my word for it. Will you help them?"

Begelman's mouth worked for a moment, twisting as if to say, What have these to do with such names? but Cnidori crowded round him and their black eyes reflected very small lights in the dim sun; they were people of neither fur nor feather, but scales that resembled both: leaf-shaped plates the size of a thumb with central ridges and branching radials; these were very fine in texture and refracted rainbow colours on brighter days.

The old man sighed and said, "Dear people, if you wish to take names in Hebrew you must take the names of human beings like those in Law and Prophets. The names of the Fathers: Avraham, Yitzhak, Yaakov; the Tribes: Yehuda, Shimon, Binyamin, or if you prefer female names, the Mothers: Sarai, Rivkah, Rakhael, Leah.

Whichever seems good to you." The Cnidori thanked him with pleasure and went away content.

Begelman said to Og, "Next thing you know they will want a Temple." Og suspected what they would ask for next, but said, "I believe we must redesign the force field to keep the Unds out of the cultivated areas. Perhaps we have enough components in Stores or I can learn to make them."

He had been scouting for Unds every fourth or fifth day and knew their movements. They had been avoiding the Station in fear of Og and the malfunctioning force field but he believed that they would attack again when the place was quiet, and they did so on the night of that day when the Cnidori took names. The field had been repaired and withstood their battering without shocking them; their cries were terrible to hear, and sometimes their bones cracked against the force. They fell back after many hours, leaving Og with earthworks to repair and two of their bodies to destroy.

In the morning when he had finished doing this he found Begelman lying on a couch in the Common Room, a book of prayers on his lap, faced by a group of ten Cnidori. All eleven spoke at once, Begelman with crackling anger in his voice, the Cnidori softly but with insistence.

Begelman cried out when he saw Og, "Now they tell me they must have surnames!"

"I expected so, Zohar. They know that you are ben Reuven and they have accepted your language and the names of your people. Is this not reasonable?"

"I have no authority to make Jews of them!"

"You are the only authority left. You have taught them."

"Damn you! You have been pushing for this!"

41

"I have pushed for nothing except to make you well. I taught nothing." Within him the Master of the Word spoke: This is true, but is it right?

Begelman in anger clapped shut his book, but it was very old and its spine cracked slightly; he lifted and kissed it in repentance. He spoke in a low voice, "What does it matter now? There is no surname they can be given except the name of convert, which is ben Avraham or bat Avraham, according to the gender of the first name. And how can they be converts when they can keep no Law and do not even know God? And what does it matter now?" He threw up his hands, "Let them be b'nei Avraham!"

But the Cnidori prime, who had taken the name Binyamin, that is, Son of the Right Hand, said, "We do not wish to be b'nei Avraham, but b'nei Zohar, because we say to you, Og ha-Golem, and to you, Rav Zohar, that because Zohar has been as a father to us we feel as sons to him."

Og feared that the old man might now become truly ill with rage, and indeed his hands trembled on the book, but he said quietly enough, "My children, Jews do not behave so. Converts must become Jews in the ways allowed to them. If you do not understand, I have not taught you well enough, and I am too old to teach more. I have yielded too much already to a people who do not worship God, and I am not even a Rabbi with such small authority as is given to one."

"Rav Zohar, we have come to tell you that we have sworn to worship your God."

"But you must not worship me."

"But we may worship the God who created such a man as you, and such teachings as you have taught us, and those men who made the great Golem." They went away quickly and quietly without speaking further.

"They will be back again," Begelman said. "And again and again. Why did I ever let you in? Lord God King of the Universe, what am I to do?"

It *is* right, Og told the Master of the Word. "You are more alive and healthy than you have long been, Zohar," he said. "And you have people who love you. Can you not let them do so?"

He sought out Binyamin. "Do not trouble Rav Zohar with demands he cannot fulfil, no matter how much you desire to honour him. Later I will ask him to think if there is a way he can do as you wish, within the Law."

"We will do whatever you advise, Golem."

Og continued with his work, but while he was digging he turned up a strange artifact and he had a foreboding. At times he had discovered potsherds which were the remnants of clay vessels the Cnidori had made to cook vegetables they could not digest raw, and this discovery was an almost whole cylinder of the same texture, colour and markings; one of its end rims was blackened by burn marks, and dark streaks ran up its sides. He did not know what it was but it seemed sinister to him; in conscience he had no choice but to show it to Zohar.

"It does not seem like a cooking vessel," he said.

"No," said Begelman. "It does not." He pointed to a place inside where there was a leaf-shaped Cnidori scale, blackened, clinging to its wall, and to two other burn marks of the same shape. Strangely, to Og, his eyes filled with tears.

"Perhaps it is a casing in which they dispose of their dead," Og said.

Zohar wiped his eyes and said, "No. It is a casing in which they make them dead. Many were killed by Unds, and some have starved, and the rest die of age. All those they weight and sink into the marshes. This is a sacrifice. They have a god, and its name is Baal." He shook his

43

head. "My children." He wept for a moment again and said, "Take this away and smash it until there is not a piece to recognize."

Og did so, but Zohar locked himself into his room and would not answer to anyone.

Og did not know what to do now. He was again as helpless as he had been on the loading dock where he had first learned to use his logic.

The Cnidori came to inquire of Golem and he told them what had happened. They said, "It is true that our ancestors worshipped a Being and made sacrifices, but none of that was done after Zohar gave us help. We were afraid he and his God would hold us in contempt."

"Both Zohar and his God have done imperfect acts. But now I will leave him alone, because he is very troubled."

"But it is a great sin in his eyes," said Binyamin sorrowfully. "I doubt that he will ever care for us again."

And Og continued with his work, but he thought his logic had failed him, in accordance with Zohar's taunts.

In the evening a Cnidor called Elyahu came writhing toward him along the ground in great distress. "Come quickly!" he called. "Binyamin is doing *nidset!*"

"What is that?"

"Only come quickly!" Elyahu turned back in haste. Og unclipped his scoops and followed, overtaking the small creature and bearing him forward in his arms. They found Binyamin and other Cnidori in a grave of ferns. They had built a smoky fire and were placing upon it a fresh cylinder: a network of withy branches had been woven into the bottom of it.

"No, no!" cried Og, but they did not regard him; the cylinder was set on the fire and smoke came out of its top. Then the Cnidori helped Binyamin climb over its edge and he dropped inward, into the smoke.

"*No!*" Og cried again, and he toppled the vessel from the fire, but without violence so that Binyamin would not be harmed. "*You shall make no sacrifices!*" Then he tapped it so that it split, and the Cnidor lay in its halves, trembling.

"*That* is *nidset*, Golem," said Elyahu.

But Golem plucked up the whimpering Cnidor. "Why were you doing such a terrible thing, Binyamin?"

"We thought," Binyamin said in a quavering voice, "we thought that all of the gods were angry with us – our old god for leaving him and our new one for having worshipped the old – and that a sacrifice would take away the anger of all."

"That confounds my logic somewhat." Og set down Binyamin, beat out the fire, and cast the pieces of the cylinder far away. "All gods are One, and the One forgives whoever asks. Now come. I believe I hear the Unds again, and we need shelter close to home until we can build a wider one."

Then the Cnidori raised a babble of voices. "No! What good is such a God if even Zohar does not listen to Him and forgive us?"

It seemed to Og for one moment as if the Cnidori felt themselves cheated of a sacrifice; he put this thought aside. "The man is sick and old, and he is not thinking clearly either, while you have demanded much of him."

"Then, Golem, we will demand no more, but die among the Unds!" The shrieking of the beasts grew louder on the night winds but the Cnidori drew their little knives and would not stir.

"Truly you are an outrageous people," said Golem. "But I am only a machine." He extended his four hinged arms and his four coil arms and bearing them up in their tens raced with them on treads and wheels until they were within the safety of the force field.

But when he set them down they grouped together closely near the field and would not say one word.

Og considered the stubborn Zohar on the one side, and the stubborn b'nei Avraham on the other, and he thought that perhaps it was time for him to cease his being. A great storm of lightning and thunder broke out; the Unds did not approach, and within the force field there was stillness.

He disarmed himself and stood before Zohar's door. He considered the sacrifice of Yitzhak, and the Golden Calf, and how Moshe Rabbenu had broken the Tables, and many other excellent examples, and he spoke quietly.

"Zohar, you need not answer, but you must listen. Your people tell me they have made no sacrifices since they knew you. But Binyamin, who longs to call himself your son, has tried to sacrifice himself to placate whatever gods may forgive his people, and would have died if I had not prevented him. After that they were ready to let the Unds kill them. I prevented that also, but they will not speak to me, or to you if you do not forgive them. I cannot do any more here and I have nothing further to say to you. Good-bye."

He turned from the door without waiting, but heard it open, and Zohar's voice cried out, "Og, where are you going?"

"To the storeroom, to turn myself off. I have always said I was no more than a machine, and now I have reached the limit of my logic and my usefulness."

"No, Golem, wait! Don't take everything from me!" The old man was standing with his hands clasped and hair awry. "There must be some end to foolishness," he whispered. "Where are they?"

"Out by the field near the entrance," Og said. "You will see them when the lightning flashes."

The Holy One, blessed be His Name, gave Zohar one more year, and in that time Og ha-Golem built and planted, and in this he was helped by the b'nei Avraham. They made lamps from their vegetable oils and lit them on Sabbaths and the Holy Days calculated by Zohar. In season they mated and their bellies swelled. Zohar tended them when his strength allowed, as in old days, and when Elyahu died of brain haemorrhage and Yitzhak of a swift-growing tumour which nothing could stop, he led the mourners in prayer for their length of days. One baby was stillborn, but ten came from the womb in good health; they were grey-pink, toothless, and squalled fearfully, but Zohar fondled and praised them. "These people were twelve when I found them," he said to Og. "Now there are forty-six and I have known them for five generations." He told the Cnidori, "Children of Avraham, Jews have converted, and Jews have adopted, but never children of a different species, so there is no precedent I can find to let any one of you call yourselves a child of Zohar, but as a community I see no reason why you cannot call yourselves b'nei Zohar, my children, collectively."

The people were wise enough by now to accept this decision without argument. They saw that the old man's time of renewed strength was done and he was becoming frailer every day; they learned to make decisions for themselves. Og too helped him now only when he asked. Zohar seemed content, although sometimes he appeared about to speak and remained silent. The people noticed these moods and spoke to Og of them occasionally, but Og said, "He must tend to his spirit for himself, b'nei Avraham. My work is done."

He had cleared the land in many areas around the station, and protected them with force fields whose antennas he had made with forges he had built. The Unds were driven back into their wilds of cave and valley; they were great and terrible, but magnificent life-forms of their own kind and he wished to kill no more. He had only to wait for the day when Zohar would die in peace.

Once a day Og visited him in the Common Room where he spent most of his time reading or with his hands on his book and his eyes to the distance. One peaceful day when they were alone he said to Og, "I must tell you this while my head is still clear. And I can tell only you." He gathered his thoughts for a moment. "It took me a long time to realize that I was the last Jew, though Galactic Federation kept saying so. I had been long alone, but that realization made me fiercely, hideously lonely. Perhaps you don't understand. I think you do. And then my loneliness turned itself inside out and I grew myself a kind of perverse pride. The last! The last! I would close the Book that was opened those thousands of years before, as great in a way as the first had been ... but I had found the Cnidori, and they were a people to talk with and keep from going mad in loneliness – but Jews! They were ugly, and filthy, and the opposite of everything I saw as human. I despised them. Almost, I hated them ... that was what wanted to be Jews! And I had started it by teaching them, because I was so lonely – and I had no way to stop it except to destroy them, and I nearly did that! And you – " He began to weep with the weak passion of age.

"Zohar, do not weep. You will make yourself ill."

"My soul is sick! It is like a boil that needs lancing, and it hurts so much! Who will forgive me?" He reached out and grasped one of Og's arms. "Who?"

"*They* will forgive you anything – but if you ask you will only hurt yourself more deeply. And I make no judgements."

"But I must be judged!" Zohar cried. "Let me have a little peace to die with!"

"If I must, then, Zohar, I judge you a member of humanity who has saved more people than would be alive without him. I think you could not wish better."

Zohar said weakly, "You knew all the time, didn't you?"

"Yes," said Og. "I believe I did."

But Zohar did not hear, for he had fainted.

He woke in his bed and when his eyes opened he saw Og beside him. "What are you?" he said, and Og stared with his unwinking eye; he thought Zohar's mind had left him.

Then Zohar laughed. "My mind is not gone yet. But what are you, really, Og? You cannot answer. Ah well ... would you ask my people to come here now, so I can say good-bye? I doubt it will be long; they raise all kinds of uproar, but at least they can't cry."

Og brought the people, and Zohar blessed them all and each; they were silent, in awe of him. He seemed to fade while he spoke, as if he were being enveloped in mist. "I have no advice for you," he whispered at last. "I have taught all I know and that is little enough because I am not very wise, but you will find the wise among yourselves. Now, whoever remembers, let him recite me a psalm. Not the twenty-third. I want the hundred-and-fourth, and leave out that stupid part at the end where the sinners are consumed from the earth."

But it was only Og who remembered that psalm in its entirety, and spoke the words describing the world Zohar had come from an unmeasurable time ago.

> *O Lord my God You are very great!*
> *You are clothed with honour and majesty,*
> *Who covers Yourself with light as with a garment,*
> *Who has stretched out the heavens like a tent,*
> *Who has laid the beams of Your chambers on the waters,*
> *Who makes the clouds Your chariot,*
> *Who rides on the wings of the wind,*
> *Who makes the winds Your messengers,*
> *fire and flame Your ministers ...*

When he was finished, Zohar said the *Shema*, which tells that God is One, and died. And Og thought that he must be pleased with his dying.

Og removed himself. He let the b'nei Avraham prepare the body, wrap it in the prayer shawl, and bury it. He waited during the days in which the people sat in mourning, and when they had got up he said, "Surely my time is come." He travelled once about the domains he had created for their inhabitants and returned to say good-bye in fewer words than Zohar had done.

But the people cried, "No, Golem, no! How can you leave us now when we need you so greatly?"

"You are not children. Zohar told you that you must manage for yourselves."

"But we have so much to learn. We do not know how to use the radio, and we want to tell Galactic Federation that Zohar is dead, and of all he and you have done for us."

"I doubt that Galactic Federation is interested," said Og.

"Nevertheless we will learn!"

They were a stubborn people. Og said, "I will stay for that, but no longer."

Then Og discovered he must teach them enough *lingua* to make themselves understood by Galactic Federation. All were determined learners, and a few had a gift for languages. When he had satisfied himself that they were capable, he said, "Now."

And they said, "Og ha-Golem, why must you waste yourself? We have so much to discover about the God we worship and the men who have worshipped Him!"

"Zohar taught you all he knew, and that was a great deal."

"Indeed he taught us the Law and the Prophets, but he did not teach us the tongues of Aramaic or Greek, or Writings, or Mishna, or Talmud (Palestinian and Babylonian), or Tosefta, or Commentary, or –"

"But why must you learn all that?"

"To keep it for others who may wish to know of it when we are dead."

So Og surrounded himself with them, the sons and daughters of Avraham and their children, who now took surnames of their own from womb parents – and all of them b'nei Zohar – and he began: "Here is Mishna, given by word of mouth from Scribe to Scribe for a thousand years. Fifth Division, *Nezikin*, which is Damages; *Baba Metzia*: the Middle Gate: 'If two took hold of a garment and one said, "I found it," and the other said, "*I* found it," or one said, "I bought it," and the other said, "*I* bought it," each takes an oath that he claims not less than half and they divide it ...'"

In this manner Og ha-Golem, who had endless patience, lived a thousand and twenty years. By radio the Galaxy heard of the strange work of strange creatures, and over hundreds of years colonists who wished to call themselves b'nei Avraham drifted inward to re-create the world Pardes. They were not great in number, but they made a world. From *pardes* is derived "Paradise", but in

51

the humble world of Pardes the peoples drained more of the swamps and planted fruitful orchards and pleasant gardens. All of these were named for their creators, except one.

When Og discovered that his functions were deteriorating he refused replacement parts and directed that when he stopped, all of his components must be dismantled and scattered to the ends of the earth, for fear of idolatry. But a garden was named for him, may his spirit rest in justice and his carapace rust in peace, and the one being who had no organic life is remembered with love among living things.

Here the people live, doing good and evil, contending with God and arguing with each other as usual, and all keep the Tradition as well as they can. Only the descendants of the aboriginal inhabitants, once called Cnidori, jealously guard for themselves the privilege of the name b'nei Zohar, and they are considered by the others to be snobbish, clannish, and stiff-necked.

1981

THE OTHER EYE

I am writing on this worn-down piece of vellum that the priests threw away. I scrubbed it with pumice and water, and stole the inkstick. If you find me and betray me be damned to you. No more waste space. This began one turn and forty stands ago, when my eye began to go blind. It is my other eye, you see, the one that turns out, and does not work too well either, showing me two of everything and different colours at that.

I used to bring the priests their water from the sluices a clockstroke away, and hard going on the rough tailings, but good and honest work for all that, as my hairy-white dam used to say. All of us do work: dig out the tunnels to reach the Great Kingdom, put up stone shorings to prop the tunnels, pick out the jewels to put on the breastplates of the priests, grow the airweed and farm the moss and whitefern for us and the beasts, tend the beasts and slaughter them.

My old sire was a tender of beasts and stank of them, and my dam filled the sconces that give our light, and smelled of oil. They would drink the grindbrew and fight over who smelled the worse, and beat each other and knock me arse over crockpot. So I lived with the priests in their tunnel and carried water. They wanted to pogue me and I said – "What will you give me if let

HYLLIS GOTLIEB

you?" – I saw them getting water carried to them, and eating the best parts of meat, sitting soft on weavings stuffed with fernstraw, and all they did was make black marks on vellum like this. They laughed and said – "Look at you, Mem, with your fur smelling of oil and your fingers leaving black soot marks, making us a price! Do you think you are worth anything?"

It is true that I could not afford much water to wash in, but they are not supposed to have women either. I only said – "Your Holinesses want us to be worthy of the Great Kingdom, and claim that we are wise trusting you to lead us there. Let me learn a little of what you know so that I will be even wiser and worthier." – How can you be wiser than sitting on your backside making black marks on vellum while others do your work for you?

They laughed and said – "Vellum and inksticks are too valuable to give you, but take this tablet of tallow wax and this stylus and make all the marks you like." – I did not care that they laughed. I did not tell them I knew that the marks meant things and I learned what. I let them do what they wanted and brought them their water too. I even picked the lice out of their fur. Then my eye began to go blind.

At first I thought: this scribe work is too hard on my eyes. But I never saw a blind priest. And then that I had a sickness of the eye because it did not move right. But it never pained me.

Two stands and three sleeps it was going dark and I was afraid to tell because you know what happens to the blind who cannot work, so I worked harder though I stumbled, drew water and stored food. Then it was blind.

I said to myself, well I will get used to this. That went on for a round of sleeps by the priestbook. And the first stand after that I woke up with my eye full of light.

54

It was like if you put together all of the lamps and fires you ever saw, and more. It was like that and full of heat too. I thought, this is some brain injury or I have gone mad. I had fallen, you know, nine stands ago and struck my head. But it did not hurt then or now.

But the light, the light was like pain. I thought I was injured or gone mad – no, I have said that – but it was like that, all confusion. All that stand I could not see for the light. Even when I shut my eye or held my hand against it was light. I thought it was burning through my head and that everyone must see it. I stumbled all day and bruised myself and cut my skin and when I slept with my eyes full of tears I had the light in it. For those two stands and sleeps it was so, I could not bear it, but when I woke –

– I have used up half my space and this is the other side of my vellum – when I woke my eye was not so much full of light but it had colours. I mean the light was filled with colours. All the colours of the jewels in the breast-plates filled the light.

All that stand I had the blazing colours in that eye and I picked my way over the stones to the sluices with my straight eye and spilt half the water and the priests cursed me. But when I went to sleep my eye went dark and slept too, except for a few little lights. It woke up with me again half green and half blue, and the light I could not stand in the middle of the blue. It was all lights and colours. It kept like that for two stands. On the third everything was clear and had edges.

The green part is some kind of plants you can stand on. There are stones here too, but they are flat enough to walk on without falling. The blue is the roof and the light in it lets you see everything. And warms the people – people? What am I saying? But there are moving figures, with pink and brown skins, not fur.

I asked myself if this place was the Great Kingdom and my eye was its opening. I saw myself standing on the green and people would look at me or through me and not notice. I did not want them to notice me, not when I was in bed with one of those on top of me, snorting foul breath in my face and hands going everywhere.

Around that time I got pregnant, but I took the pinch-herb and it bled away, it only made me sick one stand and I spent that half-asleep and being with those people in the light. I had not realized that I lived in darkness. But half darkness and half light is full of fear.

I had not told anyone at all. Sometimes I could not eat or sleep for fear. But I was sure that no one would like this vision of mine. If they did believe me they would be fearful or jealous, and if not, they would say I was out of my mind. And I thought so too. I cried so much with fear it was a wonder I could see even a vision. But I went on working and saving my food when I could not eat it. And the people in my eye began to smile at me.

That frightened me even more. I had to talk to someone. I told Eb, my friend who waters the beasts, whom I meet at the sluices. She said – "Mem, I do not believe you." – and I said – "Whether or not you do I cannot help, but it is so." I had to tell. She went back and told the priests. They came and took hold of me when I was drawing water. They took me to their chamber and said – "What is this?" – and I told them. They talked among themselves a great while, holding me with eight hands and not letting go, as if I would fly through my eye into the light. Then they began to argue and scream, and in that time the people in my eye came and said – "Mem? We have been expecting you, Mem." – I do not know whether I heard it in my ear or in my mind, whether these people really spoke or I wanted so much for them to speak.

They took my hand, and that hand of mine that I gave them had a brown skin.

The priests and the men and women who had gathered round them said – "That is an evil and accursed vision! We must pluck out that eye!" Both my eyes burst into tears for pity, and I cried – "No! No! Not my eye!" And they said – "Yes, it must be so!" – and the head priest fetched tongs. It seemed to me that they were all joyful to think of taking this eye. They were so full of rage at me, and all because of a sick eye! My eyes were weeping and I stared at those other people on the green grass, they gave me a flower and said – "What is troubling you, Mem? What do you see?" – and then my fear gave me strength.

I broke their grasp of me, baring my teeth and making the noise of a beast. I seized hold of the tongs, it was heavy, and swung out around me and the people fell away as if I was a demon. I would have hurt them to save myself. I ran to my chamber and piled stones in the entrance.

They howled around me for some time, but the priests knew I was trapped, and the people are fickle, their passions blow away. After a while I heard the picks and axes of their digging. My fear did not blow away. My eyes were swollen with crying over it, both the dark and the light. I do not know how long it was before I heard the whisper: – "Mem!" That was Eb.

I said – "Go away, Eb. How could you do such a thing?" She was whimpering – "I was afraid." Then she said – "Forgive me" – but I told her to go away. She whimpered again and said – "Let me help you find a hiding place" – and I laughed bitterly. She said – "Please, Mem, it is where I used to go with Aff the herdsman, and if his woman knew of it she would kill me. I have candles there, and food I kept." I had no choice but to trust her. I am waiting here, in her meeting-place. I hear the endless sounds of the picks, and the wafts of the airweed carry the smells of beasts and fuel oil. Ten sleeps ago my straight eye began to go blind. My tears have run dry. There is nothing to do and nowhere to go. My sight becomes dimmer every clockstroke. The people in my lighted eye are holding my brown hands, but my other eye is gathering darkness. Will the light pierce it too, while my hands are cut on the stones I cannot see? I have reached the end of my space and my good eye cannot see any m

1988

MOTHER LODE

The Amsu spend their lives foraging in a zigzag course between the ice rings and the asteroid moons of Epictetus VI, called Apikiki by most of its inhabitants. The local name provokes laughter among some visitors, but the Amsu do not. They are a kilometre in length, and occasionally the young and ignorant ones try to engulf a ship; since they are protected by GalFed, these incidents lead to embarrassing complications.

Amsuwlle was old and wise: she ate ore, drank ice and kept on course. When the Surveyor *Limbo*, a fast cruiser, docked with her on short notice, she extruded her siphon, planted it smartly over the lock door with a solid *flump*, paced the ship without wobble or quiver till the door opened, and flooded the lock with cold water.

.Good luck.: Threyha was Sector Coordinator and ESP on the *Limbo*. She sent a last picture of herself from her tank, waving a languid scaly hand.

:Thank you.: For nothing. Elena Cortez was waiting in a wet-suit with oxygen tanks; the current whirled her like a top and pulled her into the tube. It sealed behind her and retracted pleating as it went, to the vast phosphorescent chamber of Amsuwlle's gorge.

She spun in the dim turbulence, fighting ore chunks and luminous gas bubbles and trying to muffle an explosion of awful panic. *Out! Out! Out!*

:What a pity to cause you such inconvenience.:

A valve opened close by and decanted her into a spherical cavity; the rocks and liquids sucked out, the wet walls squeezed her gently — *:Never fear, Zaf is here!:* — the sinus filled with gas, and she hung in its centre, then spiralled toward the wall and landed in a puddle of silt. Amsuwlle had begun to spin.

:The air is quite good, my dear. Welcome aboard!:

She pulled off the mask. There was air all right, cold and damp; it smelled of stale water and wet metal, with an overtone of tart cool flesh like a melon's and no hint of decay. She unbuckled the tanks, shivering, scrubbing at her face with cold crinkled hands to wipe away the sweat of fear and embarrassment. She watched the faint ripples of light on the walls, listened to the whish and slap of water, the suck and blubber of valves, and seven or eight hearts going boom, whicker, thack, flub, tickatick with no ascertainable coordination, as if a clock maker had set all his timepieces going at once and the grandfathers, alarms, turnips, electrics, chronometers went on telling their own time.

A round red glow of light grew on the dark wall before her, and something like a black arm came through, tipped with two horns instead of fingers, one of them hung with a penlight.

"Well, Zaf, I am a terrible coward. Anyway, it is good to see you again."

Zaf pulled his length through the valve. He was about the size and thickness of a python, and his horns, looked much like an annelid worm. He smelled faintly of sulphur compounds.

"A great pleasure," he said, and dipped his anterior end. It had a mouth and behind that a silver light-sensitive band. The air was not good for him: he was strapped with a tank, and tubes ran into several of his gill slits; with the free ones he manipulated air into speech. He was an ESP but also the soul of tact; he used his strange warble to communicate with all speaking creatures.

A Solthree pushed his way through, a tall heavy man with red hair and beard. "I'm Roberts," he said. "I suppose Zaf's told you who we are. Jones is spraying and Takashima's sleeping. God, it's cold in here." He rubbed his hands, twitched his eyes in every direction except hers. "You'll want a change and a hot drink. No alcohol on board, I'm afraid."

"I know," Elena said. Nothing inflammable was carried on an Amsu, and foreign bodies stored and recycled their own wastes.

:What is worrying him , Zaf?:

:Dear lady, I never pry. That is your business.: Mild ESP chuckle. *:But I think he must have some idea why you are here.:*

Elena Cortez, an enthusiastic student of interterrestrial relationships, had the unhappy task of telling people where to get off. When a new colony was seriously disturbing the ecology or the native civilization of a planet, no matter how perfect it might be from the point of view of its settlers, she had GalFed authority to ask it to shift, remove, or disperse itself. She had no power to shift or remove it herself, or threaten to do so. Otherwise she would not have lived through many tacky situations. She was a distant early warning. She warned gently, listened to impassioned arguments calmly, and almost always succeeded at the unpleasant work. When she did not succeed, she accepted refusals gently. The colony, if endangered, was left to itself; if it was a danger it was left to legal, political or military authorities. Those who rebuffed Elena always lived, or did not live, to learn better.

Amsuwlle spun gently against the flow of planetary debris. Unlike her hearts, the grooved excurrents on her sides worked in coordination jetting silvering threads of vapour to keep her on course. She was shaped like a vegetable marrow, and from a distance seemed just as smooth. Closer, she was dappled with pale light-sensors and huge opalescent patches; closer yet her skin was ridged and grooved in a brain-fold pattern; it was flexible but firm. At her mouthless front end she had a sensory network fine enough to taste a single microgram, at the rear end an ovipositor, midway two intake siphons and an excretory tube. She excreted compacted nuggets of titanium, tungsten, vanadium, selenium and other useful metals. Because of that she was protected by GalFed and men rode her along her jagged path, spraying her eggs to keep down fungus and scraping calcareous deposits off her arteries.

Since she did not expect to stay long, Elena carried one coverall in her waterproof bag. It was of the good grey stuff GalFed fitted its surveyor teams with, and she had painted a pattern of leaves and flowers all over it; it was sufficiently incongruous in the tinny dayroom, lined in polythene, where one lamp hung overhead and every once in a while the amoeboid shape of a cell or parasite, swimming free in tissue fluid, flattened itself against the translucent wall.

There was room for only one more at the table; the men's heads almost knocked against hers: Roberts, the research geologist, whose beard bristled an inch away; Zaf hanging in coils from some kind of rack and looking like a caduceus; Dai Jones, a little dark wiry man, the only miner of the lot; and round-faced Takashima, the heir to an electronics firm who was taking a look at one of the sources of his components. Hearts beat around them in endless pulses of disharmony.

:You have all been happy here, Zaf?:

:Oh indeed, all Solthrees love the Amsu. For myself of course it is east, west, home it best. That is an apothegm of our philosopher-king Nyf.:

:It's well-known; his fame travels far.:

:Now you are laughing at me, Elena.:

:Never, Zaf. You know I don't behave that way. I am always happy to learn how closely distant peoples think.:

She said aloud, "Perhaps you know why I am here. You can see I have never boarded an Amsu before, but I am taking over liaison in this sector because your regular, Par Singri, is ill with fungous bronchitis and I am subbing."

"I thought Zaf was our liaison," Jones said.

"Between you and Amsuwlle, yes. Here I am liaison between the Amsu and Zaf and this end and GalFed at the other." She squeezed the last drop from her bulb of tea and refilled it.

"What's the emergency?"

"There have been delays in rendezvous with ore carriers. Amsunli was four standard days late on her last trip and Amsusdag two days."

"What's that supposed to mean? Hell, you get delays in all kinds of space shipping, and the Amsu aren't machines, they're animals."

"They have been charted for fifty years ... in the last three years more than half the deliveries have been delayed. And there is more. Twelve days ago Amsutru was going to meet with the ore carrier *Raghavendra*. Then nine days late she is found squashed in a mess against Asteroid 6337 with her crew dead, every one, and also a prematurely hatched larva burrowing through her siphon."

A small silence. Jones clasped his hands tightly. "Amsutru? My God, Jack Tanner was on her. I knew him."

"No man has ever died on one before ... and, you know, there are not that many Amsu – never more than twenty-five at once."

"A freak accident," Roberts said.

"Yes, maybe."

"But you're here. You expect something to happen here."

"Oh, I hope not. But ... you are thirteen days out and twelve to go ... you are eighteen hours behind schedule. You have been aware of that, haven't you?"

"Sure we're aware of it! We get course checks on radio from the spacelight transmitters."

"What do you expect to do about it, Dr Cortez?" Jones asked. "We can't give the old lady a kick in the shins."

"Has anything odd happened?"

"Not that we know. We figured everything was going all right."

"That's likely true. But still, Amsutru is gone, and you can understand why GalFed is concerned."

"But what do you intend to do?" Roberts asked.

"Well, no one has ever turned an Amsu around, have they? Maybe we will not have any more delay, and I will just look around and have a nice ride."

Takashima laughed. "I think you will end up doing jobs like us, Dr Cortez. Amsuwlle has no room for tourists."

"But if there's trouble?" Roberts persisted.

"I would hope, gentlemen, that we would all be able to get the hell off."

"Well, Zaf ..." They were alone, and Elena did not feel she had done very well. She was a small dark woman from Venezuela, very delicately boned, with thick black hair falling to her shoulders. Her ancestry was a mixture of all the local peoples, and her skin colour balanced light brown with terra cotta. Happily mongrelized, she had the knack of making herself at home among very disparate peoples, but she did not normally handle the complaints of ore shippers, especially ones who shipped on Leviathans. "I am a fish out of water," she said.

"I think you have another image in mind," said Zaf, as Amsuwlle's liquid pulses thudded.

"Well, I am very ... no, I am not discouraged. This is odd. I feel quite calm."

"Good."

"But I should not be. I heartily dislike this assignment –"

"Since I asked for help, I am afraid I am to blame."

"Oh no! It is Par Singri who was stupid enough to get sick. He would have done better here. I enjoy being with you, and I have nothing against Amsuwlle, but I do not like to be in places where things are always throbbing and bubbling ... yet I am calm." She clasped her wrist and studied her watch. "My pulse in normal."

"Then I suppose that is not so good."

"Now you are laughing at me ... but I admit I am being irrational." She looked around till her eye lit on the waste container with its empty bulbs. "Some kind of drug? I don't know which one of those is mine."

"There are no drugs on board – oh Roberts brought some Banaquil for his nerves, but he stopped using it after the first few days, and no one has touched it. It is a prescription drug. He considers it a weakness to take pills and had only enough to last the trip."

"I have no drugs except a little painkiller for an ear infection because I was afraid being underwater would start it again ... but I feel a little sleepy ... and a little dull. Have the men behaved strangely? Have they changed at all since they came on board?"

"They don't quarrel at all and that is strange for Solthrees — but on the Amsu they are never together long enough."

"Do you feel different since you have been here?"

He shifted his tanks. "Let me damn well tell you I miss my mud, and this synthetic stuff is wishy-washy to a disgusting degree."

Elena laughed, but when he had gone, she collect four of the discarded bulbs and took them to her cabin.

She sat on her bunk and looked at them. There was a drop or two in each. *Elena, you are just being stupid.* She turned the faucet set into the living wall, drew a little water into a cup and tasted it. It was deliciously cold and good, otherwise not unusual in any way. Yet, she did not feel quite herself. *Of course you should feel tired from what you have been through, and any other effects are probably from spinning on this creature. Even your old friend Zaf thinks you are an idiot.*

:I do not.:

:Now you are prying!:

:Elena dear, however stupid you may think you feel, it is a fact that Amsutru got lost and we are behind schedule. You were chosen to come here on very good ground and even the wildest suspicion you have must be checked out.:

:Good, Zaf. Now I may let my fantasy run wild ... you know the Limbo is pacing us?:

:I am aware of it. How long is Threyha giving us her kind attention?:

:Until I can find her an answer, querido.:

:I hope she will not be bored on such a long slow trip.:

:Ask her how to modify our equipment to test the water for Banaquil and also three of four of the main tranquillizer groups. Try out the liquid in these bulbs and also the main wa-

ter supply ... and oh yes, we do have distilled water for emergencies?:

:Indeed, but a canister will take quite a lot of your cabin space.:

:I am travelling light, and I am not expecting company.:

There was nothing else to do but try to sleep. Even with the drowsiness it was not so easy with all the distractions in the very walls.

Then think about water.

What the Amsu produced was regularly tested – between trips. On board it was Zaf's task to make sure it was maintained to GalFed specs, but he checked for substances poisonous to Solthrees and his own Yefni, not psychotropic drugs that wouldn't have any effect on him.

Roberts' Banaquil had not been touched. Outside source. She threw out politics, plots, and pirates. The arrangements with the Amsu were the results of agreements among many peoples; the profits were parcelled out equitably. She knew the sector very well; it was thoroughly patrolled, and local rivalries kept to a minimum. No one had ever stolen ore. The Amsu were happy to be well cared for; they were not particularly intelligent, but they had some ESP and knew ways of containing and rejecting substances – and persons – they thought might do them harm.

She went to sleep, finally, among the bubblings and thudding, the pale wash of phosphorescence over the walls, the huge living engine of a sentient being.

A call to the unconscious woke her, and she opened her airlock. It was a tiny chamber almost fully occupied by Zaf, coiled around a canister of distilled water.

"There is Banaquil in the water supply, five milligrams per litter, and in all the bulbs too. Nothing else, you may be thankful."

"I may, but I think I am not. Who its putting it in?"

"Elena, this is hard to explain, Amsuwlle is synthesizing it. Who could put it in when Roberts' supply has not been touched? The others don't even know of it."

"But ... why? And how did she get it? All the wastes are recycled. From sweat?"

"I can show you, I think. Will you let me squeeze into your cabin for a moment?"

Inside, he bent his head low and with the sharp tip of a horn drew a gash between two of his black rings.

"Zaf!"

"Don't be frightened. I heal fast." He pulled the cut apart with a sinuous movement, and a globule of viscous yellow blood dropped slowly to the floor. It lay there a moment, spread slightly, and in a few moments sank without leaving a mark, absorbed. "Roberts cut himself on one of his instruments. Oh, nine or ten days ago ... she know of his drugs, and his nervousness, through me, probably ..."

"And picked it up from that tiny specimen?"

"Very simply. She tracks ore files by traces as small as one microgram. She is just as sensitive within."

"But why?"

"Oh dear ... can you not guess? Because of the quality on which all of our mining operations depend." He gathered his coils together and began to move backward out of the cabin. "Amsuwlle loves to please."

"Wait!" She gave him a hard look, very difficult because the eye band ran around his head, and there was not place to bring a focus to bear. "You know of such things that have happened before."

"That's true, I don't deny it."

"And you have reported them?"

"Of course, Elena! They proved of great interest to anatomists and psychologists ... administration did not find them worrisome."

"What kind?"

"One of the first Amsu we used grew an extra heart to deliver more heat and oxygen to this part of her body for our sake – and incorporated the change in her genetic material ... would you find that worrisome?"

"I think ... one day, perhaps, it might be."

"Possibly. Now I will let you finish your sleep. I must work."

"Wait. What about the Banaquil?"

"It can be got rid of – with tact – and do you think it wise? Of course it cannot have been in the water longer than ten days, and there is no worry about withdrawal symptoms with such small amounts ... and the men are disturbed enough now. Whatever you choose."

Elena paused. "You must help me decide. If things are left as they are, we may fall further behind."

"Something must change. We have introduced a new element – yourself, my dear. And I doubt – I do not know what an opium den is, but you have a thought about men lying around asleep – I doubt that is what happened with all the other delays. The drug is only one factor in this unhappy situation." The air-lock door closed behind him.

And beyond it came a furious thrashing and thumping.

:Zaf, what is it? What's wrong?:

:She refuses to open up. I cannot get through the valve.:

:Come back in here.:

:I am required to take accounting of the stores, and believe me, you and I will not be comfortable together in one cabin for any length of time.:

:I am not very comfortable myself right now. I will come out.:

:If you wish, though I doubt it will help. Bring your oxygen.:

The crew quarters were in a storage area of the posterior intestinal canal, a blind sac divided mainly by inert plastics. A little airlock with an artificial opening had been built into each cabin. Elena's lock had two other openings: one to the great water conduit Zaf was trying to get out to.

:Go through to the other lock,: Elena said.

:That would be difficult. It opens outward and it is full of water.: He hunched up a coil and slammed it against the rubbery valve into Amsuwlle's belly. Elena ran her fingers over the puckered surface trying to find give in it. There was none.

:Why is she doing this?: She was not afraid of enclosed spaces, and for the moment was too curious to be frightened.

:I am trying to find out, if can be allowed to think.:

:Think good, Zaf. Think mud.:

:I am going to make mud if I don't get out of here pretty damn fast.:

For all that he looked like a cross between a worm and a python Zaf was vastly different from either. He could wind but not slither: his integument was a single helix of cartilage, a powerful and fairly rigid casing with not much give between its whorls. His two horns curved one to the front and one to the rear, and on his home planet he wound through the mud like a corkscrew or a post-hole digger; the muscular black spring of his body was strong enough to pierce shale and sandstone as well. He could rip Amsuwlle's internal tissues more easily than he had slit his own.

Perhaps that consideration reached some important ganglion in Amsuwlle's constitution, for after a moment the valve opened with an elastic blap and a rush of water and debris slammed against them. Zaf whirled away to his tasks. :*Not very polite,*: was his only comment.

:*But you haven't told me why!*:

:*Oh Elena! can you not understand? She needs us!*:

Elena wrung out her leotard and wrapped herself in a blanket.

She needs us. Us = Jones, Roberts, Takashima – and Zaf. They serve, she provides. She does not need me. I am the interloper (and keep it down and far back now (who may take them away)). And Zaf? He is disturbed. Can I trust him, my friend of so many years? Yet he called for help, he brought me here – and who else is there?

"There is nothing in the men's psych reports to suggest abnormal bonding with the Amsu." She and Zaf were alone in the dayroom. Since there was no real night or morning, everyone chose his own schedule. Elena drank coffee sparingly and ate something that seemed to be moistened chicken feed. She had no intention of living solely on distilled water derived from recycled wastes.

"Of course not. They are all within normal range. Roberts is thirty-eight years old, a bachelor, helps support old parents, lady friend nine years no immediate plan to marry, takes pleasure in playing music on some kind of blowpipe with group of people, mild frustration and resentment common to age and situation – among Solthrees.

"Takashima is twenty-seven, married with two children, overindulges in food, generally content, only complaint he has no one to play Japanese chess with.

"Dai Jones, forty-one, comes from large family now scattered, impoverished background, hard worker, divorced no children, unfortunate experiences with women, feels or is unattractive to them.

"Make of that what you will, I don't know what it means. I have no time to lie in loops and chatter. I must work."

"I will come with you."

She followed, bubbling and gasping in the cold vaults, while he zapped suspicious-looking amoebae with antibiotic bullets and used a strigil like a giant squeegee to scrape and collect calcium fibres from the walls of the pale blood vessels that Amsuwlle obligingly emptied for him one by one.

:*Zaf, there are no psych reports on the Amsu.*:

:*There was no need for them as long as there was no danger.*:

:*Did you never try to find out?*:

: *Oh, I ask always, but she has not much to say. No language! In feeling it is always: nice, good, or: pain, heaviness. They reproduce slowly, very slowly, and of the two eggs Amsuwlle is carrying one is malformed and will abort. Sometimes ... there is almost something like "thank you". They are not very strong for the terrible conditions they live in ... look, here is a softness in the wall.... I think she is developing an aneurysm. It may burst.*:

:*Could that kill her?*:

:*In the artery from the heart that feeds her principal ganglion, yes. This is not a serious one. We can have it fixed.*:

:*But Zaf, don't you realize —*:

:*In a moment, Elena. Come with me.*: He squeezed through a tiny opening and pulled her after.

Of the great and marvellous chambers Amsuwlle contained there was no end. For all the freakish system, she was only the elaboration of a very simple animal found in small on many worlds. She was essentially a skin on the outside and an alimentary canal within; she had no limbs to move and her musculature was all visceral: it served mainly her hearts, intestines, blood vessels, and reproductive organs. Between her gut and her horny epithelium were tremendous sinuses of almost liquid protoplasm, broadly netted with cables of nerve and vein and swimming with strange arrow-shaped creatures of pale mauve, a metre long and with luminous nuclei.

:Mesenchyme,: Zaf said. *:They do odd jobs and turn into specialized cells when Amsuwlle needs them.:*

To Elena the diaphanous swimmers seemed like choir-boys serving an altar, and the vast cavity with its glimmering lights and pumping organ hearts trembled in the atmosphere of an ancient cathedral.

:This is beautiful.:

:Yes, even a Yefni may admire it.:

:I wonder if it was an aneurysm that killed Amsutru.:

:Oh, Elena, how you must spoil things! That kind of serious malfunction never occurs except in very old animals, and we never ride them beyond a certain age. A minor one such as she has now she could heal herself.:

:Still –:

Something grabbed her hard round the middle and squeezed.

Zaf swung his lantern round. A girdle of mauve iridescence, its nucleus elongated and writhing, was doing its best to divide her in two. Zaf bent his head and hooked it off with one horn, snicked a bladed claw from his tail and sheared it neatly in half. The halves, forgetting their errand, dashed off in opposite directions.

Elena's mask had slipped, she was doubled and choking. Zaf slapped it on true, and she howled inward a lungful of air. Then he dumped his light and scraper and looped a coil around her. A flock of devilish choirboys dove at them with solid thumps. Zaf twitched his blade, the arrows retreated a space and swiftly coalesced into an enveloping mantle to engulf foreign bodies. Zaf freed Elena and butted her away; she drifted outward through the light jelly till she found a handhold on a minutely pulsing capillary. Her own pulses were roaring, and she watched the battle through sparkles in her eyes, in the light of the mesenchyme itself. Protoplasm, no matter how ill intentioned, was no worthy adversary for any Yefni. He ripped and slashed with horns and tail till they exploded in quivering spheres and expanded, a liquid nebula, outward to darkness.

Still in a fury, he found Elena, coiled her, and spun her toward the valve. It did not open at his touch; he wrenched it viciously with his horns, and it shrank bleeding milky essence.

He watched in silence as she lay twisted on the cabin floor, vomiting.

After a little while she pulled herself up and said, "I am better now. Get out and let me change."

"Change now. I am all modesty." He shoved his head among his coils.

She coughed and then sighed. "Oh, Zaf."

When she was dressed, she said, "I have started something and now it is too much, you know. I should not have come."

"Perhaps."

"But I am come, I am here. Now I better finish."

"Yes," he said sadly.

Jones slaps his hand on the cool melon-wall, no favours asked and none given, old lady ...

finning his way through nave and apse while the hearts boom like organs. Roberts does not ask whether the whale loves Jonah, or consciously wish to write a poem or hymn rather than a paper on the alchemy of its digestive processes, but he does not hurry....

Takashima, adored only son of the magnate, is free for the moment of that grim warlord of the assembly line, cheerfully navigates a monster of ancient myth and finds her curiously gentle....

Gentle.

Elena sighed.

"I must tell the men ... something. They should leave, and I have no authority to force them off. Listen – I think the hearts are changing rhythm. I must be mistaken; I could not have got to know them that well."

"Oh, but you did. Everyone does. I told Amsuwlle to reroute the blood away from her weakened artery."

"That was kind of you, under the circumstances." Elena said.

"Under the circumstances we need all the safety we can get."

"Lady, you must think we're fools. We can't leave the ore here for anybody to take. " Jones was working at keeping his voice down.

"The *Limbo* is pacing us. she'll make sure nobody takes the ore. Nobody has even tried for forty years."

"The *Limbo*? Spying?"

"No. Only making sure we are safe. We are not safe Amsuwlle has become a hostile environment. Zaf has told you."

"There was no hostility till you came," Roberts said.

"Then let us say she does not care for me. I am the wrong person for the job, and it was a mistake to send me. I cannot help that, but it seems to be true. I came in peace, but she seems to consider me a threat because I must ask you to leave if there is any danger here. She cannot bear that because she depends on you, perhaps too strongly. If that has made her hostile, then she is a threat, and I must ask you to leave even if it is my fault. I cannot force you. All I can do is ask, even beg. We must get off!"

"Even at the cost of everything we'd have to leave?"

She held out her hands. "I tell you, there is no other choice!"

Roberts gave the table a hard slap. "Get off if you like, and take anyone you want with you. I waited three years for this chance, and I'm not giving it up now." He got up and left. Jones followed with a dark angry face.

Takashima shrugged in confusion. "I don't know what is happening, but I like life. I help anyway I can."

"You can," Zaf said. "Contact the *Limbo* by radio, tell them to alert the ESP and stand by. I will instruct you, but I think it best that I don't try to do it myself right now."

"This is stupid." Elena wiped her forehead. "Threyha's one of the strongest ESPs in the galaxy. She should be alert."

"You know how Khagodi are. She is far too busy to send her friend Zaf little messages of love. I am lucky if she gives me a tenth of her mind for a moment once in a while." He did not have enough power to reach the ship by himself and was sensitive about it.

"I am foolish and ungrateful. I did not thank you for saving my life."

"Disregard it. Just arrange your mind for me, please. It is confusion."

"I would like to arrange it for myself."

"If you wish to finish the work, my dear, and give Threyha a pro tem report, you had better do it before all hell explodes."

"Yes ... I know." The pulses and their cells were butting against the walls.

Elena rapped her head with her knuckles. "When I came on board, the men realized they might have to leave, and they became quite upset ... in the case of Roberts the journey was a great privilege, for Takashima

a holiday he longed to have, for Jones his main liveli-
hood. That is reasonable. But then also, I believe, they
suffered from the last twinges of an old Solthree super-
stition that a women brought bad luck to a men's working ship ... and now, in a way, they have made it come
true ...

"Amsuwlle has just enough sense to absorb this ... and
she dearly loves, as you say, to please them. You became
the unconscious channel and reinforcement of their un-
easiness – of course you cannot help that – and she became disturbed. She finds all of this feeling an irritant
and wants to eject the cause of it, me, and the instrument, you. That is simple emotional mechanics."

"They are the ones whose emotions began this cycle,
and she is not attacking them."

"I think you have a different relationship with her.
Theirs is a more primitive male-female relationship,
based on a psychodynamic concept of Solthrees and a
few other races, they call it Edipo – oh, I am so tired I
can't remember what they call it in *lingua* – yes, Oedipus
complex." Zaf absorbed that a burble of gills. "How
amusing." He was an egg laying hermaphrodite.

"Yes, very." She rubbed her eyes. "Has Takashima
reached them?"

"He is broadcasting. Go on."

"That is all there is to say about the situation here
right now. It will clear up when we leave. But it is the future I am worried about. Men tend and use machines
and think of them as if they are female; they ride and
tend the Amsu as if they are machines – but Amsuwlle is
no machine, she is living matter, she adapts for them,
grows extra hearts, redirects her blood supply, her musculature, her liquids...not in normal evolutionary patterns, nor by the eugenic principles men use to breed
cattle, but only because their attentions give her a feeling

of well-being ... she does not adapt for her survival, but for theirs. Will a redistributed circulatory pattern improve the quality of her offspring? If she synthesizes drugs, what will that do to her heart actions?... On Sol Three they breed an animal called a dog for household pet, and sometimes a dog will attach itself so strongly to its owner that when he dies it will not eat or sleep but simply pine and languish until it dies as well. Then men write tearful songs about the faithfulness of the poor creature, but it has simply been destructive of itself and disturbed the evolutionary pattern of its species....

"Fifty years ago there were between eighteen and twenty-two Amsu circling Apikiki. Every few years the breeding cycle slows down and they conjugate to interchange genetic material – but fifty years in the progress of even such a big, slow animal should give you more than your present population of twenty-five with all the scraping of arteries and egg spraying and patching of aneurysms ... only two eggs in this huge beast, and one is malformed. What does she care? Men are caring for her, and they are satisfied with what they get. Eggs can be placed anywhere, and if necessary men will lead her to the ice and the ores –"

Before she could say another word they floated gently to the centre of the room.

What –

And slammed against the side wall. Elena cried out at the bruising of her shoulder; Zaf had been driven into a knot and was struggling to untangle himself. Vibration pushed them jaggedly to the opposite wall, then sliding into the ceiling.

:She has stopped spinning.:

Zaf untwined himself; Elena wiped blood off her mouth from her bitten tongue, droplets hovered in a cloud round her face. "What?" Zaf grabbed at his tank, floating a metre away. *:Breaking radio contact ... shooting her jets in irregular vapour pattern.:* He snorted an air bubble out of the tube. "White noise field."

"Do something, Zaf!"

"Like what?"

The hearts went boom, whicker, thack-thack; the mesenchyme cells butted their snouts on the walls; the waters roared all about them.

"Takashima?"

"He has air, but the radio is under a heap of wet gravel. The others are knocking about in the jelly near the egg chamber."

"Those things will get at them."

"She has no time to bother with that." Zaf hooked himself onto a handhold, yanked open a locker door, and got out the cauterizer he would have used to repair the weakened artery. He slipped a new power cell into it.

"What are you doing?"

Taking a precaution." He ran the white-hot beam around the frame of the plastic cabin door.

"But, Zaf, you're sealing us –"

"I am sealing her out." The valve beyond opened, and water struck like a fist. The door buckled, shuddered, and held. "Just in time."

The lights went out. "Ventilation will go to next," Zaf said. "You will want oxygen." He found tanks in the locker. The luminous arrows, colours of lightning, swarmed and swarmed outside the cabin.

Elena sucked on the dead air of the tank. *:It is a good thing you know what to do in emergencies, Zaf.:*

He said nothing to that, and perhaps it was not the time to ask how many such emergencies there had been. Amsuwlle's entire orchestration of living matter, hearts, waters, cells rock and ice fragments, was breaking against the frail plastic shell.

Another lurch and the sealed door became their floor.

:She is changing course.:

:Can the Limbo *follow?:*

:If Takashima made contact – oh, Great Heavens, she is expelling the faulty egg to lead them off course!:

A wrenching shudder filled the whole body –

:– and oh, the Heavenly Shell, the other has gone with it, it has gone....:

The light came on, the air freshened, the internal tempest died down into the endless beating of hearts. Floor became floor, and Amsuwlle spun to her own unknown destination. She had made a choice and had chosen her crew.

Zaf, in a rage, jittered up and down, bouncing on the spring of his body. "She has lost them both! She is shattered and wrenched, and I am done!"

"Zaf, please!"

"Everything is ruined, and I am lost! Oh, why could you not have stopped this?" He sprang toward her and ripped off her mask. "Why?"

"Zaf!"

"The eggs are gone, we are lost, going somewhere out into space where we will all starve before she lets us go – no *Limbo*, no radio, no base – all my responsibility – and no help! All you can do is say please, please!"

Elena, completely disoriented, could only stare at him.

His tail rose, the blade snicked and touched her chin. "Look at me. Have you ever read my psych report? You did not think it necessary? It says I am a man of great courage, intelligence and resourcefulness, very sympathetic to and fitted for work on Amsu. On Amsu. You understand? Do you see me sitting in an office at Galfed Central with my coils in knots and my sulphur mud dripping all over? Or hopping about city roads like –

like your toy, a pogo stick? or flying an airship or starship – without hands? Do you?"

She said nothing, and Zaf, her friend of twelve years, drew a light line with his blade under her chin toward the windpipe. "You do not understand."

She found a voice. "Do all those other ESP liaisons feel so lonely and unfitted on all those other Amsu, and patch them up and play down the reports, and ride them for their pride?"

"I am the only man of my world to become a GalFed official."

"And my family worked half their lives to send one of them to the stars." She put her hand on his head between the horns and pushed the sharp slicer out of her mind. "Oh, Zaf, you asked me to come."

"I asked you ..." the blade did not waver, "and Par Singri is not sick; he is only a little man who thinks little square thoughts and feels he has done something brilliant when he fits them into a big square. I persuaded Threyha to send you ... because I saw how things were going...you were my friend ... and I thought you would be able to stop it before everything got ruined."

She tried not to think of her husband at GalFed Central or her family who had worked so hard in a hard land; her hand rested lightly on his head. "I am sorry for Amsuwlle."

"I am not. She would not have cared if she had killed me, and I have thought only of myself." The blade withdrew and he bowed his head. "That is what is so terrible." He flung his head from side to side. "The eggs are lost and we are going nowhere! And – oh, Elena, the men! They are still in the egg chamber!"

Both of them were clinging to the tattered rim of the chamber wall; their oxygen tanks were nearly empty, and they were shivering almost hysterically with chill. They would not have been there, or anywhere else, if part of Amsuwlle's intestinal tract had not given way when the eggs were so violently ejected and filled the egg chamber and blocked the now flaccid ovipositor with rock, silt, and coagulating protoplasm. The stuff had not quite stopped and was still pushing outward with slow but glacial force.

Zaf wound his length about Jones and Roberts and hooked his way by head and tail like a climber of ice, in slow steps backward: his mind, wide open, broadcast his misery and despair.

Back in the day room they stared at each other with haggard faces.

"I suppose you were right," Roberts said. "We should have tried to get off earlier."

"It doesn't matter," Elena said dully. She sighed. "We'd better see if we can't get Takashima."

The room was a mess; Zaf had used his blade to re-open the door, and no one worried about locks and valves any more. Locker doors had broken open with the violence of Amsuwlle's writhings; tanks and canisters were dented or burst. "We don't have much food," Jones said. Packages had spilled, their contents fouled with splatters of mud. "It won't matter for very long, will it?"

:Oh, don't give up hope quite so soon, my dears.:

Jones yelped. "Ohmigawd, what's that?"

"Be at ease, gentlemen," Zaf said without much relief. "That is Threyha."

Once again the spin stopped, and they floated; once again the siphon extruded dutifully and down through it went the rush of waters. Amsuwlle was being obedient again.

It was not easy to be anything but obedient to Threyha. In a few minutes she gave them her image in the sinus leading from the siphon. The floor sagged from her weight, upward of six hundred kilos, and there was no room for her height of three metres. She simply nudged the ceiling with her scaly pointed jaw and it shrank away, thumped the floor with her heavy tail and it firmed and flattened under her. *:I am not coming any farther or the poor thing will have another rupture.:* She smoothed down her opalescent scales and stood properly erect. *:And I must get back to my tank.?:* She was amphibian, but preferred water. *:Collect Takashima and come to me.:*

"How –"

:Very easily. When she let go that second egg and all that loose protoplasm, she left a beautiful trail ... and when a Khagodi cannot outthink an Amsu, it will be a wet day in the desert. Now hurry please.:

While they were gathering themselves together as best they could, she got a good hard hold on Amsuwlle's ganglia and nerve networks and sent her slowly back on course. Then she flashed a few orders, and the mesenchyme slavishly arranged themselves in neat layers to replace valves and membranes. *:What a mess. She is not going to be the same.:*

"Neither will we," said Zaf.

:That can be discussed later. You are going to ride her to rendezvous.:

They left Zaf in the day room. "I suppose I will not see you again for a long time, Elena," he said sorrowfully.

:You will see each other in fifteen days at debriefing,: Threyha said from the entrance. *:Sentimental farewells are not in order.:*

There were no sentimental farewells for Amsuwlle.

Elena and the men dragged themselves aboard the *Limbo* without a word.

Threyha did not have or need a voice. Her telepathy was a stentorian bellow, but always under perfect control. While she was still in the lock of her tank, waiting for it to fill with her own world's mixture of waters, she directed a beam of thought. *:Elena.:*

:Leave me alone. You deceived me. Par Singri is not sick.: She was scrubbing herself with a cloth, trying to get off the layers of silt, sweat, dried protoplasm and other accretions of her term on Amsuwlle.

:Zaf was too proud to ask you for help personally when he was so frightened, and I wanted him on egalitarian terms with you.:

:Now you will have him punished.:

:Of course not. But I cannot allow him to make himself any sicker. I have a good psychman, a methane breather with eighteen legs and blue eyes in his knees, who will cure him of the notion that his shape is too peculiar to be of use to GalFed.....: She waved her arms through the water to freshen it. *:This stuff is always stale slop no matter how they aerate it.... Spare me from people with feelings of inferiority! Only man of his planet in GalFed! We have invited fifteen of his cousins to join us; likely they will accept, and then he will boss them unmercifully.:*

:What of me? I have not done very well.: She thought of the great wounded creature, half killed with kindness, wrenched out of shape and aching with bewilderment.

:You spoke when necessary and shut up otherwise. It's what you are paid for. I will put forward your recommendation that we implant the Amsu with robot monitors and except for emergencies service them at rendezvous. Otherwise let them take care of themselves. Now you deserve a good sleep, because in twelve hours you are going to board Amsumar: we have a low-priority emergency —:

"Oh, no!"

:– from the ESP, who happens to be my nephew; he is a bright sensible boy but a bit frantic. It will take you a day or two to cool that, and we will be back in good time to meet with Zaf and Amsuwlle. You would say there is nothing like getting into the water again to cure a fear of drowning.:

:Threyha, why do you not simply take over the universe?:

:I hate authority. And of course no other Khagodi would obey me. One last thing: aside from my nephew the crew on Amsumar are all female beetle types from Procyon-something, and you will not have to worry about being considered a – what do you call it? Jinx or Jonah?:

"One is as good as another," said Elena, and fell asleep.

1973

THE MILITARY HOSPITAL

The helicopter moved through the city in the air-lane between skyscrapers. It was on autopilot, pre-set course, and there was no one to squint down the canyons of the streets where the life-mass seethed. Children looked up at it with dull eyes; if it had come lower they would have stoned or shot at it. The armoured cars that burrowed among them were scratched and pocked from their attacks.

Fresh and smooth, dressed in crisp white, DeLazzari came into the Control Room at the top of the Hospital. He had had a week off, he was on for three; he ran the Hospital, supervised nurse-patient relationships, directed the sweepers in the maintenance of sterility, and monitored the pile. He took over this function wherever he was told to go, but he particularly liked the Military Hospital because it was clean, roomy, and had very few patients. He was a stocky man with thick black hair, broad wings of moustache, and skin the colour of baked earth; he had the blood of all nations in him. "The bad blood of all nations," he would add with a laugh if he felt like impressing one of the trots Mama Rakosy sent up to the apartment, though it was rare he felt like impressing anyone. He was sworn to forego women, drugs and liquor for three weeks, so he switched on the big external screen and dumped out of his bag the cigars, candy and gum that would sustain him while he watched the course of the helicopter over the city.

A trasher's bomb went off in one of the buildings; daggers of glass blew out singing, and sliced at the scalps and shoulders of a knot of demonstrators clumped at its base; a fragment of concrete hurled outward and grazed the helicopter, then fell to dent a fibreglass helmet and concuss the bike-rider who fell from his machine and lay unconscious under the bruising feet; the wounded demonstrators scattered or crawled, leaving their placards, and others took their places, raising neon-coloured cold-light standards of complicated symbols; they camped in the table-sized space, oblivious to bloody glass, hard-hats with crossbows, skinheads with slingshots, longhairs, freaks, mohicans, children, and above all the whoop and howl of police sirens coming up.

The helicopter moved north and away; the armoured cars butted their way through, into less crowded streets where merchants did business across wickets in iron cages in which one touch of a floor button dropped steel shutters and made a place impregnable fast enough to cut a slice off anyone who got in the way. Farther north the City Hospital and the Central Police Depot formed two wings of a great moth-shaped complex webbed about by stalled paddy wagons and ambulances.

DeLazzari grinned. In City Hospital twelve Directors manned the Control Room, endlessly profane and harried. Shop was always depleted: the sweepers rusted and ground down from lack of parts and the nurses were obsolete and inefficient. Only the Doctors moved at great speed and in Olympian calm.

He switched on his own O.R. screen. Doctors were already closing around the operating table, waiting.

They were silver, slab-shaped, featureless. They drew power from a remote source, and nobody he knew had any idea where it was. They had orders and carried them out – or perhaps they simply did what they chose. He had never been in their physical presence, nor wanted to be.

The helicopter was passing between blank-walled buildings where the dead were stored in very small vaults, tier upon tier upon tier; at street level the niches reserved for floral tributes were empty except for wire frames to which a few dried leaves and petals clung trembling in the down-draft from the rotors. North beyond that in the concrete plaza the racers were heating up for the evening, a horde endlessly circling.

But the city had to end in the north at the great circle enclosing the Military Hospital. It had no wall, no road, no entrance at ground level. What it had was a force field the helicopter had to rise steeply to surmount. Within, for a wall it had a thicket of greenery half a mile deep going all the way round; outside the field there was a circuit of tumbled masonry pieces, stones, burnt sticks, as if many ragged armies had tried to storm it and retreated, disgusted and weary.

Inside there was no great mystery. The Military Hospital healed broken soldiers from distant and ancient wars; the big circular building had taken no architectural prizes, and on its rolling greens two or three stumbling patients were being supported on their rounds by nurses. Like all Directors DeLazzari tended to make himself out a minor Dracula; like all the rest his power lay in the modicum of choice he had among the buttons he pushed.

The helicopter landed on its field and discharged its cell, a Life Unit in which a dying soldier lay enmeshed;

it took on another cell, containing another soldier who had been pronounced cured and would be discharged germ-free into his theatre of war; it was also boarded by the previous Director, pocket full of credits and head full of plans for a good week.

The Hospital doors opened, the cell rolled through them down a hall into an anteroom where it split; a wagon emerged from it carrying the patient and his humming, flickering life-system, the anteroom sealed itself, flooded with aseptic sprays and drained, washing away blood-traces; the O.R. sweeper removed the wet packs from the ruined flesh and dropped them on the floor, which dissolved them. In the operating room the i.v. system was pumping, the monitors pulsed, the Doctors activated their autoclaves in one incandescent flash and then extruded a hundred tentacles, probes, knives, sensors, and flexed them; their glitter and flash was almost blinding in the harsh light. DeLazzari was obliged to watch them; he hated it, and they needed no light. It was provided on demand of the Supervisors and Directors Union, though if machines chose to go renegade there was very little the Supervisors and Directors could say or do.

Doctors had never gone renegade. Neither had sweepers or nurses; it was a delicious myth citizens loved to terrify themselves with, perhaps because they resented the fact that madness should be reserved for people. DeLazzari thought that was pretty funny and he was scared too.

The O.R. sweeper sprayed himself (DeLazzari thought of it as delousing), the doors opened, the sweeper pushed in the body, still housing its low flicker of life, removed the attachments and set it on the table. The Doctors reattached what was needed; the sweeper backed into a corner and turned his own power down.

DeLazzari flicked a glance at the indicator and found it correct.

One Doctor swabbed the body with a personal nozzle and began to remove steel fragments from belly and groin, another slit the chest and reached in to remove bone slivers from the left lung, a third trimmed the stump of the right forefinger and fitted a new one from the Parts Bank, a fourth tied off and removed torn veins from the thighs, all without bumping head, shoulders, or elbows because they had none, a fifth kept the throat clear, a sixth gave heart massage, the first opened the belly and cut out a gangrened bowel section, the third sewed and sealed the new right forefinger and as an afterthought trimmed the nail, the fifth, still watching every breath, peeled back sections of the scalp and drilled holes in the skull. All in silence except for the soft clash and ringing of sensors, knives, and probes. Blood splashed; their body surfaces repelled it in a mist of droplets and the floor washed it away.

The sweeper turned his power up on some silent order and fetched a strange small cage of silver wires. The fifth Doctor took it, placed it over the soldier's head, and studied its nodes as coordinates in relation to the skull. Then he spoke at last. "Awaken," he said.

DeLazzari gave a hoarse nervous laugh and whispered, "*Let there be light.*" The boy's eyelids flickered and opened. The eyes were deep blue; the enlarged pupils contracted promptly and at an equal rate. DeLazzari wondered, as always, if he were conscious enough to be afraid he was lying in an old cemetery among the gravestones. Silver graves.

"Are you awake?" The voice was deep, God-the-Father-All-Powerful. The Doctor checked the nose tube and cleared the throat. "Max, are you awake?"

"Yes ... yes ... yes ..."

"Can you answer questions?"

"Yes."

"Recording for psychiatric report." He extruded a fine probe and inserted it into the brain. "What do you see? Tell me what you see."

"I see ... from the top of the Ferris wheel I can see all the boats in the harbour, and when I come down in a swoop all the people looking up ..."

The probe withdrew and re-entered. "What do you see now, Max?"

"My father says they're not sweet peas, but a wild-flower, like a wild cousin of the sweet pea, toadflax, some people call them butter-and-eggs.... '*Scrophulari-aceae linaria vulgaris* is the big name for them, Max, and that *vulgaris* means common, but they're not so common anymore....'"

Probe.

"... something like the fireworks I used to watch when I was a kid, but they're not fireworks, they're the real thing, and they turn the sky on fire...."

"Area established."

Probe.

"One eye a black hole and the kid lying across her with its skull, with its skull, with its skull, I said Chris-sake, Yvon, why'd you have to? Yvon? why'd you have to? why? he said ohmigod Max how was I to know whether they were? Max? how was I to know whether?"

The probe tip burned, briefly.

"Yes, Max? He said: 'how was I to know whether' what?"

"Know what? Who's he? I don't know what you're talking about."

DeLazzari watched the probes insinuate the cortex and

withdraw. The Doctors pulled at the associations, unravelling a tangled skein; they didn't try to undo all the knots, only the most complicated and disturbing. Was the act, he wondered, a healing beneficence or a removal of guilt associated with killing?

After four or five burns the cage was removed and the scalp repaired. Surprised, DeLazzari punched O.R. Procedures, Psych Division, and typed:

WHY SURGEONS OMIT DEEP MIL. INDOCTRINATION?

NEW RULING ONE WEEK PREVIOUS, the computer said.

WHOSE AUTHORITY?

BOARD OF SUPERVISORS.

And who ordered them around? He switched off and turned back to the Doctors.

After their duties had been completed they followed some mysteriously developed ritual that looked like a laying on of hands. All probes and sensors extended, they would go over a body like a fine-tooth comb, slicing off a wart, excising a precancerous mole, straightening a twisted septum. DeLazzari switched off and lit a cigar. There were no emergencies to be expected in the next ten minutes. He blinked idly at a small screen recording of the flat encephalogram of a dead brain whose body was being maintained for Parts.

The Doctors had other customs that both annoyed and amused him by their irrationality. Tonight they had been quiet, but sometimes one of them, sectioning a bowel, might start a running blue streak of chatter like a Las Vegas comic while another, probing the forebrain, would burst out in a mighty organ baritone, "Nearer My God to Thee." On the rare but inevitable occasions when an irreparable patient died with finality they acted as one to shut down the life-system and retract their instruments; then stood for five minutes in a guardian circle of quietness, like the great slabs of Stonehenge, around the body before they would allow the sweeper to take it away.

The big external screen was still on and DeLazzari looked down into the city, where a torch-light procession was pushing its flaming way up the avenue and the walls to either side wavered with unearthly shadows. He shut off and called Shop. He peered at the fax sheet on Max Vingo clipped to his notice board and typed:

YOU GOT A CAUCASIAN TYPE NURSE APPROX 160 CM FAIR HAIR QUIET VOICE NOT PUSHY MILD-TO-WARM AND FIRST RATE?

2482 BEST QUALITY CHECKED OUT LIGHT BROWN WE CAN MAKE IT FAIR HAIR.

LIGHT BROWN OK HEALING UNIT 35.

He yawned. Nothing more for the moment. He dialled supper, surveyed the sleeping-alcove and bathroom, all his own, with satisfaction, checked the pill dispenser, which allowed him two headache tablets on request, one sleeping pill at 11:00 p.m. and one laxative at 7:30 a.m., if required. He was perfectly content.

All nurses looked about twenty-five years old, unutterably competent but not intimidating unless some little-boy type needed a mother. 2482 was there when Max Vingo first opened his eyes and stirred weakly in his mummy-wrappings.

"Hello," she said quietly.

He swallowed; his throat was still sore from the respirator. "I'm alive."

"Yes, you are, and we're glad to have you."

"This is a hospital."

"It is, and I'm your nurse, 2482."

He stared at her. "You're a – a mechanical – I've heard about you – you're a mechanical –"

"I'm a Robonurse," she said.

"Huh ... it sounds like some kind of a tank."

"That's a joke, baby – God help us," said DeLazzari, and turned her dial up half a point.

She smiled. "I'm not at all like a tank."

"No." He gave it a small interval of thought. "No, not at all."

It was the third day. DeLazzari never bothered to shave or wash on duty where he didn't see another human being; his face was covered with grey-flecked stubble. Outside he was vain, but here he never glanced into a mirror. The place was quiet; no new patients had come in, no alarms had sounded, the walking wounded were walking by themselves. Besides 2482 there were only two other nurses on duty, one with a nephritis and another tending the body soon to be frozen for Parts. Still, he did have 2482 to control and he watched with weary amusement as she warmed up under the turn of his dial.

"You're getting better already." She touched Max Vingo's forehead, a non-medical gesture since the thermocouple already registered his temperature. Her fingers were as warm as his skin. "You need more rest. Sleep now." Narcotic opened into his bloodstream from an embedded tube, and he slept.

On the fifth day the people of the city rose up against their government and it fell before them. Officers elected themselves, curfews were established, the torchlight parades and demonstrations stopped; occasionally a stray bomb exploded in a call box. Packs of dogs swarmed up the avenue, pausing to sniff at places where the blood had lain in puddles; sometimes they met a congregation of cats and there were snarling yelping skirmishes. DeLazzari eyed them on his screen, devoutly thankful that he was not stationed in City Hospital. He filled City's requests for blood, plasma and parts as far as regulations required and didn't try to contact their Control Room.

At the Military Hospital the nephritis got up and walked out whole, the deadhead was cut up and frozen in Parts, an interesting new malaria mutation came in and was assigned a Doctor to himself in Isolation. 2482 peeled away the bandages from Max Vingo's head and hand.

He asked for a mirror and when she held it before him he examined the scars visible on his forehead and scalp and said, "I feel like I'm made up of spare parts." He lifted his hand and flexed it. "That's not so funny." The forefinger was his own now, but it had once belonged to a black man and though most of the pigment had been chemically removed it still had an odd bluish tinge. "I guess it's better than being without one."

"You'll soon be your old handsome self."

"I bet you say that to all the formerly handsome guys."

"Of course. How would you get well otherwise?"

He laughed, and while she was wiping his face with a soft cloth he said, "2482, haven't you ever had a name?"

"I've never needed one."

"I guess if I get really familiar I can call you 2 for short."

"Hoo boy, this is a humorist." DeLazzari checked the dial and indicator and left them steady on for the while. The malaria case went into convulsions without notice and he turned his attention elsewhere.

She rubbed his scalp with a cream to quicken regrowth of hair.

"What does that do for a bald guy?"

"Nothing. His follicles no longer function."

He flexed his new finger again and rubbed the strange skin with the fingertips of his other hand. "I hope mine haven't died on me."

By day seven DeLazzari was beginning to look like a debauched beachcomber. His hospital whites were grimy and his moustache ragged. However, he kept a clean desk, his sweeper cleared away the cigar stubs and the ventilators cleaned the air. Two badly scarred cases of yaws came in from a tropical battleground and two Doctors called for skin grafts and whetted their knives. In the city a curfew violator was shot and killed, and the next morning the first of the new demonstrators appeared. One of the Doctors took the chance of visiting Max for the first time when he was awake.

The soldier wasn't dismayed; he answered questions readily enough, showed off his growing hair, and demonstrated his attempts to use the grafted finger, but he kept looking from the Doctor to 2482 and back in an unsettling way, and DeLazzari turned up the nurse's dial a point.

When the Doctor was gone she said, "Did he disturb you?"

"No." But his eyes were fixed on her.

She took his hand. "Does that feel good?"

"Yes," he said. "That feels good." And he put his other hand on top of hers.

DeLazzari ate and slept and monitored the screens and supervised the duties of nurses and sweepers. Sometimes he wiped his oily face with a tissue and briefly considered rationing his cigars, which he had been smoking excessively because of boredom. Then three cases of cholera came in from the east; one was dead on arrival and immediately incinerated, the other two occupied him. But he still had time to watch the cure of Max Vingo and by turns of the dial nourish his relationship with 2482. He thought they were a pretty couple.

Max got unhooked from his i.v., ate solid food with a good appetite, and got up and walked stiffly on his scarred legs, now freed of their bandages. His hair grew in, black as DeLazzari's but finer, and the marks on his skin were almost invisible. He played chess sometimes with 2482 and didn't make any comments when she let him win. But there was an odd sadness about him, more than DeLazzari might have guessed from his Psych report. Although the ugliest of his memories had been burned away, the constellations of emotion attached to them had remained and the Doctors would never be able to do anything about those during the short time he stayed in the Hospital.

So that often at night, even sometimes when he fell into a light doze, he had sourceless nightmares he couldn't describe, and when he flailed his arms in terrified frustration 2482 took his hands and held them in her own until he slept at peace.

DeLazzari watched the TV news, followed the courses of battles over the world and on Moonbase and Marsport, and made book with himself on where his next casualties would be coming from. Not from the planets, which had their own Hospitals, or from the usual Military Base establishments. His own Hospital (he liked to think of it as his own because he was so fond of its conveniences and so full of respect for its equipment) was one of the rare few that dealt with the unusual, the interesting, and the hopeless. Down in the city the fire marchers were out and the bombs were exploding again. He knew that soon once more the people of the city would rise against their government and it would fall before them, and he kept check of blood and parts and ordered repairs on old scuppered nurses.

Max Vingo dressed himself now and saw the scars fade on his newly exposed torso. Because he was so far away from it he didn't think of the battle he might be going into. It was when he had stood for a long time at the window looking out at the rain, at how much greener it made the grass, that 2482 said to him, "Max, is there something you're afraid of?"

"I don't know."

"Is it the fighting?"

"I don't even remember much of that."

"The Doctors took those memories away from you."

"Hey!" DeLazzari growled, hand poised over the control. "Who said you could say a thing like that?"

"I don't mind that," Max said.

DeLazzari relaxed.

"Don't you want to know why?"

"If you want to tell me."

"I'm not sure ... but I think it was because the Doctors knew you were a gentle and loving man, and they didn't want for you to be changed."

He turned and faced her. "I'm the same. But I'm still a man who has to dress up like a soldier – and I don't know when that will ever change. Maybe that's why I'm frightened."

DeLazzari wondered for a moment what it would be like to be sick and helpless and taken care of by a loving machine in the shape of a beautiful woman. Then he laughed his hoarse derisive crow and went back to work. He had never been sick.

On the eighteenth day five poison cases came in from a bloodless coup in a banana republic; DeLazzari sent a dozen nurses with them into the Shock Room and watched every move. He was hot and itchy, red-eyed and out of cigars, and thinking he might as well have been in City Hospital. They were having their troubles over there, and once again he sent out the supplies. By the time he had leisure for a good look at Max Vingo, 2482's dial was all the way up and Max was cured and would be going out next day: day twenty-one, his own discharge date. He listened to their conversation for a while and whistled through his teeth. "End of a beautiful interlude," he said.

That evening Max ate little and was listless and depressed. 2482 didn't press him to eat or speak, nor did DeLazzari worry. The behaviour pattern was normal for situation and temperament.

Max went to sleep early but woke about eleven and lay in the darkness without calling or crying out, only stared toward the ceiling; sometimes for a moment he had a fit of trembling. 2482 came into the room softly, without turning on the light. "Max, you're disturbed."

"How do you know?" he said in an expressionless voice.

"I watch your heartbeat and your brain waves. Are you feeling ill?"

"No."

"Then what is the matter? Do you have terrible thoughts?"

"It's the thoughts I can't think that bother me, what's behind everything that got burned away. Maybe they shouldn't have done that, maybe they should have let me become another person, maybe if I knew, really knew, really knew what it was like to hurt and kill and be hurt and be killed and live in filth for a lifetime and another lifetime, ten times over, I'd get to laugh at it and like it and say it was the way to be, the only way to be and the way I should have been...."

"Oh no, Max. No, Max. I don't believe so."

Suddenly he folded his arms over his face and burst out weeping, in ugly tearing sobs.

"Don't, Max." She sat down beside him and pulled his arms away. "No, Max. Please don't." She pulled apart the fastenings of her blouse and clasped his head between her tender, pulsing and unfleshly breasts.

DeLazzari grinned lasciviously and watched them on the infrared scanner, chin propped on his hand. "Lovely, lovely, lovely," he whispered. Then he pre-set 2482's dial to move down three points during the next four hours, popped his pill, and went to bed.

The alarm woke him at four. "Now what in hell is that?" He staggered groggily over to the console to find the source. He switched on lights. The red warning signal was on over 2482's dial. Neither the dial or the indicator had moved from UP position. He turned on Max Vingo's screen. She had lain down on the bed beside him and he was sleeping peacefully in her arms. DeLazzari snarled. "Circuit failure." The emergency panel checked out red in her number. He dialled Shop.

RE-ROUTE CONTROL ON 2482.

CONTROL RE-ROUTED, the machine typed back.

WHY DID YOU NOT RE-ROUTE ON AUTO WHEN FAILURE REGISTERED?

REGULATION STATES DIRECTOR AUTONOMOUS IN ALL ASPECTS NURSE-PATIENT RELATIONSHIP NOW ALSO INCLUDING ALTERNATE CIRCUITS.

WHY WAS I NOT TOLD THAT BEFORE?

THAT IS NEW REGULATION. WHY DO YOU NOT REQUEST LIST OF NEW REGULATIONS DAILY UPDATED AND READILY AVAILABLE ALL TIMES?

"At four o'clock in the morning?" DeLazzari punched off. He noted that the indicator was falling now, and on the screen he could see 2482 moving herself away from Max and smoothing the covers neatly over him.

DeLazzari woke early on the last day and checked out the cholera, the yaws and the poison. The choleras were nearly well; one of the yaws needed further work on palate deformity; one of the poisons had died irrevocably, he sent it to Autopsy; another was being maintained in Shock, the rest recovering.

While he ate breakfast he watched the news of battle and outrage; growing from his harshly uprooted childhood faith a tendril of thought suggested that Satan was plunging poisoned knives in the sores of the world. "De-Lazzari the Metaphysician!" He laughed. "Go on, you bastards, fight! I need the work." The city seemed to be doing his will, because it was as it had been.

Max Vingo was bathing himself, depilating his own face, dressing himself in a new uniform. A sweeper brought him breakfast. DeLazzari, recording his Director's Report, noted that he seemed calm and rested, and permitted himself a small glow of satisfaction at a good job nearly finished.

When the breakfast tray was removed, Max stood up and looked around the room as if there was something he might take with him, but he had no possessions. 2482 came in and stood by the door.

"I was waiting for you," he said.

"I've been occupied."

"I understand. It's time to go, I guess."

"Good luck."

"I've had that already." He picked up his cap and looked at it. "2482 – Nurse, may I kiss you?"

DeLazzari gave her the last downturn of the dial.

She stared at him and said firmly, "I'm a machine, sir. You wouldn't want to kiss a machine." She opened the top of her blouse, placed her hands on her chest at the base of her neck and pulled them apart, her skin opened like a seam. Inside she was the gold-and-silver gleam of a hundred metals threaded in loops, wound on spindles, flickering in minute gears and casings; her workings were almost fearsomely beautiful, but she was not a woman.

"Gets 'em every time." DeLazzari yawned and waited for the hurt shock, the outrage, the film of hardness coming down over the eyes like a third eyelid.

Max Vingo stood looking at her in her frozen posture of display. His eyelids twitched once, then he smiled. "I would have been very pleased and grateful to kiss a machine," he said and touched her arm lightly. "Good-bye, Nurse." He went out and down the hall toward his transportation cell.

DeLazzari's brows rose. "At least that's a change." 2482 was still standing there with her innards hanging out. "Close it up, woman. That's indecent." For a wild moment he wondered if there might be an expression trapped behind her eyes, and shook his head. He called down Shop and sent her for post-patient diagnostic with special attention to control system.

He cleaned up for the new man. That is, he evened up the pile of tape reels and ate the last piece of candy. Then he filched an ID plate belonging to one of the poison cases, put everything on AUTO, went down a couple of floors and used the ID to get into Patients' Autobath. For this experience of hot lather, stinging spray, perfume and powder he had been saving himself like a virgin.

When he came out in half an hour he was smooth, sweet-smelling, and crisply clothed. As the door locked behind him five Doctors rounded a corner and came down the corridor in single file. DeLazzari stood very still. Instead of passing him they turned with a soft whirr of their nylon castors and came near. He breathed faster. They formed a semicircle around him; they were featureless and silver, and smelt faintly of warm metal. He coughed.

"What do you want?"

They were silent.

"What do you want, hey? Why don't you say something?"

They came nearer and he shrank against the door, but there were more machines on the other side.

"Get away from me! I'm not one of your stinking zombies!"

The central Doctor extruded a sensor, a slender shining limb with a small bright bulb on the end. It was harmless, he had seen it used thousands of times from the Control Room, but he went rigid and broke out into a sweat. The bulb touched him very lightly on the forehead, lingered a moment, and retracted. The Doctors, having been answered whatever question they had asked themselves, backed away, resumed their file formation, and went on down the hall. DeLazzari burst into hoarse laughter and scrubbed with his balled fist at the place the thing had touched. He choked on his own spit, sobered after a minute, and walked away very quickly in the opposite direction, even though it was a long way around to where he wanted to go. Much later he realized that they had simply been curious and perplexed in the presence of an unfamiliar heartbeat.

He went out in the same helicopter as Max Vingo, though the soldier in his sterile perimeter didn't know that. In the Control Room the new Director, setting out his tooth-cleaner, depilatory and changes of underwear, watched them on the monitor. Two incoming helicopters passed them on the way; the city teemed with fires and shouting and the children kicked at the slow-moving cars. In the operating theatre the silver Doctors moved forward under the lights, among the machines, and stood motionless around the narrow tables.

1972

BODY ENGLISH

Now what happens?

Just lie still sir, just, that's it, relax while I set the controls – don't move, don't move at all, one minute and you get the run of Chuck's body, you ca –

Hi, Chuck.

Yo.

Easy, just stay ... ready, OK?

Sure.

Zzt

Oh. Easy. Just easy. Ah, this is good, one step, two step ... run now, not too fast ... running. See Dick, see Jane, see Spot. Run. Oh my Lord this is good! Feet pounding, knees like pistons in oil, strong and heavy and the weight bearing itself, no pain in ankles, knees, hips, pelvis, spine, ribs, shoulders, neck, arms, elbows, hands, fingers, skull. None. Run!

Everything all – what? time?

Got your money's worth there, fella.

Time? I must have more! Please give me, I'll pay –

Sorry, mister, we're booked up. Maybe, uh, next month?

Hey, Chuck, that one really made you sweat. You OK?

Yeah. I guess.

Lemme wash you down ... feel better?

I hurt, Jacko.

It'll pass, kid. Just take a few minutes.

Awright now. Ready?

Oh yes.

You ready, Chuck?

Sure.

OK, Missus, take it easy. Don't be scared.

There's no way I would be scared of losing this pain.

Zzt

You got fifteen minutes. Enjoy.

One quarter hour. Ah, dear God, thank you for this much. No I don't want to run, you damned fool, I saved for this too long to waste.... Just let me sit and look and breathe. Just let me. Look around. Breathe. There is the sunlight. Breathe. In and out ... oh yes, I know, time. And I'm not ready. I'll never be ready. And I saved. I'll never have another. I wouldn't last until.... Thank you, young man.

I hope it helped you, Ma'am.

Oh yes – but you don't look very well. Did I do something awful to your body?

Not a thing, little lady, don't you worry about that! Chuck's fine.

Let him tell me. What is it, young fellow?

You didn't hurt me, ma'am. But I had to wait ... in – in your body, you know.

Oh. I never thought of that.

You goddam stupid shmuck, what the hell'd you have to go and say that for? They're supposed to come for relief and go away happy! You'll have them reporting me for cruelty to dumb animals – for a thousand bucks a fifteen minutes!

You can go screw off. I don't care. I can't take much more of this.

What's the matter with you? Doctor says you're in good shape.

Yeah. And little old ladies ride me Sundays. Listen, Jacko, I don't just feel their pain when I'm in their bodies – I feel it now – and it doesn't stop.

That's all in your head,

I don't care where it is. I feel it all the time. The fella with canes, every joint screaming, old lady with the cancer eating into her shoulder-blades, girl you couldn't look at with every part of her going wrongways. all she could do is cry – maybe I only got them up here in my head but they hurt me. I've got to stop.

Okay. Fine. You think I care? I got washed-up jocks waiting in line out there to do twice as much as you for half the money.

That's good. If they're dumb as me they deserve it.

Aw Chucky, we go back a long way, you and me. The machine's paid off, business is good ... hell, we're free and easy.

Yeah. Sure.

Listen, do you think you could work in one more, now you're rested? Last of the day? Little crippled kid?

Why not? It's a living.

Hi kid.

Hi yourself. Is this the whole machine? It looks kind of beat up.

It's good enough.

You got a license to work it?

Yeah I got a license to work it. Look, kid –

Hey Jacko, you're getting sweaty. What's your name, kid?

Barrie, with an i.e.

You scared, Barrie?

Yeh. A little, I guess. So many people put in so I could have this....

OK, take it easy. Let Jacko fix the electrodes ... comfortable?

Uh....

Take it real slow at first.

Zzt

Hey ... awright, this isn't so tough.

Remember, easy. Step at a time. Just take it around the park, not too fast, smell the flowers. OK?

Sure. Oh yeah, sure.

Yeah. You just lie there and be me, Chuck, right? Hey, goddammit, I can run! Jeez, I could live with this, I could have girls, I – oh hell, thanks Ms Parsons and all you jerks, why did you, oh God, scrape up all that money, gonna take my life away again in a couple minutes – shee-it I could take this, run and run, nothing in the pockets, don't care, sun and trees, people on the Ferris wheel and in the fun house, and there's the gate ... lost, hidden ... a thousand dollars, nothing left for a ride on the Ferris wheel – yeah, yeah! I know it's time, you don't have to bug me!

Kiddo, you sure made every minute count.

Hey you, Mister Chuck, how'd you like being me?

Same as all the others I've been. Glad you had a good time.

Yeah, sure. I almost ran you right out of the park and got lost.

Nope. If you get much farther away the radio field breaks and just leaves you here and me staggering around kind of dizzy.

Oh. I see. Well, thanks for everything, Mister.

Hey Chuck, baby, that's it for today.

I got to get out of this while I can still walk.

You'll feel better tomorrow. Let's go have a beer and count the money. Look at it this way, Chuck, you're doing a real humanitarian service for these people.

Ah shut up, Jacko. Just shut. Up.

1986

MONKEY WRENCH

The network of spacelights is spread throughout the Galaxy, its orbit pacing the stars; it has not yet completed one twenty-millionth of that orbit. There are holes in it, where Galactic Federation has not yet reached, but where it is established spacelights guide GalFed starships through dark nebulae and the blackest spans between the stars.

In Local System GF3284, Spacelight 599 is small and looks insignificant; there is a lot of blackness beyond it, and it is known as "the one on the edge of nowhere". But, second only to Base, it contains the biggest information bank in the sector. From local traffic and the nearest station it receives, stores, relays and answers five hundred requests during every twenty-four Sol3/Standard hours – requests for maps, coordinates, medicines, doctors, plasma, whole blood, ship parts, human body parts, police, repair men, priests; data from every branch of science, art and history – from a thousand races; homanid, arthropod, arachnid, avian, ichthyoid – whatever classification there is.

And it answers them all, unless something goes wrong.

Five-ninety-nine was invisible in the dim-lit sky.

If it could have been seen from the supply ship, it

would have seemed a huge black ball like an anarchist's bomb, with a complex fuse of antennas for radar, maser and radio.

Bugasz closed with it as if it were a bomb. Every once in a while, in a tic, he lifted a hand and bit skin from the sides of his nails. He was a big man with crisp yellow hair and a face red and vein-webbed from the unshielded glare of a thousand suns, no one's idea of a nervous wreck.

"Take it easy, Bugasz," Stannard said.

"I can't. I dunno what's wrong there, and I'm scared."

"The signal's eccentric; that means the antenna, and it probably knocked out the radio with it. What else can be wrong?"

"Crazy signal, dead radio? What else does it have to be?"

"They could be out checking the antenna."

"She does that. He wouldn't know how to go near an antenna. He's a computer man."

"Maybe she ran out of oxygen and got him to bring her a fresh tank. For God's sake!"

"They can do that from the inside ... why didn't they use the boat's radio to call 588, at least? Not a word!"

"Look, Bugasz, will you shut up already? The Hendrickses can take good care of themselves. There's about three hundred yells for help backed up in that computer, and Base is howling blue blazes. That's what *I'm* worried about. So call it off! Anyway, we'll be there in fifteen minutes."

Dr Ramcharan quietly folded and put away the gauzy silk square she had been embroidering with gold thread and bent over to open her instrument case and check the contents.

Stannard blinked at her. "Now don't tell me you've forgotten something."

She smiled and said in a gentle voice, "I never forget. It is like, you say, always with a woman? If I sometimes wonder, oh, did I remember to turn off all the robots when I came from home?" A small beautiful woman, she had teak-coloured skin and blue-black hair coiled in a knot at the base of her neck. Though she wore the crisp white red-crossed surcoat and narrow trousers of Med/Tech, there was always a small glint of gold about her: in the cloth of her inner sleeves, in her filigree earrings, her sandals.

The ship moved gently against the spacelight; the magnetic grapples clamped on its flanks with a reassuring *klung,* and the entrance shaft connected onto the lock with a barely perceptible suction thump. Bugasz handed out suits. Dr Ramcharan squeezed her sandals into a small chamois bag and hung them around her neck.

Stannard dragged on his suit and immediately started to sweat. Light made him sweat; heat made him sweat. He was a middle-sized man with thinning brown hair and glacier chips for eyes. He did not care for the outdoors or convivial company or comfortable travel. On a ship he was happiest when he was looking for the source of the trouble below decks where the wiring boards were racked. Sometimes he whistled to himself a bit in the dark pits of orbital stations and spacelights, back of the glittering multi-eyed panels where the questions were asked and answered. Especially if there was a good refrigeration system cooling the air around him. On leave at Base he looked for no other society than that of a silent embittered old decontamination-man, an ex-spaceman with whom he played endless games of *go*, his only recreation.

He picked up a bag much bigger than Dr Ramcharan's. "Come on, let's get over. I don't want to cook in this thing."

The locks closed behind them and opened before. Their boots vibrated silently against their feet in the dark cavern of the antechamber. They stepped before the inner door.

"It's supposed to light up in here when these doors open," Stannard said.

"Yeah." They turned questioningly in a silence broken by the faint rustle of static at the earphones. Bugasz peered at the florescent manual-control panel. "That's funny."

"What? Air's coming in; gravity's Earth-normal."

Bugasz muttered, "I dunno ..."

"Try the switches."

Bugasz pulled down OPEN, LIGHT, ALARM. Nothing happened. He plunged them back and forth, without result. "The grapples worked, so did the outside door," Stannard said.

"I used the ship's controls for that." He got out his flash and aimed the beam at the control panel. "Look. There's a couple scratches and dents around the edge there. I could see black marks on the flourescent. There." He switched the flash off and on. "Looks like it was pried off and put back.... I bet the wires are ripped behind that thing...."

Dr Ramcharan's breath quickened. Stannard felt hairs rising in a prickling wave up his legs and back and a drench of sweat running down to meet it. He squatted and opened his bag. "Find me the serial number on that panel."

"Here – 7X724."

"Get the light down here." He pulled out on of a dozen neatly racked miniature control boards, pressed a stud, and the out-lock door slid open again. "Get back in the shaft. I don't know what's in there, but if it isn't anything good we're getting out of here fast."

They backed away.

"Ready?" Stannard touched another stud.

The inner door opened. There was a short hallway and yet one more door of clear Lucite panels before them. Light blazed in their faces from the room beyond. There was nothing in it but a man crumpled on the floor and a computer humming softly to itself.

Only twelve hours before, they had set out from 601, a much bigger spacelight with enough crew to maintain a social structure that included several families. Stannard had been overseeing the maintenance staff on a tricky repair problem; he was a travelling trouble-shooter and did not live there. News of the irregular signal and the unanswered SOSs had relayed back to Base on a long chain of lights and out again to Stannard, along with microfiles on all aspects of 599, including its occupants, a married couple. This last because Stannard doubled in a police capacity – he reported to hundreds of GalFed agencies on jurisdictional and insurance matters. He loathed the extra work; but space is vast, and lives by comparison are few and short. There was a chronic lack of manpower whether it came from Sol or Betelgeuse.

The job involved endless duplications of forms he sweated filling out under hot lights with a pen gripped awkwardly in his wire-threader's fingers. There was rarely any excitement. Once he had subdued a crewmen who had gone spacemad and was laying about him with a wrench; but he never spoke of the incident, because it made him uneasy that a good, level-headed man could go wild working in the cool, quiet conditions he himself loved so well.

He had taken the risk of delaying a couple of hours to send for information about Bugasz, because the supplyman was the only person who visited 599 regularly and knew it and its occupants well. He had been on 601 when the call came, with his ship fuelled and ready, about to take off for his next stop. He had been more than willing to change course for 599.

Stannard had spent a couple of hours with the microreader on the way out, so he knew the contents of the three dossiers. And the subject of one of them was lying dead on the floor.

"That is Cornelius Hendricks, isn't it, and he *is* dead?"

Dr Ramcharan was kneeling beside him. "Very much so, I am afraid."

Once they had checked that gravity was Earth-normal inside and air and temperature were standard, Bugasz had ripped off his helmet and run through the station yelling, "Iris! Iris!" There was no answer, and he came back with his shoulders sagging, his face both anxious and defeated. "She's not here! Where can she be?"

Stannard muttered, "We'll find her. Don't worry...." He was looking at the body of Cornelius Hendricks. Age fifty-three, a quiet solitary, like Stannard, who had married Iris Cullen, a woman in her twenties, two years before. Now he was lying dead, with an empty spray can of deadly vermicide in his hand. Stannard decided that he was never going to make either of those mistakes. "How long?"

"He is very stiff. Twelve hours, perhaps?"

"That's five-six hours after the signal started going ..." So Hendricks had been alive when they got the news. And he had delayed. But nothing would have saved Hendricks; he had sprayed the stuff into his mouth, and death must have come in a few minutes.

Dr Ramcharan picked up the can by the nozzle. "Excelthion. This kills all the vermin in the local sector – but I won't allow it on 601 because of the children. You cannot go into a room for six hours after you use it."

"I got some on board," Bugasz said.

"Get rid of it. There are other effective things you can use with less trouble."

Stannard was thinking of those twelve hours. But from 601 to 599 it took just over twelve hours, and there was no shorter way. And he was thinking of Dr Ramcharan. It was Bugasz who had suggested she come, just as they were leaving; she lived on 601, one of a huge team of resident spacelight doctors who rotated every two standard years. What kind of trouble had he foreseen, that he wanted her here?

Dr Ramcharan was packing her instruments. "Are we to leave him here?"

"Did you get pictures?"

"Yes."

"Wrap him up and we'll take him along."

She took a thin transparent plastic sack out of her bag, unfolded it and began pulling it over the body. "Did the stuff do that to his face?" Stannard asked.

"Just the purple," Bugasz said. "That's what his face was like."

Even discounting the cyanosed skin, the dead man was peculiarly ugly. Not in the features themselves; but in a certain asymmetry and lack of alignment. It was as if a noble marble head had been smashed by a child and glued together to escape detection. One eye, one brow were lower than the others, the nose twisted, the mouth jagged into a sneer. "It doesn't tell what he was like, really," said Dr Ramcharan. "What was he like, Bugasz?"

"I didn't have much to do with him. I didn't know him that well."

"Doesn't look like we will, either," Stannard said. "I better look at the radio. If I can get it to work, whom do you call from here, 588?"

"Yeah. It's as far as we can get. They relay."

It was a small place, 599, a spacelight for two. The communications room was next door.

"Bugasz!" Stannard yelled. Bugasz came running. "Why didn't you tell me about this?"

The radio was smashed, staved in, a wreck of coils and wires. It looked as if the madman with the monkey wrench had been at it. There was in fact a wrench on the floor.

Bugasz gaped. "Honest to God, Stannard, I didn't even see that. All I was looking for was her."

Stannard had bent over to stare at a red-lit indicator on a panel beside the radio. "The boat's not in dock. It's gone."

"Do you think she −"

"How far could she get in that?"

"Only to 588. But the lock controls are bust!"

"Not from the inside. I checked."

"I can call 588 from the ship −"

"Not yet."

"But Stannard −"

"She'll keep, Bugasz! I'm worried about the orbit now! All this smashing, if the pile's been touched −"

"But that's sealed! Even you haven't got high enough clearance −"

"He did all this. Someone did. If he wanted to foul up the pile bad enough he could manage that too. Let's look at the antennas." He trotted down the short hallway to the antenna-control room. It was a small, narrow place with one end wall taken up by instruments, and the other by a little spiral staircase leading to the hatch that gave access to the antennas. The antennas themselves folded into recesses with translucent walls in the centre of the spacelight. Now they were partially retraced, the

117

switches jammed. "God, what a mess! That bastard didn't leave much," Stannard said. "This is going to be a hell of a repair job. Try the locks ... they're gone too?"

"You can use the remote to open them – I'll go out and see what's doing."

"No, wait a minute." He was reluctant to let Bugasz out of his sight. Mrs Hendricks was gone, and so was the boat; Bugasz was edgy and overeager. Stannard wanted to know if these facts were connected. "If she did leave the boat, is there any place she could have got to besides 588?"

"Hell, no. This light's out in the butt end of nowhere. Hendricks wasn't any ordinary dispatcher or lighthouse-keeper. He was a research man with special grants. All he wanted was to be alone with his computer."

"And his wife," Stannard added, startling himself because he hadn't meant to speak. Bugasz hadn't even heard; he was staring up at the antenna hatch. Stannard Sighed. "Gotta get that machine going, if he didn't bust it too. Come on, let's unsuit. I'm boiling."

"I'd like to have a look –"

"Leave it alone! You don't know which way it'll collapse if you touch it. Come on."

Dr Ramcharan used a small pump to extract air from the bag before she sealed it. Stannard took a last look at the face half obscured by plastic folds. "A girl twenty-six? Why'd she marry him?"

"Maybe she thought no one else would have her," Bugasz said.

Stannard took his own and Bugasz's suits and hung them in the locker near the doorway. "There's only one suit here. It must be his. Well, doctor, if you're through with that I'll call the drone." He used one of his control boards; the locks opened again, and a small squat loading wagon trundled in from the ship to pick up the body.

"I'll wash up now," Dr Ramcharan said and went off to find the bathroom. After a moment she came to the doorway and said, "Bugasz, there's a three-d portrait here, is it Mrs Hendricks?"

"Yes." He went over, and Stannard followed him into the bedroom, hesitantly crossing the threshold into privacy.

The bedroom was spare as a monk's cell, what one would have expected of Hendricks. But on a small table there was a Lucite block, measuring perhaps fifteen centimetres each way, and containing a three-dimensional portrait photograph, head and shoulders, of an extremely beautiful woman. Her hair was long and so fair it was almost white, shading deeper into gold nearer the scalp. Her features were classic and regular, and everything else humanity calls beautiful, but the truest beauty was in the joyousness and vitality of her laughter, even in the frozen silence in which it had been preserved.

Dr Ramcharan said slowly, "Why would *she* think no one else would have her?"

"That was before," Bugasz said. "She got sick."

Stannard said, "I heard of that. She dropped out of sight for a couple of years, didn't she? Nobody said what it was, though."

Bugasz shut his mouth stubbornly and turned back into the computer room.

"Not going to get much out of him." Stannard stood looking at it a minute, then left the bedroom. Past the doorway he stopped dead in his tracks. There was no one in the computer room. Bugasz was gone.

"Bugasz! Bugasz! Damn it, what –"

The drone was gone; the lock doors were closed. Stannard had a sick glimpse of himself and Dr Ramcharan stranded here without radio, Bugasz flown with the evidence. He ran to the locker. Bugasz's suit was still there, but he would not need it simply to get into the ship; he could risk leaving without it.

Stannard grabbed his own suit, fumbled it on, sealed it, sweating, and dragged at the lock control, almost praying. The door slid aside.

Bugasz was standing in the shaft, the open ship behind him. He was suitless, weaponless, shamefaced. His arms hung at his sides.

Stannard snarled, "What the hell you think you're doing?"

"I had to ..." Bugasz muttered. "I had to radio 588 ... to see if ..."

"What is it? Hey?"

Bugasz shook his head and licked his lips. "The boat reached there ... empty. They're sending it back."

Stannard looked at him. Bugasz swept an arm back toward the shaft. "It's the truth. Call them yourself if you want."

Stannard hesitated a moment and said, "I'll take your word."

"Thanks."

Anger mounting, Stannard wrenched at his suit-clamps. "Just don't, Bugasz, don't try it again!" He was humiliatingly aware of how ludicrous he looked when he was angry: red splotches flecked out on his white skin. "You hear me? Don't try it!" He hung up the suit once more. "We stick together till we find out what's up here. You understand?"

He turned and stood staring at the computer; it hummed, the ready light pulsed; the stillness beyond it was heavy.

"There it is. Everything's gone but that. It's the only thing that didn't get bashed in. Why?"

"Maybe it's booby-trapped."

"It's a nice thought."

"Or – he didn't leave any note ... maybe he left a message in it."

"Yeah." He went over, reached out a hand toward the microphone, and let it fall.

"You scared, Stannard?"

"What do you think, you fool!"

Dr Ramcharan said quickly, "Stannard, if you have any doubt, seal this place and let us leave. The police will take care of it."

"Right now, *I'm* the police," Stannard said. "I have to see this thing gets working, if I can; I have to get that back-up cleared, because there'll be people lost or dead; they may be already, because he didn't get the stuff out to them." He wiped a hand over his face. "I don't know everything that's been done here. The man was mad. If he's monkeyed with the pile and the orbit's shifted, we may really find out where nowhere is when we try to take off."

"If the orbit had changed we'd never have got here."

"He could have timed it to veer off at a certain point. He could have booby-trapped it, like you say, or even timed it to blow up ..."

"Then why don't we just –"

"Look, you don't understand! If this place blows up we're not only short one spacelight, we'll have hot asteroids shooting all over. It's a godawful hazard to anything running in this district! Use your head!"

"I don't want it blown off!" Bugasz yelled. "You're the police, the techman, the authority – you get us out of this!"

"All right! Take the doctor and get on board ship. Take her out a thousand kilometres and pace the light. If nothing happens in two hours, you can come down with your head intact. Okay?"

Dr Ramcharan said, "Please, Stannard, let us not have heroics. If we were to blow up, I think we would have done so as soon as the locks were opened. I don't think it was meant to happen."

Stannard considered a moment. "Yeah. I guess you're right." He swallowed, picked up the microphone and said, "Paul Stannard, GF/Tech Supervisor, Sector 3284, Security clearance B."

The machine said, in a machine's voice, "IDENTIFY."

Stannard allowed himself one breath of relief and pressed his thumb against a small sensitive plate.

"PROCEED."

"What is your orbit, number, class, generation?"

"MY GENERATION IS THIRD, MY CLASS IS LV MOD 85, MY NUMBER IS 1526 AND MY ORBIT IS THE NINTH CIRCLE OF HELL."

Stannard jerked back, Bugasz gulped, and Dr Ramcharan's breath shuddered between her teeth. The computer screen flashed to life, suddenly, in a flickering pattern of concentric circles.

"What in hell's going on here?" Stannard hung up the microphone and stepped back, shivering a little. Then he grabbed at it in a fierce snatch. "I said, give me your orbit, your position!"

"THE QUESTION IS ALREADY ANSWERED. MY ORBIT IS THE NINTH –"

"Shut up! Stop!" Stannard knew his face by now was brindled as a Biblical calf. He said through his teeth, "Ask a stupid question, you get a stupid answer."

"Stannard –" Dr Ramcharan hesitated, then said, "Tell him – tell it – is it speaking for Hendricks, do you think?"

"Looks like it – I wish I knew why. What did you want?"

"If it is Hendricks, tell him – tell him he is not in the

Ninth Circle, but in Circle Seven, Ring Two."

Stannard blinked at her. "Why?"

"Please. I think it will do no harm."

Stannard picked up the mike slowly and said, "You are in Circle Seven, Ring Two, not the Ninth."

The machine hummed a moment, and said, "I STAND CORRECTED."

Stannard said to the woman, "I gather we're talking about Dante and the *Inferno*, but I don't get what that was all about."

"Circle Seven, Ring Two is where the suicides are."

Stannard grunted. "That means he set all this up before he died. He went to a lot of trouble."

"He meant to hinder us. This is his booby-trap."

"Yeah, but why? Breaking everything I can understand; that's anger, and it took a lot of anger for him to kill himself ... but this? It's stupid. He didn't even know ..." He had been going to say "us", but stopped. Hendricks had known Bugasz. He resisted an impulse to turn and look at Bugasz. He didn't want to start another fight. Not right now. He spoke into the microphone again. "All right. What game do you think you're playing?"

"WHAT GAME DID YOU WISH TO PLAY? CHESS? GO? TOSS FOR WHITE?" The screen swirled into the image of a coin, spinning dizzily.

Stannard hung up in disgust.

Bugasz muttered, "He was a computer nut."

"I gathered that." He tried again. "Does your memory contain the coordinates of the present orbit of 599?"

"YES."

"What is the orbit?"

"CORRECTED ORBIT: CIRCLE SEVEN, RING TWO."

"Forget the theology. I am not concerned with the orbit of Cornelius Hendricks but of 599."

"NO INFORMATION AVAILABLE."

"But is the information contained in the memory store?"

"YES."

"Good. Do you have a protect on that information?"

" YES."

"I see. Is that information available with the use of a code-word?"

" YES."

"Hah. I'm just one rung too low to clear the code by priority. Let's see, signal started going eccentric between twenty and twenty-two hours ... were all requests answered and dispatched up to day 226, hour twenty?"

"ALL REQUESTS ANSWERED AND DISPATCHED UNTIL DAY 226, HOUR SIXTEEN."

"He must have been doing a lot of sitting around brooding ... were no questions answered at all after hour twenty?"

"QUESTIONS ANSWERED, BUT NOT DISPATCHED UNTIL HOUR TWENTY."

"I guess he started laying about then. That means nothing's been coming in since twenty hours, if the radio wasn't working. All right, give me a printout of all requests and answers between hours sixteen and twenty."

"REQUESTS ARE AVAILABLE; ANSWERS ARE NOT."

"Hm, we could have been sending the stuff out by ship radio ... that guy really knew how to hold a grudge. Tell me, are the answers tied to the code-word?"

" YES."

"Give me a memory map."

The map spread itself out on the screen, beautifully marked and spaced. He searched it. There was one huge area of blank spaces, with no indication of what was stored in it, no hint to allow him access. And he was afraid to tamper with it.

"That does it. Hendricks was the only one who would

have known the code-word, and Hendricks is dead." He bit his lip. "Damn, there must be something we can do ... give me hard copy on your undispatched questions. At least I'll know what's been going on."

The printer started racketa-tacketing, and a tongue of paper began to extrude from the slot. Stannard switched on the monitor-recorder, and the transcoded voices whispered across space:

"Urgent alert GalFedPol 500 kilos heroin in bauxite cargo cruiser Winged Star en route ..."

"They'd be landed by the time we got that one out."

"Urgent 527 ready receive three cases radiation poisoning treatment begun at ..."

Dr Ramcharan shivered, and they were silent.

"Kaghouro Clearing Company announces completion of program as indicated ..."

Stannard groaned to himself. The careful phrases meant that, after nine standard years of labouring the Kaghouri had finally composed a program to translate the language of the alien raiders who had been stripping them for twenty-five years; there would be plenty for GalFed to do about that. He couldn't even mention it to the others because it was highly classified, and he was the police, the Security man or what passed for one ... and the answers were sitting there in the machine. He tore off the printout and scanned it. He couldn't read encoded program, but he knew something of what it involved: thousands of lives, uncounted wealth, millions of hours of desperate, patient drudgery. He could feel his whole skin twitching at the thought, and he had to keep his mouth shut. And he had to have the code.

He started when Bugasz asked, "Why all this fancy business with code words?"

"That I don't know, but he could have erased the whole thing, answers, orbit and all ... he could have done a dozen different things to destroy us if he'd wanted, but he didn't. Dr Ramcharan was right – that wasn't the idea. But there's something else behind this, and I'd sure like to know what it is."

"What are you going to do for us now, Stannard?"

"I think it's a matter of what you're going to do, Bugasz. You knew the man, at least to some extent. What do *you* think he'd have chosen for a code word?"

"You crazy? What do I know about computers?"

"You knew a computer nut. Did he have any favourite expressions or mottoes?"

"None I ever heard. He was so close-mouthed I never even heard him say gee whiz."

"I need that thing. We've got to get past this ... maybe we can work around him, try another subject...."

"Ask him where Iris Hendricks is, for a start. I'd like to know that."

"Fat lot that's – I guess it won't hurt to try." He raised the mike. "Where is Iris Hendricks?"

"IRIS HENDRICKS IS WHERE IRIS HENDRICKS SHOULD BE."

Bugasz whispered, "I don't like that."

"I'm not too keen on it myself. Fifteen-twenty-six, is Iris Hendricks alive?"

"IRIS HENDRICKS WAS ALIVE WHEN LAST SEEN BY COR-NELIUS HENDRICKS."

"Is Iris Hendricks now alive?" Stannard pressed.

The machine blared, "FAITHLESS, FAITHLESS, FAITH-LESS!" The screen splattered with red stars of pain. Pause, click, whirr. "NO INFORMATION ON THAT SUB-JECT."

The three of them looked at one another. Stannard said again, urgently, "Is Iris Hendricks still alive?"

"NO INFORMATION ON THAT SUBJECT." The screen sparked.

"What happened there?" Bugasz asked.

"I'm not sure. I think it's some kind of automatic switch-off ... I'm scared to monkey around with anything, because I don't know how he's got it set up here, and I might wipe off something we need." He stared at the humming mass for a moment, thinking of the Kaghouri waiting for the results of their nine years' effort. "Maybe ..." His fingers tightened on the mike. He said in a reasonable voice with an undercurrent of tension, "Paul Stannard, GF/Tech Supervisor, Sector 3284, Security Clearance B." He whispered, "Cross your fingers."

"IDENTIFY."

He thumbed the plate once more.

"PROCEED."

"What is your number, class, generation?"

"MY GENERATION IS THIRD MY CLASS IS LV MOD 85, MY NUMBER IS 1526."

"Fifteen-twenty-six, will you play a game with me?"

"CERTAINLY. WHAT KIND OF GAME DID YOU WISH TO PLAY? CHESS? GO? TOSS FOR WHITE?" Once again the coin spun on the screen.

"*Go*," said Stannard.

Bugasz snarled, "Stannard, what do you think you're doing?"

"Playing *go*."

Bugasz glared at him, and Dr Ramcharan said with a touch of dryness, "I didn't know you played games, Stannard."

"It's the only one I know," said Stannard, and he addressed the machine: "I'll take white."

"YOU ARE THE PAUL STANNARD, WHO DEFEATED ZANGZX OF EUROPA AT THE PAN-SOL FESTIVAL, 2577?"

"Yes."

"I AM NOT PROGRAMMED TO PLAY WITH A FIFTH-CLASS PLAYER."

Stannard grunted. "Done his homework." He hung up and turned to the others. "I wanted to get back my access to the memory store, or the part of it we were dealing with when it cut off. The part he kept for himself, to play around with. This was the only way I could think of to do it. This part ... looks like he implanted a bit of his personality into it some way ... it's not uncommon, I guess, with people who love computers...."

"Do you do that, Stannard?" the woman asked.

"It's not one of my games."

Bugasz moved restlessly. "What's that got to do with the orbit, or where Mrs Hendricks is?"

"Mrs Hendricks certainly has to be tied in with his personal life – and the rest is, in some way, too, I'm sure of it. I know we won't get the orbit till we find out how. Now ... if you have any better ideas, spit them out."

"The machine won't play," said Dr Ramcharan.

"That doesn't matter. It was willing to talk about playing, and that was all I needed to get back to where I wanted to be." He went back to the microphone. "Do you have information on Iris Hendricks?"

"YOU WISH VITAL STATISTICS?"

"I guess so."

"CLARIFY."

"Yes, go ahead." A picture of Iris Hendricks flashed on the screen, and he waited glumly while the machine reeled off everything he already knew. When it stopped, he asked, "Can you tell me where she is now?"

"LAST SEEN LEAVING 599, NO DEFINITE INFORMATION ON PRESENT WHEREABOUTS."

"I think this thing's waffling," Bugasz said.

Dr Ramcharan said, "You may find out something if you ask about Hendricks himself."

"I'll try it – but we'll have to go all the way through

another damn dossier. Fifteen-twenty-six, can you tell me anything about Cornelius Hendricks?"

"YOU WISH VITAL STATISTICS?"

"Yeah, I – I mean, go ahead."

The picture of a man appeared, and the machine began, "CORNELIUS HENDRICKS, BORN 2529 –"

"Hey, wait a minute!" Stannard yelled. "Who's that guy in the picture supposed to be?"

"THAT IS A REPRESENTATION OF CORNELIUS HENDRICKS."

Regular handsome features? Firm clean jaw-line? Perfectly arched brows?

"The hell you say! That's not Hendricks!"

"Yes it is," Dr Ramcharan said softly. "It is."

It wasn't, and it was. Each brow, each half of the mouth, each eye belonged to Hendricks. To the handsome man he would have been if his well shaped but badly arranged features had been squared off and symmetrical. "It's the way he wanted to think of himself," she said.

Stannard sighed. "Yeah. .. I guess so ..." He remembered the dead empurpled face and set it beside the vital Greek ideal.

"How'd he do it?" Bugasz asked.

"Oh ... probably fed the machine a picture of himself and told it to beautify or de-uglify or symmetrize him or something."

Dr Ramcharan said, "You think it is disgusting."

Stannard shrugged uncomfortably. "I dunno ... something ..."

"It matches the picture of Mrs Hendricks."

"Yeah," Stannard said. "Better get on with it." He addressed the machine again. "Did Hendricks say he was going to kill himself?"

"YES."

"Why?"

"CLARIFY."

"All right. Why did he kill himself?"

There was a blank hum for a moment, and the wait was long. The machine said with a subtle but definite change of intonation, "BECAUSE I WAS BETRAYED."

The others moved away a little, and Stannard broke into another sweat. He swore to himself. Hendricks, damned fool, tangling himself up with his machine. People crying out of space for help. I, I, I. Hendricks, the I, was dead. Hendricks the ugly man, Prince Frog, twisting his absurd passion for a beautiful young woman into the clean skeins of wires and transistors that belonged to Stannard. And to the urgencies of a thousand races. "Who betrayed you?" he asked.

The machine said in its curious stilted voice, "MY WIFE AND BUGASZ WERE PLOTTING AGAINST ME."

It was out, what he had been waiting for. The explanation for all of Bugasz's moods, nerves, surliness. The missing piece that fit only to add greater complexities.

Bugasz yelled, "He's a goddamn liar! I never —"

"Shut up. What were they planning to do?"

"PLOTTING, PLOTTING, THEY DROVE ME TO THIS, THEY DROVE ME ..." Silence. Stannard waited for the sudden shift of the cut-off, but there was none, only the silence around the hum. He hung up and turned to Bugasz.

"You have anything to say?"

Bugasz was almost speechless. "Say?" His face was magenta, his voice strangled in his throat. "You think that mad fool is telling the truth?"

"I'd say ... he's telling some kind of truth — what it looks like to him. I know he was crazy. I can't take his word. But you've been a mess of nerves; you've been running around yelling for Iris Hendricks like a dog who forgot where he buried the bone ... there's something in it somewhere. You didn't kill him – but he claims you gave him a push. If it's true, you were the cause of the mess we're in, and you ought to have something to say about it."

"Say? What can I say when *I'm* going crazy? *He's* the one doing all the talking. Ask him!"

Stannard turned back to the mike. "How were they plotting? What did they intend to do?"

"THEY WERE GOING TO LEAVE ME ... WITH NOTHING TO DO BUT KILL MYSELF, BECAUSE SHE WAS ALL MY LIFE. NOW THEY ARE GONE, AND THERE IS NOTHING TO DO BUT DIE."

"Bugasz is here," Stannard said dryly.

"STATEMENT INCOMPREHENSIBLE."

"Here, Bugasz, speak for yourself."

Bugasz grabbed the mike and yelled, "Hendricks, you goddam liar –"

"IDENTIFY."

Bugasz's lip curled, but he controlled himself long enough to answer. "Laszlo Bugasz, Supply Agent 72, Sector 3284, Security clearance C3." and jabbed the plate with his thumb as if he were gouging an eye.

The machine stammered. "BUGASZ? BUGASZ? NO, NO, NOT COMPREHENSIBLE, NO ANSWER POSSIBLE, DATA ARE NOT, NOT NOT, N ..." The screen flickered with a thousand mad images, blanked and finally, "DO YOU WISH TO PLAY A GAME?" The coin spun.

"Hang up," Stannard said. "I don't' think we better try anything else for a while."

"Stannard –" Bugasz choked. "You really believe that – that –"

Stannard found a chair, sat on it and let his hands drop between his knees. Dr Ramcharan gave him a long look and said gently, "Bugasz, I think he would like to know what was between you and Mrs Hendricks."

"Nothing."

Stannard raised his head.

"I'm not lying. I haven't even spoken to her since I started servicing this light."

"Then where the hell'd he get all his crazy ideas? Tell me that!"

Bugasz shook his head. "I don't know."

"But you knew her before, back on Base! Well enough to call her by her first name –"

"All right! But that was back on Base. This is different!"

"Whatever it was, it was enough to send Hendricks off his head. What happened back there, then?"

Bugasz sat down. "I did love her, once."

"Once! It looks like that's all Hendricks needed!"

The red-veined face twisted. "I wasn't *in* love with her, you fool! I loved her. Everybody did. You saw what she looked like."

"But you knew her very well –"

"You saw the dossier. She was in starship communications, and I'd just joined up with GalFed ... we took a couple of courses together in emergency procedures, shipboard stuff."

"Shipboard stuff? And she came here?"

"She'd been going out to Tau Ceti – before she got sick."

"Go on."

"With what?" Bugasz shrugged. "She married Hendricks and came out here."

"And stopping here every two months, you never saw her? Not once?"

"A blink of her, going round a corner. That's all."

"Hendricks wouldn't let you ..."

"He had nothing to do with that."

"But you said you'd loved her ..." he swallowed.

"Didn't you even take her out, ask her to marry you, anything?"

"You kidding? She had all those young guys hot out of the academies crawling around her; she was having a good time. Look at me," he slapped his chest. "What would she want with me? My big dumb head? My ugly red face? My pilot's pay? I was ten years older, I had no future ..."

"And Hendricks made all this mess out of that? Come on, Bugasz! And if age mattered, Hendricks was twice her age."

"That was after she got sick."

"So she was sick. But she got better. What's that got to do with all this?"

Bugasz sighed and shook his head. "She didn't get better. She had Schoebl's disease."

"I never heard of it."

"It didn't have a name when she got it. And they kept it off the records as much as they could. Just said 'unspecified disease' without even a description."

"Why?"

"It's – it's a horrible, godawful – if it leaked out they'd have had a panic blow-up and maybe have had to close down half the lights in the sector."

"But you knew – with your security rating?"

"I knew. I used to have lunch with her about once a week. One day she didn't turn up, so I asked around for her and got all kinds of dumb excuses ... maybe they thought I was a deadhead, but a supply man gets to know all kinds of people, all kinds of things. So I found out."

Stannard crossed his arms. "Bugasz, this sounds like a lot of –"

Dr Ramcharan interrupted, "I know of Schoebl. An alien-parasitologist. I studied from one of his texts, but I never knew he had a disease named after him."

"You'll hear about it. They named it after him because he isolated the parasite and found a cure – three weeks ago. This doctor, a young guy who told me about it first, back then on Base, well he got kicked out for shooting his mouth off – not about this, just generally; and he was sent out to the sticks. I ran into him, and he tipped me off they had a cure ... a couple weeks ago. Still shooting his mouth off, I guess."

"It sounds plausible," Dr Ramcharan said.

"It would if we knew who this guy was."

"You're not gonna. I don't want to get him bumped again."

"What kind of disease was it, Bugasz?" she asked.

"You know that tropical Earth disease, something about an elephant?"

"Elephantiasis?"

"Yeah. The one where you swell up in the feet, and –"

"Yes. That is also a parasite. Filaria. It blocks the lymph glands, sometimes causes lumps under the skin ..."

"But that's mostly the feet, or ..." he rubbed his forehead. "This one – this one you can get anywhere ... shoulder, hand, lips, cheeks, nose ..." His face screwed up like a child's who was about to cry. "I saw her ... I got in and saw her."

"Your blabbermouth doctor friend," Stannard said.

"Yeah. But nobody saw her after that. She didn't want people to ..."

Dr Ramcharan said, "I believe the disease exists. I heard rumours of it, but it had no name then."

"It's got one now. Schoebl's disease. They caught three cases of it on Base, altogether, and isolated them before it got around; but they didn't know what it was."

"You went to see her – you might have caught it."

"It stops spreading when the nodes ripen. I didn't

know that then. But I saw her." He put his head in his hands.

"But Hendricks never kept you away from her when you dropped off supplies," Stannard said.

"No, but she wouldn't look at anybody. She –"

"Bugasz! Did you know you had two unauthorized visits marked down on your record in the last two weeks?"

Bugasz jerked up. "Hendricks!" he snarled. "He said he'd tell on me, that sonofabitch!" He slumped again. "There's my job."

"So you've been lying all along."

"Damn you, I never lied! Not once!"

Stannard poured a sweat of fury and impatience and frustration. "Then why were you out here?"

"I wanted to tell him, for God's sake! Can't you understand? I wanted to tell him she could be cured! He wouldn't even let me in. I thought, so help me God, I thought he'd be glad; I thought he'd be jumping up and down cheering his head off! He wouldn't even let me in! I had to talk to him on the radio. I was yelling at him –" Bugasz held his hands before him, stretched and trembling, "yelling at him, 'Hendricks, I only want to tell you they got a cure for the damn thing; it's Schoebl's disease, some kind of bug, if you'll only take her into Base they can –'" His hands fell to his knees. "He cut me off. I couldn't even get him to talk to me. I came back a week later and tried again, and he said he'd report me. That's it."

"This cure could be only a rumour."

"No. I checked with another guy I know. It's classified, but it's no rumour."

"Huh. I didn't know Security was that full of holes."

"I wouldn't tell you if my job wasn't shot."

135

"This makes everything even more complicated."

"No, Stannard ..." Dr Ramcharan shook her head sadly. "That poor man ... you remember, he took her when she was hideous. He was ugly; perhaps there was no one else in the world, he thought, who would have him ... such a man would be an ugly person inside, too, I think?" She looked at the blank screen where the picture had flashed Hendricks' idealization. "Or too shy and self-conscious ... or he would see that ugly people also live and are loved in the world. It was his mistake that he took her because she had been beautiful. But he took her, and she was grateful, and perhaps even loved him for it ..." She ran her eyes over the plated walls. "You have this garden, a place for two, like in the silly songs, only lined in steel. And then Bugasz, the outside world, comes pounding on the doors with the news that she will be beautiful again, with a miraculous cure, like being freed from an evil spell – and he is only an ugly man. Would she look at him after that? And as an irrational man, would he not be angry at Bugasz and do his best to strike back?"

"He might," said Stannard. "And Bugasz could have explained some of this before, too."

"How could I? He swore he'd have my job. There's nothing in the universe I'm fit for except shoving this old scow back and forth, and now I haven't even got that. I'll end up in decontamination spraying Excelthion on Schoebl's bugs, and if there's a leak in the dickey-suit I'll get my lungs burnt out like Hendricks got his."

"Yeah, it's sad," Stannard said and watched Bugasz stiffen. "If all this is true, if there is such a disease, if she had it, if Schoebl found a cure for it, why in hell did you come out here if you knew it meant your job? Whatever it was, something about your coming out here triggered him. Why didn't you just sit tight and wait and let the news of the cure leak out, through the news reports? Having radio contact, he couldn't have missed them. Even if he was such a hermit and didn't listen to news, the Base hospital, knowing her case, would have got in touch with him. He couldn't have avoided it. And then he'd have had to do something, probably something constructive because he'd have got a slow solid push – he couldn't have ducked out; he'd have been ashamed. But he wouldn't have flung himself around and smashed everything up."

"I know it was dumb." Bugasz cracked his knuckles. "I didn't want him to – I didn't do it to make him act like that. I didn't know it would happen...."

"You were the one who wanted Dr Ramcharan to come."

"Sure, I figured if there was something wrong with the antenna, he'd have to let us in – and if I had a doctor with me I could force him to let her examine Iris and maybe make a case out of treating her. I didn't know my coming here before would have started ..." He moved his hands helplessly.

"Then why –"

"Give me a minute, for God's sake! It's hard to say this." He fumbled in his pockets for a tissue and wiped his forehead. "I could have married her, after she got sick. She would have had me. I'm better looking than Hendricks, anyway, and younger. Women don't scrunch their faces up when they look at me, and I've had what I wanted – all except her. She'd have come to love me, and I'd have loved her, because there was nothing twisted about her, inside. But I got in to see her ... and they hadn't even let her have a mirror – and – and she looked at me, and – the look in my eyes told her what the thing had done.

"*He* looked right in her face, and he married her. I could have had faith a cure'd be found ... it was a parasite, not a thing like cancer. Cures for this kind of thing turn up fast enough when they're needed as much as this one was."

"You cannot blame yourself for choosing not to marry an ugly women," Dr Ramcharan said. "It has happened a few times before."

"But he gave her his love and a marriage ... all I gave her was the sick look in my eyes that told her for the first time what a horrible, godawful thing she'd turned into." He raised his head. "That's why I came out. I wanted to be the one to give her the news, like giving her back her beauty ... because I felt I was the one who took it away. I wanted to make up –"

"But she's gone," Stannard said. "Even granting Hendricks was nuts, and I grant it willingly, there's nothing to prove you didn't lift her off this place and leave her somewhere, having a good idea what Hendricks would do, and then come back with us, all innocent, bringing Dr Ramcharan so she could testify he killed himself. You could even have smashed the radio yourself, so he couldn't send out a call and head you off. You could have dispatched the boat to 588 so he couldn't get out of here and have ripped off the outside controls – or even rigged the antennas so we couldn't reach here very easily.

"And there's nothing to prove Mrs Hendricks was deformed, even if she did have something wrong with her at one time. You may not have known Hendricks very well, but you knew enough of him to predict he might just kill himself if you were trying to take his wife away from him or if he thought you were ... why didn't you blow up the pile already, Bugasz? Then there would have been no evidence at all."

"You crazy fool!" Bugasz screamed, "That's what that sonofabitch wants you to think! You're playing right into his hands!"

"Maybe I am." Stannard turned to the humming machine. "But I don't trust that thing any more. Whatever kind of nut Hendricks was, he made his biggest mistake when he got that computer tangled up with his feelings. I'm going to shut this whole operation down and take you with me to Base. Let those poor fools out there answer their own questions – it's better than having them trust people like you and Hendricks. And we'll take the tapes and recordings and let the police listen to them and ask you their questions and knock their heads over what to do about the whole thing. I don't want to touch it any more. I'm tired."

"Stannard, if you do that we'll never find her! Stannard! She'll stay lost somewhere out here. I don't know where she is, I swear! I haven't done any of the things you think. And I haven't touched this machine, you know I have C3 clearance – it's shut off, I couldn't get near it. I couldn't have got near the pile even if I'd wanted to; I couldn't have monkeyed with the orbit – I'm a pilot, and all I can do with machinery is pull switches – maybe I can tighten a screw, but even then I wreck the thread." He slapped the console. "Hendricks set things up to make this happen – it's the way he figured he'd get even. Stannard!" he begged. "Please! Ask him! Ask him if she had Schoebl's disease. It's the only way I can think of that'll prove I told you the truth."

"Why should he have put that in?"

"I don't know! Chances are he didn't, and it's just one more damn dumb idea – but I'm willing to take even a one-in-a-million chance. Please!"

Stannard regarded the machine with loathing. Madness in its twisted wires. He got up slowly, his shoulders weary. He went over and picked up the microphone. "More damn idiotic ... Hendricks –"

The screen stayed blank. "NO DATA, NO DATA, NO DATA –"

"Stop." He swabbed his forehead. "I don't know if I can get anything out of this thing now ..." He began wearily for the last time, "Paul Stannard, GF/Tech Supervisor ..." and went through the rigmarole. "No, I do not want to play a game. I want to know if Cornelius Hendricks knew that his wife had Schoebl's disease."

"I READ YOU, TECHMAN. THE PROTECT IS DISSOLVED. ALL DATA ARE NOW ACCESSIBLE."

They stared at it in silence for a full minute, and Stannard whispered, "Is 'Schoebl's disease' the code word?"

"YES."

Taking no chances, Stannard grabbed his bag and pulled out his own recorder. "Give me the orbit! Gimme the stores!"

Bugasz yelled, "Ask him where Iris is, goddammit, ask him!"

"All right, give me a minute! Now, Hendricks, you damn well better tell me where your wife is!"

The screen flashed in mad succession with the picture of Iris, the reconstructed image of Hendricks, the *go*-board, the spinning coin, the concentric circles, a nebula, a map of the spacelight network, the memory-map – now filled, an unspecified flow-diagram, a monster – real or imagined – a hideous caricature of Hendricks' actual face.

The sound rose blaring till the metal voice rebounded endlessly from the steel walls.

"DEAD, DEAD, DEAD. YOU FOOL! UNDER THE ANTENNA! DEAD! NOBODY WILL HAVE HER! NOBODY!" The voice died abruptly into a wail. "OH IRIS IRIS IRIS, I DIDN'T MEAN IT, IRIS, FORGIVE ME, IRIS, I DIDN'T MEAN IT – IRIS

IRIS IRIS IRIS ..."

On and on and on – but Bugasz, with a cougar's ripple of movement, had slid into his suit, grabbed Stannard's bag, and was racing for the antenna room before Stannard could as much as turn around and blink.

The machine went on, "IRIS IRIS IRIS –" but Stannard made no move to shut it up. He stood waiting till a few minutes later when Bugasz came back, carrying the woman's limp body. He took her into the bedroom and laid her gently on the bed. Dr Ramcharan was in there already, and Stannard came after.

She started to undo the spacesuit, but as they moved closer, she said, "Please don't look."

Stannard went back to where the machine was still wailing. Bugasz knocked back his helmet and ran after him, twitching him round by a push at the shoulder. He roared, "You! You wouldn't let me check the antennas!" and swung a back-hand blow to the side of the head that sent Stannard flying.

"IRIS IRIS IRIS –"

After a moment, Stannard dragged himself up, staggered over, pulled down the mike. "Stop it," he said. "You can stop now. She's alive."

Stannard ran diagnostic tests and satisfied himself that 1526 was no longer a jealous liar. There was nothing wrong with the orbit; the answers for hours sixteen to twenty were there for the picking. And Iris Hendricks was alive, but only just. In gasping whispers she was able to add the few details they needed to know. Hendricks had sent her out to check the antennas and simply retracted them. Although they moved very slowly, not in one quick collapse, there was no way for her to escape. The hatches were locked, and she couldn't dodge out of the way without ripping her air-hose; she had no oxygen tanks. She had been carrying a heavy lantern; all she could do was jam it under the angle of one of the descending arms and lie trapped in the narrow space it left her. She had lain there for eighteen hours. "I thought it was a mistake at first – I was going to call him through the suit-radio ... but he started screaming things – he thought I was dead – and – and –"

Dr Ramcharan drugged her into relieved sleep, and Bugasz called in the drone.

"Will she live?" Stannard asked.

"Oh, yes. She would have weakened and died soon if we had not found her, but now she is only bruised." She turned to Bugasz. "How will they cure her?"

"The way I heard it, there's drugs to kill the parasites and dissolve the nodes. Some of them will probably have to be cut out. She won't be – everything she was, but ..." He watched the drone trundling toward the shaft with its burden, and Dr Ramcharan gave her attention to Stannard's battered cheekbone and the cut on the corner of his mouth.

"You are determined to stay?" Stannard winced a little at her touch. "It is not good for men to be alone in these places."

"The police will be here within a day, and I can clear things up faster. I'm not a lonely type. Besides, I won't even be alone." He cocked his head at the machine, and grimaced. "I've got him."

Bugasz tore his eyes away from the disappearing drone, came over to Stannard and gave a couple of preliminary swallows. "I'm sorry."

Stannard, bruised, thin-haired and cold-eyed, feeling a little sorry for himself and ridiculing himself for it, looked up at Bugasz and took one small flicker of enjoyment from the big man's humility. "Forget it."

Bugasz, with a slumping of the shoulders, went into the ship.

"The poor man will lose his job," Dr Ramcharan said.

Stannard said, "Not through me. I'll do my best to help him keep it. But he took a swing at me, and I'm not gonna let him off the hook." He grinned at the expression on her face, even though it hurt his mouth. "You'll tell him, anyway, as soon as you get on board."

"You are hard on the feelings of a person, Stannard."

"I'm a techman. I never wanted to be a policeman."

She took his chin in her hand and looked down so there was no escaping her eyes. The shadow of her sleeve glittered with gold, and her fingers laced his jaw like hot gold wire. "You are not lonely and you do not need to be loved. I think someone forgot to teach you how."

He sat unmoving, hands resting on his knees. "Are you lonely, Dr Ramcharan?"

"My husband is treating tentacle paralysis on Barnard Nine, and my children are home in New Bombay with my mother. But I will have a sabbatical soon, and I hope to see them all."

"Good luck," he said.

She packed her bag quietly and left, going down the shaft with the slipping glide of a woman who has learned to keep a sari from sliding off her shoulder.

The locks closed.

Stannard called for a tape printout of the Kaghouri data first and then for the rest of the answers. It would save time for the police, and he would have at least one neat package to hand over to them. Then he turned down the thermostat, dimmed the lights and sat down. He began to shape in his mind the explanations he would have to lay out; but there was plenty of time for that, and he left it. He meditated briefly on the complexities of men and the machines that served them. His thoughts, his eyes, drifted back to the computer. He sighed.

Part of Hendricks' tormented spirit was still twined in its guts. The man had had no right to do that, to force his machine to lie, deceive, conceal, accuse ... but it had been done. The psych-police would unreel the situation hour by hour from its stores, would report, judge and close the case. Still unresolved forever because a machine may not expiate nor a man absolve it.

He got up very slowly, went over and picked up the mike.

"Fifteen-twenty-six, this is Stannard again ... will you play a game of *go* with me?"

"I AM NOT PROGRAMMED TO PLAY WITH A FIFTH-CLASS PLAYER."

"That's all right," he said. "I'll take white and give you a four-stone handicap. It'll even us out okay ..."

He waited, almost tensely, and after a moment the *go*-board appeared, white-hatched against the grey, black-dotted at the D and Q cross-points of 4 and 16.

"Fine." He took a deep breath. "My first move is R 14 ..."

1968

SUNDAY'S CHILD

The cloud lowered till it rested on the tips of the scraggy pines; lightning forked through it and thunder ricocheted between cloud and ground.

Nadja's eyes sharpened out of their stupor. She lay unmoving in the bunk and stared upward through the dome roof: a few autumn branches tapped it, beckoning. The Plexiglas triangles stared back at her. Their shutters had been folded back because of the darkening sky, and the sharp locking triangles became one faceted eye. One became many and many became one and again many. Eyes.

They watched. Eyes. I's. Eye. Watch.

She screamed. "Stop!" And again, "Stop! No, no!"

She leaped and ran screaming through the partition doorway, down the hall, out the door, Mandros gaping. David frozen with a hand reached to grab her. Barefoot in the cold wind, the wet earth; her tattered nightgown billowed and her feet splattered mud at every step. "No! Don't!"

Lightning probed before her eyes, split a dead tree that burst into flames. Weeping, Nadja flung herself in its crèche, fainted, and lay like an animal roasting in coals.

David and Mandros pulled her out and dropped her on the ground; her hair was burning, and David tore off his jacket, squeezed out the flames with it. She lay snorting with her face half in mud, the rags of her black hair tangled in white ash.

"God damn it, never know what she'll do." David shoved his arm into the muck under her shoulders and lifted her.

Mandros took her by the stick legs and said nothing. The downpour began again, drenching the fire, and combed the thin dark hair straight down Mandros's skull, caught in globules through David's hair and beard. They hauled her inside, a dead weight, bruised and filthy.

Stella was waiting. "She badly hurt?"

"A few bruises, her hair got burned," David said. "I think she fainted."

He took the weight from Mandros and carried her to the small infirmary in the service complex. The skinny body hung over his shoulder; tears and raindrops fell from Nadja's face, with a flake of ash, a drop of blood from the bruised cheek, saliva from her open mouth. One wet red leaf was plastered on the side of her neck. He put her on the bed, took off his glasses and wiped them with thumb and fingers. "She shouldn't be here."

"Yeah." Stella ripped off the old nightgown in one powerful sweep. "Wash that and save it for patches."

"That *is* patches." He touched Nadja's face, gently turned her body over and back again. "Just needs a bit of antiseptic."

They bathed the gaunt pale shape, trimmed the singed hair, daubed the bruises. Nadja stirred and muttered, protested with feeble hands.

When she was settled they stood looking at her for a moment without pride in their pathetic handiwork. There might have been beauty in her with health and vigour. And sanity, Stella said to herself. That's not asking much. "You're right. She shouldn't be here."

David said morosely, "Try moving her and she'll fight like a cat in a sack." He left, and Nadja lay as she had done most of the days and nights, shifting sometimes to short intervals of lucidity or bursts of mania.

She had battered the door one midnight a couple of years earlier, howling a tale of beating, rape, pursuit. No one had pursued. David and Joseph Running Deer had picked up her trail through mud and scrub for a kilometre, and except for a fox and two rabbits no other tracks had crossed her path. She was haunted down the crazy labyrinth of her mind by imaginary furies; because of her terror they had let her stay, and she had never left.

"What is it?"

Nadja was trying to whisper. She licked her lips and swallowed.

"What?"

"Send ... send ..."

"What?" Stella lifted the blue-veined wrist, its pulse thready and vulnerable.

"Send Mandros. Here." Nadja's head whipped from side to side. "Mandros!"

"Him? Why do you want −"

"Mandros!" Her voice rose to a shriek.

"All right. Stay quiet and I'll get him."

She opened the door and stepped back. Mandros was standing there, waiting, hair still falling in lines down his forehead, lower lip hanging loose from his teeth. His brown eyes narrowed, shifted from side to side like Nadja's head. Stella licked her lips. "She wants you."

"Alone," Nadja croaked.

Stella looked at her, and then at Mandros in the checked flannel shirt still so wet it clung to his shoulders. "Try to keep her calm." Mandros said nothing. She passed him, the door closed. She pulled herself away from it uneasily and through the triangles watched David outside in the rain rescuing what was left of his jacket.

In the common room Ephraim Markoosie was sorting out his tackle box. His hair too was black, but his slant brown eyes were merry. "She gone wild again?"

"Yeah. Burnt half her hair off this time."

He shook his head. His wife Annabel was warming her feet by the tiny gas heater, knitting a scarf from yarn scraps; she had tied the ends of her braids with blue and red strands. Because they lived less outdoors, the Markoosies did not have the deeply weathered faces of most Inuit.

Stella sat on the braided rug, picked pieces of yarn from the tangle in the sugar sack, and began to splice them.

After a long silence, Ephraim asked, "You not feeling well?"

"I was wondering where Mandros came from."

"Better not ask," said Annabel. "You make yourself sick with too much of that."

Stella shrugged. She had no memory of anything before finding herself in front of the dome five years ago, and no strength of will or tortuous effort could push her memory further. She crossed her legs and kept on splicing.

David flung the sodden tattered jacket in the middle of the floor. "Have I got a job for somebody!"

Ephraim put aside the tackle box. "Ha. Mister Medicine Man, how come you sew up people all right and you can't fix clothes?" He picked up the jacket and began to pluck at the charred edges of the holes. "We got plenty of rabbit skins."

"I'm not a plastic surgeon."

Ephraim chuckled. Stella got up and took her coat off the hook.

"You going outside?" David asked.

"A few minutes. The rain's let up."

"There's a rough wind."

"I won't be long."

To the church again? he asked with his eyes. She lowered her own.

Joseph Running Deer was setting out on his patrol of the power line, and nodded as she passed. Pushing aside thorny bushes and whipping branches, she went a score of metres along the path to the church, a path she had worn mainly by herself, and paused to look back.

The dome's triangles reflected the sullen sky. Joseph in his yellow slicker, pieced into the shapes of leaves through the black branches, receded and dwindled. Five kilometres southward, Leona Cress from the next dome would be patrolling the line to the transformer; when they met they would make the small exchanges for which they did not waste radio time or helicopter fuel: greetings, gossip, letters, packages. Across the boreal forest stood dome after dome.

From the zenith of each a watchtower rose: its inhabitant read pollution monitors and pressed reports on button panels. Sometimes a mine, well, or processing plant fifty or a hundred kilometres away would shut down for a day if the air got too thick. Whatever the reading, the air stank excrementally of sulphur and caught the throat; on blue days the grey always bordered the horizon.

The machines did not grope, crush or boil as frantically as they had once done. There were fewer people and fewer demands. Southward the cities on the lakes sat choked in their own detritus and their inhabitants lived in domes much larger than the ones manned by the northern watchtowers, but still in domes with filtered air; every year fewer children were born in them, and every year more young adults lifted off Earth for the bleaker domes of planets and moons. The equatorial zones rippled with sands and sparse grasses, most of their lung-plantations hacked away, the rest withering. The lakes shrank and thickened with algae and the watersheds leached the increasingly treeless soil and carried the salt of the earth and its pollutants into more and more bitter seas. The icecaps had diminished, and the forests pulled their borders back from the temperate zones and retreated toward the tundra, narrowing and thinning over the Precambrian shield; the trees gnarled.

No starships lifted.

Five years earlier the first tentative but desperate few to break the boundary of the solar system had reported a ring of alien ships appearing without warning from the void. Then in turn the radio of each venturer blurted half an hour of garbled hysteria and went dead. Tracking satellites lost them. Twelve strange ships orbited the system half a million kilometres beyond Pluto. Signals beamed at them in millions of combinations were unanswered, and after seven or eight months Earth gave up. Three new ships lifted toward the Pole star and died.

Earth sat and considered herself, walled-in and choking. Astronomers considered the ships and asked themselves: Alpha Centauri, Sirius – or Procyon? The ships had appeared instantly in orbit. There were no directions to adduce. One day someone said, as if it were a datum: Procyon – why, when the others were nearer? – and the twelve had become the aliens of Procyon, hostile by nature but of what shape no one could guess, except in the wild imagining of the newly formed sects that prayed to them.

Stella climbed the path to the clearing where the church stood on a rock of pinkish granite, one of many that rose from the soil, some angular, deep red or grey, some like the heads or limbs of giants waking to split the thin skin of earth like an amniotic membrane. The church had been built by some group long vanished; it was a weathered shell, outer paint worn off, shingles falling or askew, steeple frail with rust. There was nothing inside: some believer had stolen the crucifix, and the pews and panelling had been removed for use in the dome. It had no denomination, no creed, and Stella did not know why she came there, because she did not pray, but she stood in its windy doorway and watched the land from the height of the rock, rather than from the dome's tower with its winking lights and smutty windows.

Sometimes, with her inner eye, she watched herself from the ships of Procyon: through telescope, past port or view-screen, cutting silver circles of orbit· Pluto, Neptune, Uranus, Saturn, past looping comets and asteroid gravel to the third planet, the dying world: stratosphere, atmosphere, cloud, and Stella. Big woman with a weathered granitic face and body solid down to the feet flat on bone-coloured rock, the multibillion-year-old granite. She had long fair hair of the sort that grows grey imperceptibly, a wisp gathered from each temple and drawn back into a thin braid tied with string. Ephraim had made her a long sky-blue buckskin coat lined and bordered with rabbit fur; she rubbed cornmeal on it to keep it clean, a small vanity.

"Here I am," she told the Procyons. Because of her amnesia she often had the terrifying fantasy that the

151

aliens had formed her and set her in the dome for some awful purpose; she spent black hours scouring her mind and driving her memory; she went at her tasks with almost as much mania as Nadja's to drive out irrational guilt. One midnight in bed she had forced herself to tell David of the fear, shaking and sweating, pushing the words out.

He had lit the lamp and stared at her for a long while, and she crouched before him in her naked soul, jeering at herself because her hands were trembling. "No, I'll never believe that," he said at last, and turned out the light. The black hours separated themselves and diminished. She accepted them.

The hour was blue now, evening rising under the shadow of the world. The dome was lit in a filigree of light through its shutters.

Branches crackled: David came up the path, stumbling a little and cursing under his breath. His hands and arms were the essence of grace, and the rest of him heavy and clumsy as a dancing bear. He stopped at the base of the rock and looked up at her. "You all right, love?"

"Yes. I'm all right."

He reached out his hand and she came down and took it. A fine soft rain began.

Nadja's appetite improved; she ate broth, bread, stew. The hollows of her body filled out a little. She did not sleep quite so much, and her mania became subdued, but she giggled often on a note just below hysteria, and spoke in rhyming snatches.

The winter closed down.

The men set traps and caught lean foxes and their prey, the scrawny rabbits. The flesh of the foxes was left to placate the wolves and wild dogs who had joined the packs; the bigger animals had been overhunted and were scarce. The women chopped firewood and burned charcoal for the water-filter. Snow turned dirty before it reached the ground and glittered only in the brightest sunlight.

David, coming back with a brace of rabbits hung over his shoulder, stopped to watch Stella chopping wood; his hands were too valuable to gather calluses from an axe handle. "It makes me sweat to look at you."

"I'm sweating," she said between hacks.

Nadja drifted through the half-open doorway, singing and twirling to some imaginary orchestra.

"Oh God, there she goes again." David started toward her and paused.

She was standing, arms stretched high, face to the sun and full of ecstasy.

"At least she put on some weight," said Stella.

"Yes ... she has ... hasn't she?" David was staring at the slender ankles in the snow, the thin arms rising from the sleeves of the shapeless faded gown. He dropped the rabbits and approached her with a stalker's caution. "Nadja dear, come inside with me. It's too cold for you...." He pulled down one of her arms slowly and gripped her hand. "Come on, sweetheart." She went with him, skipping barefoot in the snow, singing one of the odd little tunes of the young child or the mad.

Stella's sweat turned cold. She put the axe on the stacked wood and followed.

David persuaded Nadja to lie on her bunk, squatted beside her and put his hand on her belly. She giggled and tickled his neck. He raised his head to Stella and the flat outer planes of his glasses shone with sunlit triangles. "How long since she menstruated?"

"I don't know ... she's so irregular – we keep her

clean, but it's hard to keep track." Her voice rose. "You think she's pregnant?"

"Don't get excited! Look," he smoothed the cloth over Nadja's stomach, "not much swelling, but it's where she put most of the weight. You can feel –"

"No –" she stepped backward. *Send Mandros.* "You're sure."

"Yes. I'm sure."

"You knew it outside. You saw something."

"Yes," said David. "I saw it move."

The fire had not yet been built, and the common room was cold and bleak. David knocked his pipe on the fender and stuffed it with tobacco. "Last ten years, only three babies in the domes I know of ... two of them taken south...."

Stella rolled a cigarette she did not want because she felt nauseated. "How far gone is she?"

David struck fire from a lighter, touched it to the kindling, and lit pipe and cigarette. "Three months and a bit. Early for it to move, but not impossible."

"She didn't throw up or anything."

"It's not necessary."

"You think she was raped?"

"I doubt it. She'd have probably raised hell and been knocked around."

"How could it happen, then? Who would do that?"

"I don't know. I haven't seen any of the men hanging around her."

"Mandros ... when she ran out in the rain – 'Send Mandros,' she said – oh God, I wish I hadn't ... but he was waiting, I was afraid she'd go wild again ... and – and David, I think he's impotent."

"Yes ... I've thought that. He doesn't go near anyone, seems to be shrinking inside. Gives everybody the same

look, blank. I'd swear he has no sexual feelings at all –
but he's the only man we know who was alone with her."

"Maybe he had feelings, once."

"Or somebody else did, on some wild impulse, when
nobody was looking...." He shuffled his feet. "It wasn't
me."

"I know that ... I can read your face too." She licked
her lips. "Should we ask her?"

"What's the use? It could be God, the devil, the Procyons, the Sasquatch, the Wendigo ..."

"If we tell the others they'll be upset and insulted, a
woman so sick being victimized. The men will be tense,
and the women will start wondering...."

"No, we'd better not tell. She's hardly showing, and
she wears those loose nightgowns....We'll have a fuel al-
lowance built up soon and we'll call for the chopper,
send her off on some excuse. It'll take a lot of doing, but
we can't care for her properly up here anyway."

"We'll have the man here. It'll still be a horrible
puzzle."

"I don't think we'll solve it."

She dropped her cigarette into the fire. "The atmosphere will be poisoned."

"It *is* poisoned, love."

Mandros went about his work: patrolled the line,
butchered meat, took his turn at the cooking pots and in
the tower. Said perhaps ten words a day, mainly *yes, no,
okay, uh-huh;* his eyes were blank. He did not go near
Nadja.

Nadja ate heartily; her weight-gain balanced out the
slow thickening of her belly.

Once, on a clear day, she said, "I like the blue sky,"
and smiled.

Stella's heart clenched, and relaxed. Maybe it would

be all right; in the south Nadja would become well, the baby would be loved. Her black hour paled a little.

The dome's life went on quietly as ever with its slow air of winding down. The radio brought no news of great disasters and did not mention the Procyons. In the evenings, tasks done, Billy and Clyde sometimes put away their checkers, Billy brought out his battered fiddle and he and Clyde played and sang the old loggers' songs; the flames shook to the stamp of their feet. They were wiry men with red weathered faces and cross-hatched necks, friends for thirty years and perfectly suited to each other, without heat or passion. The late March snow thickened on the windows.

"It's like this, Dave, eh?" Clyde scraped one sole on the side of the other boot and stared at the worn leather. Billy stood half behind him, nodding at every phrase. "We used to work in the woods, eh? an there ain't been no fuckin woods since we were young bucks, so we come out here, eh?" Billy nodded and Clyde paused and looked up as if he expected David to read his mind.

"What are you getting at, Clyde?"

Clyde tightened his fists, twisting the question between them. "Up here we been workin, doin whatever had to be done. I think we pulled our weight, eh?"

"You mean you want to go? Clyde? Billy?"

Billy nodded.

"Yeah. I didn' want to say it just like that."

"After twelve years ..."

"Then I guess it's about time, eh? We're gettin older ... if there's a place that's clean enough we'll fish an trap, an if not they need manpower down south with all them leavin an dyin off."

"But –"

"You wouldn feel bad if we left, Dave? We done our share an all."

"You're my friends! I can't help feeling bad. And – and I just – God damn it, I just don't understand!"

"Well ..." Clyde struggled and Billy pursed his mouth and shook his head. "It's a queer thing, Dave, and I don't think I understand either. We been talking about it, ain't we, Billy? Something here doesn't feel right, we dunno what, but we want to leave." He added, simply and with finality, "That's all it is."

David gave in. "At least let me call for the helicopter. We'll have enough fuel soon."

"No thanks, Dave. We got snowshoes. If we can take a hatchet an a frypan an maybe a couple of lighters, we'll make it on our own."

Fiddle, stamping feet, bawdy song ... those long-time friends.

But – Nadja ... could they? No, not those old bachelors, bent and dry as the wood they stacked.

The early April snow fell thickly and melted fast. In two weeks David would send for the helicopter. He set trap lines with Joseph and Ephraim. They spoke of Clyde and Billy with mild regret.

Stella found it strange that no-one seemed to notice how swollen Nadja was becoming. Perhaps they were occupied with their own thoughts.

One evening Joseph calmly announced that he and Anna-Marie Corbière were leaving in two days for Manitoulin Island to stay on the reserve with his family. Jenny Bellisle, whose father lived in the Métis commune there, said she would go with them. Once again David offered the helicopter, and they refused.

PHYLLIS GOTLIEB

"I didn't even bother asking them if they felt funny."
David turned the pipe in his fingers; flecks of ash scattered on the floor.

Ephraim sat punching holes in a piece of leather.
Annabel squatted on the floor, propped against his back,
knitting. Except where it concerned Nadja, David did
not guard his tongue with them; he was tired of strange
feelings.

Stella was sewing moccasins from cut pieces prepared
by Ephraim. "Annabel, what's that you're knitting?"

The scarf had been finished long ago; Annabel held
up a small multicoloured piece. "Second sleeve of jacket.
For the baby. Nadja's."

"Annabel," Stella whispered, "who else knows?"

"Maybe everybody. Or nobody. They don't talk.
Maybe they don't want to know." She turned the needle
and started a new row. "She's getting pretty big ... you
think it's Mandros?"

"We don't know. We didn't want to talk about it because we'd upset everybody."

"They got upset from something, eh? Mandros, he
don't look like he's leaving."

"I wish he would," said David. "Oh God, I wish we'd
never kept her here!"

"Ephraim? Annabel? How about you?"

"I don't feel funny," said Ephraim. "Yet."

Stella ploughed through the wet snow to the church and
stood in its door frame under the dripping eaves and rotting shingles. Through the branches she saw David as a
shadow in the tower, Ephraim beginning his long walk
down the line, Joseph with Anne-Marie and Jenny
shouldering their packs and moving away forever.

"David, Ephraim, Annabel, Nadja, Mandros, and I.

Procyons, why are you waiting?... and why did I say that?"

"David, let's all leave in the helicopter." She was curled about his body, breathing against his warm stout back.

"Zat?" He jerked awake in the middle of a snore.

"I said let's get out of here in the helicopter."

"Unh. Won't take all if dome's empty."

"Who cares about domes? We're just puppets pushing buttons. We can't be kept here."

"Maybe don' wan' all go ..." Not having been quite awake, he slept.

Maybe. Ephraim and Annabel who had come here to ease their old age a little – settling in the barren south? They would rather go north and die.

If we leave now it will be like sending them north to die.

The thaw quickened and little rivulets stirred, waiting for black-flies. The snow turned to grey rains that streaked the glass.

On the day David planned to call for the helicopter the cloud lowered and lightning forked it. Stella shuddered; Nadja had run out into the fire on such a day. She kept close watch, but Nadja was quiet, kneeling on the rug in the common room building towers with Clyde's abandoned checkers, red upon black upon red. The child kicked visibly in her belly, her own movements were slow and deliberate.

"You won't get the copter today," said Stella.

"Yeah." David tugged fingers through his ginger beard. "They couldn't reach here before nightfall even if the storm let up."

Nadja grinned, swiped wildly at the tower and checkers flew everywhere. Her face shifted abruptly, mouth turned down at the corners, and her eyes filled with tears.

"All right, Nadja...." David squatted, gathered the checkers with his quick hands and rebuilt the tower.

Nadja clapped her hands and laughed, the child writhed in her belly and he turned his eyes away.

Ephraim came and sat down, unrolled a piece of leatherwork; he was ready to take his place on the line as soon as Mandros returned.

Silently Mandros appeared in the doorway watching Nadja. Water ran down his face, dripped from his oilskin and pooled at his feet.

For a moment the room seemed to echo with the banter of lost friends, filled with their shadows.

David's eyes were fixed on Mandros. Words came without control. "You see her, Mandros? Do you? A madwoman? Why? Why her? Tell me, hey?" His voice was almost pleading. "Mandros?"

"I don't know what you are saying," said Mandros. He stood, boots puddling the floor, a glove held in each upturned hand like an offering. "What do you mean?" His eyes were blank, not shifting, his lower lip hung.

He turned and left.

Nadja, unmoved, went on playing with checkers.

David rubbed sweat off his forehead with the palms of his hands. "I shouldn't have done that."

Ephraim sighed and got up, rolled his piece of leather and put it on a table. His jacket was checkered in red and black like a big game-board. He zipped it, took his oilskin off its hook and shouldered it on. The sky was darkening, wind whipped rain against the glass.

"Ephraim, don't bother about the line," Stella said. "Nobody's going to be attacking it tonight."

Ephraim shrugged. "I promised Tom Arcand some

skins and I'll have a talk with him down there. In here is cold as Ellesmere Island." He took mittens from his pocket. "Maybe I'll go there."

"I'm sorry, Ephraim," David whispered.

Ephraim grunted. The outer door thudded behind him.

David pounded his fist on his knee in an agony of embarrassment.

"What's the matter, David? There was nothing wrong in asking."

His shoulders twitched. "We've lost the others.... I don't want Ephraim to ..."

Nadja looked up, and her hand, in the act of placing the last checker, paused above the tower. Her eyes were calm. She was bent forward slightly, and the drape of the gown over her belly hid the child's movement. She had been well cared for; her hair was clean and fell in soft waves to her shoulders, her dark eyes were unshadowed, her skin smooth; the bone structure of her face showed clearly, but without gauntness.

She's pretty, Stella thought. At last, and so what? "How's the baby, Nadja?" she asked, to fill the silence. "Which do you want, a boy or a girl?"

Nadja looked, somewhere, not at her. "It is a male. Its name is Aesh." She placed the last checker. "In our language."

"In our language? What ..." Stella and David stared at each other in a strange fear.

David raised his hand as Stella was about to speak again. "That's enough," he said. "Forget it."

Annabel came down from the tower and headed for the kitchen, and Stella in turn climbed the iron spiral.

The tower stood much higher above ground than the church, but Stella had never found it peaceful. Lights flickered over the panel map, the radio whispered of the deaths of continents; the stars had been obscured by pollution, and at night nothing could be seen through the windows except sometimes a dirty moon. The panes reflected the watcher and the objects inside, and Stella, who never flinched before a mirror, did not like the grim face the glass returned to her.

The shades and frames on the roof got in the way of the light below, but Stella in imagination observed David smoking his pipe by the fire and trying to find reason in Nadja; Annabel moving about among the cooking pots; Mandros perhaps sitting on the edge of his bunk sewing up the split finger of a glove....

White light slammed the dome, the rock, the world.

From the sudden darkness came a hiss intense as a scream. Stella cried out in echo....

When her blinded eyes cleared she saw the small beam of the emergency lantern, grabbed it out of its clamp with one hand and with the other dragged down on the switches of the wind generator and its power line.

The lights trembled and then surged.

"Stel-ell-ellla!" David was yelling over the intercom.

"I'm all right!" She was gripping the lantern, thoughts ricocheting wildly; the flash-beam swung over the dead blank panel, her heart jumped in rhythm with *no-loss, no-loss, no-loss*, beating so fiercely it took her a moment to realize that the radio had also gone dead. Wireless. She said confusedly, "But how –"

"–ella!"

"I'm coming!" She ran down the stair. "David, the radio's dead! The line –"

He was in his coat, cramming his hat down over his ears. "Ephraim! If he was around when it blew –"

Nadja was hunched on the floor, weeping. Annabel, in silence, watched David yanking on his boots. Mandros was waiting, dressed for outdoors. Stella found that her hand was locked around the lantern. She held it out, Mandros took it and went into the darkness with David. The door thudded. Annabel picked up the scroll of leather and gripped it with both hands. Rain swept against the glass.

Nadja flung herself into a rigid backward arch as if she were in tetany and began to scream.

The power line was laid along the ground, flowing between hewn rock faces and over old stream beds; it was cased in flexible plastic; a twenty-centimetre cable that shifted naturally with seasonal erosion and withstood flooding and rock-falls. It could not break and had not been broken. It had been sheared by a terrific force that left the ends ten metres apart, coiling like pythons, wiring fused into lumps of solder.

Ephraim was lying in the pounding rain beside the charred track of its furious burning. He was dead, one arm rag and bone, one side blackened to cinder. The bag of skins for Tom Arcand lay beside him.

David doubled up, vomiting, and wondered dimly why he was not surprised.

He straightened, spat, turned his face away from Ephraim, and Mandros. "Too far ... to bring him in ... until the rain ..."

"I'm sorry," said Mandros.

David shook his head.

Mandros said, "Tomorrow I will make a travois."

"Yes," said David. "You do that." Blindly he headed north against the rain.

As they came within sight of the dome they heard the muffled screaming under the driving wind. David ran ahead, sloshing, dragged the door open. "Stella! Annabel!"

"Infirmary, David!"

They were holding the screaming Nadja down on the bed, one to each pair of limbs as the body arched, the child writhed inside her. Nadja's gown was flecked with blood.

"You give her anything?" David struggled with soaked clothes.

"Only the usual. I was afraid, I didn't know what –" Her voice was trembling. "I'm afraid the baby –"

"I'll hold her, you give her a double dose, intravenous."

Nadja did not turn quiet under increased medication; her voice sank two octaves into a steady moan. Her body flattened on the bed. Annabel let go of the small tight fists and raised her eyes to David.

They were very still; they were the stillest things in the room.

"Ephraim is dead," he whispered. "I think lightning ..." Lightning? Whatever tore that line apart like a piece of string.

Annabel looked down and brushed the hair from Nadja's wet forehead. Her hand moved in a series of little jerks. "You bring him in?"

"Couldn't ... half a kilometre away ... tomorrow –" He pulled in a deep breath, exhaled on half a sob and hurried to the lavatory to wash.

Nadja's moan shifted to a sound that was half giggle and half snarl of pain. "Ephraim's away," she croaked, "he's gone to stay, he won't be back another day...."

Annabel pulled back her hand as if it had been burnt, and stared at the twisted face. Then slowly reached out again to lift the wrenching body so that Stella could change the gown and bedding. Nadja was bleeding in a thin steady stream.

David's primitive hospital gave him a few drugs, instruments, bandages, a clean shirt and surgical gloves.

"Only six months, David! Is – is she –"

"Aborting, maybe ... can't be sure it's six, though...." He rested his hand on Nadja's belly. "Or whether it happened that day...." The dome shape tightened itself into a peak. "But it's way low down, contracting and ..." one hand on the humped curve, he explored with the other, "my God, fighting like hell – dilated – head's right up at the top –" Blood spurted around his hand. The red stream ran off the bed and dripped on the tile floor. "Got to bring it on, it's the only way to stop –"

The screaming rose.

"Another needle?"

"Not yet. We'll need the –" sweat ran down his face and caught in globules through his beard, "need the – the –"

"Christ, David, the blood!"

"I know, God damn it! Need anaesthetic and we've hardly got –" bearing down on the squirming hump with one hand, he forced with the other, "never had such a tough ... ah ..." The waters broke and flowed, the red paled for a few moments, and deepened again. David's face was so dark red it seemed he would sweat blood. "Never had such a – get the instrument and anaesthesia packages off the shelf above –" groping through blood, heaving desperately at the hidden shape in the flesh envelope to bring the head on aim with the world. "That's it – first the relaxant ..."

And fighting like hell. Why does he?

He?

All right, then, pull him out hind-end first, anything to make the womb tighten and close, stop the blood.... "That's better ... place the cone so she can breathe, and tape it – Jesus, we've got enough equipment to pull a hangnail!" He was panting. He knew what to do well enough, and had almost nothing to do it with. "See if you can get Mandros to raise Central Eastern Hospital."

"I told you, David, the radio's dead."

He said nothing, aimed his blade to enlarge an opening for the stubborn and furious child. His teeth were chattering. Annabel wiped his face. Nadja was quiet and pale.

"Her pulse is weak," Stella said.

"She has a murmur, I'm scared of that – oh, I can't go on this way, it has to be caesarean."

He raised the blade.

The belly humped and a red bubble swelled out of its peak and broke; from within a sharp thing had punctured it. "What's that?" The pointed thing caught the harsh light, began to tear a ragged line down the skin. A claw.

"Oh, my God!" David howled, and sliced. Divided the shredded membranes, reached in and pulled away the dark squirming creature, held it up, it was received.

Deaf, dumb, blind, David. Knife on floor in darkening red.

Stitch on stitch, he sewed.

"David ... she's dead, David...."

Tears joined sweat rivers falling in blood.

"I know," he said, and kept on sewing.

It was male. *His name is Aesh.*

"In our language," David muttered. In our language, what?

Aesh was covered with fine dark hairs, not thickly, but like the arm of a hairy man. Ears very small, high on the head, eyes sharp and black, slanting a little. His nails were sharp translucent claws with a fine blood vessel running through each almost to the tip. In his armpits were small webbings of hairy goose-pimpled skin extending from halfway down the inside of the upper arm across to the vicinity of the sixth rib. His penis was short and tubular, without glans, like a section of aorta, and his one testicle was the size and colour of a chestnut, covered with the long dark hairs that reminded Stella, hysterically, of the hair plastering itself in straight lines down Mandros's head in the rain.

"A mutant," she whispered. "The pollution ..."

"No," said David. "I think he is as he was meant to be."

Swaddled in a blanket, bedded in a crate, Aesh slept.

Stella had sent Annabel to bed with sleeping pills; washed David as if he were the baby and propelled him into the common room; found the bottle of whiskey inherited from some transient, pushed it into his hands with a glass. Wrapped Nadja's body in rubber sheeting and placed it in the storeroom. It was very light. Cleaned the infirmary with mop and bucket until the only blood that remained was left crusting on the tied-off stub of the child's umbilicus. Because she was going to sleep here this night, with him. He mewled and snuffled a little, Aesh.

"The power line is cut," said David, tilting the glass. He was nowhere on the way to becoming drunk. "I wish I liked this stuff. The power line, the wireless ... the others are gone or dead."

"Tomorrow we'll go down to the transformer."

"We'll try it.... I wonder if we'll reach it."

"Why, David? Who will stop us?"

"Whoever, whatever cut the line. You'll realize when you see it."

"I'm not sure I understand what you're getting at." She was afraid she did.

"The power, the radio," he repeated. "The others – Clyde, Billy, and the rest – felt funny, and they left. Ephraim refused to feel funny – and he's gone. Nadja ... isn't needed anymore. Is she? Could she bring up? that? child?"

"David, I think you're getting –"

"I wish I could. Oh God. But there was nothing. Even if we could have taken her south. Not with that. But we were kept here. The ones who were kept here were the ones necessary to make sure that child got born alive. In good health. That six-month full-term child." He looked at her as he had looked when she told him of her terrible fear. "It didn't all come into my head this minute. There were wisps of it before. I wouldn't let it come together and now I can't stop it. The ones who were needed were you and me and Annabel."

"And Mandros."

"Him."

"But – what is he? He's not – not like that child."

"Maybe he is, under a mask. I don't know."

"A ..." she pushed the word out. "Procyon?" – *horrible fear that I was – oh it's so goddam silly, so irrational – because I can't remember – that the Procyons had, had made me and put me here for –* "David, you don't think –"

"– that he's the construct, what I was so afraid I was ... but why?"

"Maybe I am drunk," said David. He capped the bottle and heaved himself up. "We have things to do, in the morning."

There were not many places in that rocky land where the earth lay deep enough for burial, but Mandros found one, and before the sun rose he had dragged Ephraim's body back on a travois. Annabel bandaged it and dressed it in the old fur-lined parka Ephraim's father had made for him; he and Nadja, having had nothing in common in life, shared a grave.

David watched. His cheeks sagged, his eyes were red behind the glasses. By the time the last shovel was tamped the sun was half-up, and the baby began to wail in a treble piping like the squeak of a bat.

Mandros swung the spade up so that its handle rested on his shoulder. "He wants feeding, that one."

"Babies don't get fed the first day," said David.

"That one does," said Mandros.

Without a word David went indoors to instruct Stella and Annabel in mixing boiled water with sugar and powdered milk.

"You don't know if it will take this," Stella said.

"It's all we've got." From the stores where everything was saved to be reused he had gathered small bottles and was putting them to boil in a pot of water. "Cut off the fingertips of some of my surgical gloves for nipples. They won't hold up well –" he bent over the shrilling, whimpering child, set in his crate-cradle by the stove for warmth, and ran his thumb over the red parted gums," – but this one looks as if he'll be wanting solid food very soon."

"David – if we're closed in, as you say, line cut, no radio – where will we get it?"

"I don't know that either." He lifted a tiny wrist, noting that the fingers did not curl into a fist but clenched back on themselves so that the claws did not dig into the palm. "Those will bite, these will scratch, can't be cut because of the blood vessels ... webbing here – vestigial wing? – don't think he'll fly with that ... wonder what his insides are like."

Annabel looked down at the baby and away; her tearless eyes were dull. "Spirit-child," she muttered. "Witch-child."

169

The rising sun caught two shining spots on the small tight belly, and David bent closer. On each of the tiny crinkled nipples a white drop had risen. "He's got witch's milk," said David, "but that's a human phenomenon. Whatever else he is, Aesh-in-our-language is half-human." He put on his jacket again and paused in the doorway. "Mind the claws when you feed him."

The earth outside was like a soaked rug: water pressed out of it at each step. Too shallow to allow water to drain, it would pool into sickly marshes in summer.

David followed the line, squelching in rotten leaves and soggy twigs. The sky was grey-blue, the sun smoky; he detoured around the break. The baby's cry seemed to be within him, a ceaseless mourning for Ephraim, that joyful friend, and Nadja ... because I kept letting it go when she should have been sent away ... and oh God, Ephraim and Annabel, why didn't you leave? It would have hurt so if they left – and now it hurts so much more.

He walked and walked. The sun rose.

It seemed so clear last night. Now it's broken into a kaleidoscope.... Mutation? Procyons? Why did I say that? Because Stella was so afraid of ... *Mandros is the construct....*

He trudged on, head down. The sun rose.

What is a construct? A made-up thing. Why that term? *Under a mask.* I said it. What did I mean?

He glanced at his watch, at the sun, and stopped. He had been walking for two hours, in soaked earth, through gullies, over swelling rock-faces. The transformer was across the valley on the hilltop. Or should have been. There was no transformer.

He felt as if he had the kind of disturbance of the ear

that creates dizziness with every head movement. Trees and rocks were ahead, and the line dipped into a hollow and disappeared. The familiar terrain warped around him, and he closed his eyes, turned carefully to mark his progress by some landmark on the way he had come.

He opened his eyes and found it. The tortured snake-ends of the broken line rose with their splayed wires forty metres back. He had walked half a kilometre in two hours.

He bit hard on the gloved knuckle of his forefinger and refused to tell himself that he was crazy. He wheeled about and pushed foot before foot, holding hard to the central crystal of his being while the thoughts around it fragmented into wild patterns and the ground seemed to run under his feet like a treadmill. After a couple of dozen steps he gave up and turned back.

As soon as he took the first step toward the dome his mind started to clear and arrange itself into the well-known lattice of his personality.

And, again, he was not surprised.

He stopped for a moment. The sun shone, the sky was hazy and grey on the horizon. The earth accepted the weight of his step, the rock was solid.

"We are in quarantine," he said aloud. The squawk of a crow answered.

"You too," he said. He giggled. "Rabbits, foxes, worms, you – and us."

Shut up, you fool, and hold onto your head!

A bit dizzy still.

Think! reason! *cogite!*

Leona Cress, Tom Arcand and the rest will want to know why. What happened to Ephraim and his skins. Ephraim's gone, he won't be back ... there's his skins, lying beside the burnt patch, soaked.

No, they won't. They won't ask. Here or down south. Dome NE73, last on the northeast roster, has disappeared from register, record, memory. Leaving seventy-two. Much nicer number, 72, even, neat, divisible by 2, 3, 4, 6, 8, 9 ...

Ask Mandros.

But he would not. Ask that. Thing? So many things they had not asked, all these months, of anyone. They had got into the habit of not asking.

Tell me, hey, Mandros?

I know.

This is a crèche. They chose it, unspeakable T,H,E,Y, chose this foul ungiving place, for him to be born in.

Stella was on her knees inside the doorway, slitting cords from one of several bales. The same kind they had always received, but without markings. From the packing she was pulling bottles, blankets, clothes, food.

"How did that come here?"

"I don't know – it was just there. Outside."

"Ah. We are being provided for." He stopped himself from giggling.

Aesh screamed for three solid weeks. The shrill whine echoed through the empty spaces of the dome and killed sleep. Stella and Annabel took turns massaging his belly, David changed the formula a dozen times.

"What in God's name does he want?" Stella held the jerking, twisted child at arm's-length; her face and neck were criss-crossed with scratches.

"To hazard a guess, meat," said David. He growled, "Maybe blood." Haggard, he stumped off to tell Mandros the goddam powers-that-be had better send lactic acid. He got it.

The thick curdy stuff silenced the child for an hour or

two after feeding. "Why in hell should we have to ask? You'd think they'd know what to feed the brat."

"Maybe ... maybe it's an experiment they haven't tried before," said Stella.

It was cold in early May. The knobby buds pushed out of the trees, but did not open. Aesh discovered the power of his nails, shredded his blankets and clawed splinters of wood from his crate. David coated them with the plastic used for temporary tooth-fillings and while it was still wet bandaged them.

The mittened hands, unexpectedly, did not make Aesh scream. Surly-faced, he gnawed at them with his toothless gums.

"Keep him busy," David said, "till the teeth grow in."

Stella picked him up and held him close, though he fought like a bobcat.

"What do you want to do that for? Think he'll be grateful?" The goblin face snarled.

"I don't know. I think somebody should." She patted his cheek and he tried to bite her. "Aren't there mothers for this kind of child, somewhere?"

David shuddered. "I hate to think."

Aesh would not tolerate clothes. Stella wound him in a blanket and carried him outside with her blue coat wrapped around him. Sunlight made him whimper and he turned his face against her neck.

"Better learn to like it, Aesh. It's your sun now."

She glimpsed a movement from the corner of her eye. Mandros, standing by the burial mound, had turned to face her. He was holding something unrecognizable in his hands, and she moved closer to see what it was.

A wood carving, or a natural growth of roots and

branches twisting in and among each other in knots; he parted his fingers and held it in cupped hands for a moment, a convoluted flower of wood. It was attached to a pointed stake, and he bent and pushed it into the earth at the head of the grave. A marker. As he stood again he raised his face to the sky, hazed over and thick at the horizon; a few dewdrops sparkled on the branches.

Stella watched, though the child squirmed and water was seeping into her moccasins. The idiot face was expressionless.

"This, here, is a paradise," he said.

This here. This, here? A world of difference in a catch of breath.

"Paradise, he said."

"Paradise! What does that mean? They've got a world, dying even faster than ours.... They think they'll people it, with more of Aesh. I guess it's the only place they've found compatible."

"But why would they pick Nadja, when there were Anne-Marie, Jenny, so many other healthier ones?"

"Perhaps something in her genetic makeup. They'd probably find enough like that. There may be more – of these babies – in the world."

"I don't think so ..."

"Why?"

"I just don't."

"You surely have odd ideas, Stella."

"No odder than what's happening."

"One of a kind – who would he find to mate with?"

"It may not matter, just so they can be bred."

The child's demanding cry rose again. David tipped the last of the whiskey into the glass. "My short career as a drunkard. No radio. If there's a radio here it's probably embedded in Mandros somewhere, unless he's a telepath. If we tried to attack him or the kid they'd be down on us like – like that lightning."

"Have you thought of it, David?"

"What?"

"What you said about attacking. I don't think they mean to keep us alive if they succeed."

"Ha." He shrugged. "I'm a coward."

"You may be a bit of a liar. You're not a coward."

"No? Well ... if I'd have known what it would be, I'd have aborted ... and if she'd miscarried, okay...." He turned his face into his shoulder in the odd gesture he always made when he was about to give something of himself away. "I'm on the earth to save lives and I'm willing to die doing it."

"That's probably why they chose us, then."

Always asking why. Why it happened. Why they chose. Why – *you surely have odd ideas, Stella* – why I think there's only one, plus Mandros. I don't know. Why Procyons?

"One is enough of you, Aesh." She held the clawed hands down across the tight belly. Thin dark lips drew back from the gums. At one month the eye-teeth had come in, tiny pointed things like the claws.

"Fangs, for God's sake," said David. "I wonder what it's going to be when it grows up."

"I wonder how old it will be when it's grown." The bandages had been removed from the claws. "Aesh, you do not scratch people. You keep your hands to yourself and hold things with them." He kicked out with his feet. She grabbed them and knelt over him, hands grasped in one of hers and feet in the other. He shrilled. "I'm still stronger than you, Aesh."

"You mean," said David, "how long we have."

"Yes, and how much of the place they want, and what we can do." Aesh squirmed and shrilled in the double grasp.

"He needs a new crate. Or a cage."

She pulled her hands away quickly, and Aesh, finding his limbs free, waved them aimlessly and stared at them in silence. "Annabel ..."

"Not so good. I know."

"She doesn't answer when I speak to her. This morning she put salt in her coffee and didn't notice when she drank it."

"Yeah. Another one."

Annabel had aged immensely. Her hair remained black, but her face thinned into harsh lines and her eyes were dull. She slept long and she did not knit or sew. Stella took over the cooking and cleaning. The Procyons were generous. Food and fuel appeared at the door as it was needed, and there was no more hunting or wood-cutting to be done. Stella and David were left between the silences of Mandros and Annabel, amid the turbulence of Aesh, without hope to find whatever strength they could.

At six months Aesh crawled, and at eight he walked. His nails scraped the floor, and David made him clogs of wood covered with leather and deeply scored with grooves to accommodate the claws. "Stell-la!" he shrilled. "Da-veed!"

He hardly spoke to Mandros at all, but it was Mandros who caught him as he fell, or pulled him down from shelf or mantel when he climbed. His clogs racketed, his shrill cry echoed in the spaces.

As winter closed down David and Mandros cleared pieces of old furniture from the annex adjacent to the common room, moved the bunks there, and partitioned off some of the unused areas of the dome. Annabel whimpered when her bed was moved, and again when she saw Ephraim's tackle heaped on a pile of useless stuff in the storeroom. She walked ceaselessly among the echoes, her hair uncombed, her hands clasped before her. The stillness of hands once so busy wrenched at Stella, and when she sat the old woman down and combed and braided her hair, the submissiveness of those bent shoulders drove her to a fury at the universe. But she had no claws, and no one to scratch.

What we can do....

The snow fell heavily, the tree branches cracked in the driving wind.

One blue morning, Annabel combed and braided her own hair, bound the braids in blue and red strands of wool; she put on parka, boots and mittens, and stood before the doorway of the dome, hands clasped.

Stella, Aesh clattering behind her and grabbing at her shirt-tail, found her there. She stopped. "Annabel," she whispered.

Annabel stared at the wind-drifted snow.

"Annabel –"

"I'm going into the north." There was no inflection in her voice.

"There is no place to go."

Annabel turned her head and looked at Stella. I know, her eyes said.

Stella dragged Aesh into the common room and sat down. The door slid open and thudded closed.

She covered her face with her hands. "Stell-la! Stell-la!" the child whined.

Some feeling made her raise her eyes to the light. Annabel, already half-whitened by driven snow, had stopped and was looking in at her. She smiled once, her face crinkled in the old way, and went on.

Go, Annabel, go and be free. The snow is full of peace. Go on, God forgive me, I love you, Annabel, go on....

"David, what can we do?"

"Nothing, sweetheart."

"There is peace – somewhere."

"Not for us yet."

"Hold me, I'm so cold ... you're good and warm, like a great old bearskin. So good."

"Ha. I always knew you wanted me for my body."

Two rows of small pointed teeth filled the spaces in Aesh's gums, and he ate meat, first cooked and then raw; sometimes a little cereal; drank water, sucking with his lips as if it were flower nectar. He slept deepest toward morning and napped for an hour at noon; if allowed, he would have been nocturnal, but shamelessly David drugged him every night. No retribution struck.

He spewed urine and faeces unreservedly on carpet and floor. Stella and David battled him up and down the days, and bleeding from scratches wrestled him to the toilet bowl. After months he gave in. In revenge he screamed his fury every time he used it. Mandros watched. Sometimes, it seemed, in wry amusement.

He grew, hardly changing the shape he was born in, bent stick limbs and tight round belly; snarling face with sharp teeth, small hairy ears, black malevolent eyes: he hated light and his ears were so sensitive he went into fits of trembling at the sound of raindrops or scraping branches on the glass. He was ugly. The long shining hairs on his red-brown skin thickened and he would not accept the touch of clothes. When he went outside he allowed David to tape slit-eyed snow goggles to his head.

It became apparent early that his function was to break. From outside he threw stones at the glass; when it would not give he set about breaking all the branches he could reach. One time David pulled him inside and he tore the carpet with his teeth and nails.

Stella sat on him.

"Maan-dros!" he wailed.

"Shut up, you little bastard! He knows I'm not going to hurt you! You've done too much damage to the things made by people I cared for and you're going to stop if I have to sit on you twenty days and nights!"

Released, he jumped to the mantel and tried to wrench it from the wall. That was too much for him; he dropped to the floor and slept. Stella watched him. The fluttering of his bird-like heart raised the hairs on his chest a hundred and twenty times a minute. Little beast.

Mandros kept him from harming himself and was rewarded with arrogance and contempt. He allowed David to treat his scratches and bites, to release a foot caught between stones, to pick out burrs so that they did not tear his skin, but he hated being touched. Toward Stella he was violently contradictory. Sometimes he cursed every word she addressed to him, for he had learned to speak well, had gathered David's and Stella's curses and even seemed to pick some out of the air. Other times he ran after her plucking at sleeve or hem, whimpering, "Stell-la!" as he had done when he was a baby.

"What do you want, Aesh?"

"I don't know."

She reached out a finger to touch his cheek, gently. He pulled back shrilling, and ran.

Stella thought of the ones who had left and the ones who had died, watched David's worn face, considered her own imprisonment, and cursed.

Years passed.

Stella stood in the church doorway. "Do you know how years pass?" she asked the Procyons. "Like weeks. All the years I can't remember are lost, I don't know how many, and God damn you, you've taken away the rest."

She pushed and pushed at the wall in her mind, tortuously following the pathway back, to salvage some area of hope and freedom, and always the track stopped short one grey morning before the dome.

David grew somewhat thinner and white streaks ran down his beard. Stella hardly glanced at herself in the mirror and could not tell whether she seemed older. Mandros did not change at all.

Near ten Aesh was the size of a boy of seven or eight; his limbs thickened and his belly drew in; he had powerful shoulders and walked straight-legged instead of scuttling like a lizard. But he would not sit still long enough to learn anything, and on dull days that were not too cold he moved ceaselessly in the confines of the force field, climbing trees, squirming among bushes and rocks, rolling in the mud of stagnant pools undeterred by mosquitoes and black-flies.

In the August heat Mandros sat outside on a stone with his hands folded, staring at nothing. Aesh was rampaging nearby.

Stella squatted on a hummock in front of Mandros; she knew that he was the agent of her death, but she did not yet see death before her, and she was no longer repelled by his dark oily skin, scraggy hair, loose mouth that opened on stained yellow teeth.

"Mandros, you are from Procyon, I don't have to ask. What is your planet?"

"The fourth." He did not look at her.

"What are your people called?"

"Shar. In your language."

"But you were made to look like us —"

"That is true."

"And Aesh looks like other Shar."

"Not completely. He looks somewhat like his mother."

She said faintly, "I hadn't noticed."

"His legs are abnormally long and his face is narrow."

"Your men and women, do they have the differences we have?"

"Of course not. The women are only womb-casings, without head or limbs."

She swallowed to avoid retching. "Then no child can love its mother, or be loved."

"Why should it? It is not necessary. We worship."

"Dear Lord," she murmured, "fruit of the womb. Mandros! You say this is paradise, but we are infertile and the world is dying."

"Not so fast as ours."

"For the same reasons?"

"I know what I am told: the wombs are scarce and sterile; the world is barren. Perhaps we are cursed."

He made a quarter turn away from her, and she fell silent.

Aesh appeared before them, eyes slitted against the sun, the claws of his feet pressing into damp earth. "Why are you talking to this thing?"

Stella said, "I was speaking to Mandros because I wanted to learn about your people."

"This has nothing to teach you. Thing!" He flicked a claw near Mandros's eye. Mandros did not blink or flinch.

"Stop that!"

The claw paused in mid-air. He was looking at her strangely.

"Mandros is here to take care of you in this place and you will have to answer to your people if you hurt him."

Aesh's laughter could crush bones. "I don't have to answer to anyone because my father is the Emperor. Do you think this thing can be hurt?" He dug claws into Mandros's forehead and began to pull down.

"No!" Stella grabbed his arm. She was not stronger than Aesh anymore, but she was a good match. She caught the other hand aiming for her eyes, hooked his feet from under him with her heel, they went down, rolling in the mud. Mandros sat unmoving on the rock.

They fought over rocks and brambles and splashed in pools, scattering clouds of insects; Stella protected her eyes with an arm and he bit, she grasped one of his and held it with her teeth, his feet clawed her legs, his shrilling made the air tremble, his nails hooked in and pulled out in a hundred places, reached again and again for her eyes, her sleeves shredded protecting them, his teeth tore at her ear, he ripped out a handful of her hair, and finally butted her belly with his head, left her flat on the ground and breathless, stood over her laughing for a moment, then climbed the framework of the dome, leaned against the tower with his arms crossed and laughed.

Mandros moved, then. He stood up and called, "Aesh! Come down, you will hurt yourself!"

Stella sat up, gasping, pulled herself first to her knees, then to her feet, pushed the hair out of her eyes. She panted. "Sonofabitch! Him hurt!" She was bleeding from dozens of punctures and scratches. David, on a distant rise holding a basket of berries, was standing in a shocked stillness like a tiny figure in a great painting.

Aesh scrambled down the dome, laughing, and ran up the path to the church.

Her church. Stella followed, stumbling. A cloud had covered the sun and the sky was thickening. She was dizzy, held her head to steady it.

Mandros came after her, caught hold of her arm, and pulled her back a few steps.

"You idiot!" she snarled. "I'm not going to hurt hi –"

A bolt of lightning struck a metre before her.

She screamed in fury, wrenched away and leaped over the charred ground toward the path.

In the church Aesh had his legs hooked round a rafter and was swinging from it. He shrilled and laughed and shrilled.

"Get out of here!"

He laughed, caught the next beam with his hands, and grasped it with his legs.

Stella let her breath loose and lowered her voice. "Get out of my church. I'm not going to hurt you."

"Hurt me?" He laughed and swung.

"Come down!"

He sang, swinging, chorused by echoes:

"Damn the poor, for they shall be trampled!
Damn the mourners, they shall have more to mourn!
Damn the meek, they shall be driven from Earth!"

"Come down!"

He swung to the next beam and sang:

"Damn the peacemakers, they shall be wartorn!
Damn the merciful, they shall be –"

"Aesh!" David's voice. "Stella, for God's sake –"

Lightning struck and shivered a beam above her head. She jumped forward and the timbers missed her. Aesh screamed.

The fearful noise had sent his arms and legs flying out convulsively.

As he fell, Stella, without thought, leaped once more. When he hit, she blacked out.

She opened her eyes. David was rubbing ointment into her wounds.

Headache. Head-quake, maybe. About seven points on the Richter scale, she thought. "What's the damage?"

"There's a hole in the church roof."

"There's a few in me."

"I gave you a shot of antitet."

"Maybe it should be antirabies."

He looked at her wisely. "Mild concussion. Likely your backside aches too. That was where his head hit, and it drove your head onto the floor. Otherwise his skull would have cracked. He broke a humerus and three claws; he bled more than you did."

"Too bad. Oh well. I guess I should have let him take it out on Mandros. It was just the funny look he gave me before he did it. As if he was daring me to intervene."

"He was testing. To see how far he could go. All kids do that."

"I should have known after all these years. I just haven't had a wide experience."

"I had a kid once," he said.

Don't ask, Stella!

Okay, I won't.

"Mandros saved me. They were trying to kill me with one of their bloody lightning bolts. He pulled me back."

"I saw. I wonder whose rules he's playing by."

"I don't think I'll ask. I'm alive. I wonder for how long...."

"The second one missed."

"Did it? Who do you think it was meant for – me or him?"

"Mandros?"

"No. Aesh."

His brow puckered. "Him, Stella? Why?"

"I don't know. I get these feelings...." She began to pull herself up.

"Hey, you better not do that! You've got to rest."

"David, I don't think it matters at this point." She lowered her feet to the floor. He was right. Her backside ached. Her head roared; her teeth felt loose, probably they had cracked together when her head hit.

"Where are you going?"

She staggered drunkenly to the door. "To see him."

Aesh had three expressions: rage, sulks, and unholy glee. He was sulking. His arm was in wired splints, his nails had been cemented.

She looked down at him in the bed where he had been born out of Nadja's screams and blood.

He looked away first, and then at her. "You saved me." Probably he would never forgive her for it.

"Mandros saved me. One good turn."

"You wouldn't let me hurt him."

"And he wouldn't let me hurt you. That's the house that Jack built."

"That is nonsense talk. You would never have hurt me."

"No, I wouldn't." His eye membranes were red and so were his lids. She had never seen him cry. "Did David give you something to take away the pain?"

"Yes." His left arm twitched in its sling.

"Do you read books?"

"No. That is nonsense too. Why do you ask?"

"I was wondering where you got the anti-Beatitudes."

"I don't know what that is."

"Damn the meek and damn the merciful. That's much like something written in a book of ours. Did you make it up?"

He shook his head impatiently. "Why are you bothering me with that? I don't know. Perhaps someone told it to me."

"Maybe," she said. "But in our book we bless them."

She turned to go, but he grabbed at her nightgown. "Stella!" he wailed.

She faced him again.

What do you want, Aesh?

I don't know.

Something new in his eyes, now, a little like fear.

"What is it?"

"Stell-la! Do you love me?"

Her mind went blank.

Love?

Aesh?

That is nonsense talk.

Stell-la! a cry ...

The pain roared in her head. Her mouth worked. "My friends died so you could be born. I took care of you –"

He was trembling.

" – when I knew that I would die for it, and David too...." And the rest of the world. I am the agent of destruction.

His eyes begged.

"They could have cared for you, couldn't they? No, I guess not. You were half born of this world, a different chemistry, a different mind...."

"You are not saying!"

"I swear I don't know why I did it. You were a newborn baby, and a child. You needed care. I gave it."

"But that *is* love, Stell-la! Da-veed said it is love!"

"All right." She nodded. "David's a truthful man, and if he said it, it's so. I love you, Aesh."

"Good," he said. "I will sleep now." And closed his eyes.

She stood before the blasted church, reeling.

"Shar!" she screamed. "Damn you! No," she lowered her burning head and crouched on the rock, "forget I said that. I take it back. There's been too much damnation."

A hand touched her arm. She was beyond flinching.

"You must go in and lie down," said Mandros.

"I won't damn you either," she said thickly. The insects hummed in the shimmering air, and in her head. "Mandros, why did you save me?"

Inside the church a charred beam cracked and fell, splinters bounced on the floor.

"So that you could save him."

She saw him double. Her voice was so slurred her ears hardly registered it. "They fight among themselves, then, those Shar of yours?"

"Who does not? More than one would wish to be Emperor."

"What do you mean?" A wind rose and chilled her sweat.

"The Emperor died ... a few hours ago, by your time."

She lay on the bed and dreamed. Sometimes David washed her face, and occasionally tested her reflexes; she felt his thumbs raising her eyelids. In those seconds of vision she saw Mandros standing at the foot of the bed, or thought she saw him.

In her dream she got up and walked out of the door.

David went on tending the body on the bed, but Mandros followed her with his eyes.

The sky was lead. The trees straightened and turned to iron, with burning sconces in their centres. In the shadow of each was a Shar, squat and crook-legged. Their eyes were like pomegranate seeds, black pips in red membrane. Crêpey skin hung from their armpits in folds, vestiges of a once-winged people. The swampy pools became basins where females, dark hairy lumps of flesh, lay in nutrient baths: unwomen with receptacles into which men might empty their seed without joy; black crinkled teats to be mindlessly sucked by their infants.

Mandros, when will they come?

In twelve days, when the child is healed. Shar heal fast.

And kill us then?

They will take him to the ships. The Emperor Aesh will lead them.

The Shar came forward with hands cupped. In every cup of hands lay a stone, a flat pebble washed endlessly by rain and sea.

Her feet were in wet earth, the wind raised her hair; the air, as always, stank of sulphur.

The cupped hands waited. She picked up a stone: *when the planet was in eccentric orbit, half the time in a void so deep it deadened the soul*

The black pips swam in the red membrane, glittering with fire.

She picked a stone: *and men learned to shift it in its course, to bring it toward the sun*

A stone: *but had not waited long enough to learn to do it well*

:and the world drifted into the orbit of the void they hated Stone.

:and the hatred perverted itself and became pride

:for what they had not done except build towers of iron and stone

Beyond the arches she saw the walls of the towers, iron and stone, glittering with flame and carved with warped and tortured flowers.

:so that they hated themselves and each other, in treachery, deceit, torment, murder; often out of spite they would not beget and when they did found over the millennia

The last stone: *that their seed, which not only contained sperm, but gave the ovum its female fertility as well, was losing its quality because it too needed light*

Her hands were full of pebbles; she skimmed them in a sulphur sea.

And all the other planets of Procyon?
:burning gas or thin crusts over fire
Mandros, why are you telling me all this?
:because –

"Christ, I thought you'd never come out of it!" David was gripping her hand.

"What have I done now?"

"Caught a fever from running around outside, on top of everything. For God's sake, don't do that again, eh?"

She scratched the scab on her ear where Aesh had bitten it. "How long?"

"Four days. Mandros and I have been switching between you and Aesh the whole time. It would be nice to have both of you in good health."

Eight days more. "David, will you send Mandros here?"

"Stella! What –"

"No, no, David! I'm not going to conceive another one. Bring Mandros here and stay. There are a lot of questions I have to ask."

Mandros stood at the foot of the bed.

"When I was delirious it seemed to me that you were telling me many things about the Shar. Was it only my fever or were you really telling me those things?"

"I was. Your brain was more receptive when it was feverish."

"Now I'm well. I think." She sat up. "But I remember. You were going to explain why you had told me."

"Because I was made to serve the Emperor and no one else."

"That's not an answer." He was silent. "I suppose I'm to pull an answer from that?" She sighed. "The Emperor is dead, the Shar will be here in eight days to claim their new one and then decide whether to claim this world. How long will that take?"

"I don't know."

"But he's a child," said David.

"It doesn't seem to matter to them. The Shar ... they want to exchange one dying world for another, and I suppose they will kill us all if they take it. That's pitiful as well as horrible. But Shar are horrible –" Mandros did not blink, " – and I used to think you were too, Mandros. All those hundreds of people in the starships were killed, over fifteen years ago. But ... after Nadja conceived, Billy and Clyde, Anne-Marie and the rest were sent away. Was Ephraim killed on purpose?"

"Oh no," Mandros said. "He happened to be at the place where they broke the line. That was unfortunate."

David growled, "And I suppose Nadja was unfortunate too, hah?"

"No. That was." He was silent for the moment it took him to find the word. "Shameful. Of Ephraim I have said I was sorry, and I am still. I am not a true Shar. I have been made like a man and like a man I can be sorry."

"And a few *were* saved," Stella said. "The world is dying, but it might be possible to make it live and grow again. If the Shar leave us alone perhaps people will have new hope – but they must have searched a long time among their nearer stars before they came here, and they won't be willing to go back. Still, there are other places in this system beside the paradise they think they want – planets, moons they could make liveable with their technology. Bargains, Mandros. We could make bargains. And they would have their light."

"Their minds are very dark," said Mandros.

"*Theirs?* Clyde and the others were freed. You saved me. Aesh demands love.... I think, Mandros, that you and Aesh ... and ... and even perhaps the old Emperor, if he was watching ... have been corrupted by our paradise. By our light." She added, "In your language."

Mandros stood without a word. His eyes were blank.

Across the hall, Aesh began to cry. "Maan-dros!" He turned and left them.

"Eight days, Stella? Travelling out beyond Pluto? He won't be well by then."

"Mandros says he will."

"Emperor! My God, even for a quick-growing Shar he's young for that."

"He'll have advisors."

"Yes, and I can guess what they'll advise, if they don't kill him first. Mandros isn't all that effective a guardian. I still don't understand why he told you."

"I don't either. All I know is – David!" She took his face in her hands and drew it to hers. "There *is* very little time!"

His arms went round her. "You're not well," he whispered.

"Oh, I am now – but does it matter?"

Aesh the emperor gave no orders, climbed no walls. He kneeled on a settee made from a church pew and stared out through the triangles at the rain, the sun, the blowing trees. He let David coat his claws with the plastic filling so he could not scratch his splinted arm. At night he walked the spaces of the dome; his noisy clogs echoed and no one reproved him.

Stella, David and Mandros went through the motions of life, and did not speak much. Mandros became again the automaton he had been in the old days. Stella mopped and swept, paused to finger the rugs she had braided with Annabel and the others, refolded shawls and sweaters. They were torn and ravelling.

She felt, not quite fear, but something she could not name. A heaviness in her belly, as if she were about to give birth, or else a pressure at the top of her head as if she were a foetus butting at the amniotic membrane, about to be born. At times she thought she must be going back to her old neurosis, or still suffering from concussion, because the weight shaped itself into WHY DID HE SAVE THEM? and the pressure into WHY DID HE TELL ME? Then she felt a stab of fear. She pushed it away, and made love with David in quiet and powerful tenderness.

On the eighth day the sky was dark, and they moved like sleepwalkers.

"You haven't eaten," said David.

"I'm not hungry." She went into the common room to have a smoke and found Mandros standing in front of the fireplace.

He was holding something, and staring at her.

"What is that?" she asked dully.

He held it out to her.

She had thought at first that it might be a wooden

flower, like the one with which he had marked the grave, but it was a stone sphere.

It was heavy, she had to grip tightly to keep from dropping it.

Black stone, with a few bright crystals embedded in it like stars; marked off in triangles and hexagons, in each a small perfect carving. A sun and the eccentric orbit of its planet, a Shar with crooked body and pitted eyes, a warped and tormented flower....

"The Emperor's seal," he said.

"But why give it to – Mandros!"

He had sat down on the floor and was taking off his boots. Then he crossed his legs, rested his hands on his knees.

"It *is* time," he said. His face was pale, but his eyes were clear and alive, there might have been a glint of humour in them at the expression on her face.

"For what?"

"To destruct. Please don't be offended. It is not ugly. Though," he cocked his head, "I am glad I was not made more beautiful or I might not be willing to go."

"Destruct!"

"Yes." He was becoming translucent. He said gently, explaining to a child, "To dissolve and – go."

She saw the shadows of skull and bones. "But Aesh –"

"I was made to last until the son of the Emperor could be delivered. I had the honour of helping to prepare the Emperor himself."

"You can't! You –"

His flesh was a skin of water around the bone. But he was right. His dissolution was not ugly, but had the beauty of a fine anatomical drawing. "I have no choice. I was timed for this." She bowed her head to the sphere. "I was the seed-capsule of the Emperor. I did what was required. But I had feelings, once, and I was a man." She

193

closed her eyes. "Listen!"

She raised her head. The bone hands lifted and turned up, in offering. The skull said, "I did not want them to die, and that is the truth, I swear...."

A dwindling, a crumbling into whiteness.

A few scattered crystals among the clothes.

David's hands came round her shoulders. "What did he give you?"

"A stone."

From behind them came a whimper. Aesh was standing in fearful loneliness.

David removed the metal splint and sealed the small wounds it had made. Aesh flexed his arm. "That will be stiff for a while," David said. His hands, once they had finished their work, began to shake.

Aesh knelt on the window seat and looked out. The sky was clearing.

Stella, still gripping the sphere, was looking down at Mandros's bunk. The bedding had been stripped and piled, neatly folded, in its centre. Except for his clothing, Mandros had owned no object. His place was bare.

Aesh too had owned no toy or keepsake, and Stella herself was holding the only thing that was due to him. She held it to her forehead, and once again it told its story.

Why did you save?
Why did you tell?
Why did you give?
I suppose I'm to answer....

Her head butted against the membrane, and forced.

The sun was westering.

"Maybe they won't come today," David said.

"I think they will."

There was a roaring in the sky. Aesh trembled. He was holding the seal.

Stella took her coat from the hook. It would be a cool evening. The blue coat was very old, very worn. She had given up her vanity, the cornmeal, and the nap was worn down, the edges grimy, the fur matted. Only Ephraim's stitching remained sound and beautiful. It had been the colour the sky should have been, and became the colour the sky was. She held the coat and listened to the roar. Her body felt like phosphorus, pale and burning.

"Stella?"

She turned.

"You can't go out now, it's dangerous! Did you think you could take him to the –"

"I'm going with him."

"*With him!*" The implication struck. He stood up, his face darkened and burst into sweat. "No," he whispered.

"If Aesh wants."

She looked at the Emperor. His lips were quivering. He pressed the seal against them and nodded.

"Why, in God's name, why, Stella?"

She moved close and met his eyes.

"Stella ... good Lord, *what are you?*"

Her breath caught on a sob. "Don't look at me like that!"

"I can't help it!" He palmed the sweat from his face. "You're not – you're not –"

"I'm not a Procyon, David! I'm not!"

"No...." He seemed to be speaking without breath. "And you're not Stella either."

Her voice shook. "I'm as much Stella as I ever was."

He stood with head bowed, arms hanging. "Bargains. You really believe –"

"David! Are you sorry you loved me?"

His head and arms rose, she dropped the coat and flung herself against him, his fists knotted behind her back, she could not tell whether the burning tears between their faces were his or her own.

The noise stopped.

She turned once for the last sight of David before the dome. His glasses flashed stars from the setting sun.

Aesh, gripping his seal, huddled against her body beneath the coat, and their faintly luminous shape moved over earth darkened with broken twigs, mouldering leaves, and the shadow of night. She followed the path she had taken so many times and remembered the steps she had retraced endlessly toward the past, when in truth her life had begun at the farthest step to bring her here.

"Are you afraid?" Aesh whispered.

"No." She was full of sorrow, and if she had looked at David one more time or one moment longer she would have been in torment.

The shuttle, a sphere, had landed on the rock; its fires had exploded the church into blackened fragments, a final obscenity.

Aesh moved away from her, kicking off his clogs, and she waited. She felt the dampness of the soil through her moccasins; the wind lifted her hair, for once swept away the drench of sulphur and brought the sweetness of the earth.

A lock door opened, a ladder descended. Three Shar stood in the shadow of the opening, and though their mouths and noses were masked in the alien atmosphere she could see their eyes, like pomegranate seeds, catching a flicker of red sunset, and the dark drape of the folded skin in their armpits. Their bodies were thick and crook-legged, and Aesh's arrow-slender body seemed very vulnerable facing them. He climbed the rungs lightly, and she did not hear, but understood the word that greeted him.

Majesty.

It was heavy with irony.

Aesh, on the threshold, nodded, and with deliberation turned his back on them. On the fingers of one hand he balanced the seal lightly as a bubble, and with the other beckoned to Stella. Whatever his back may have told them, his face, in the last light, was filled with unholy joy.

He was after all not alone.

Stella placed a foot on the first rung, and the three voices struck like brass bells in her head:

Who/who are/are/you?

Why are/what for/are you/are/here?

She climbed the second rung. "I am ..." She paused for the word of the maker, the bargainer, the most delicate word in the world.

messenger

"I am a messenger of the Adversary," she said.

1976

WE CAN'T GO ON
MEETING LIKE THIS

He buys a single ticket. It is a mid-week day in early spring when the weather is mild and the children are not yet out of school; the visitors have come out to the zoo for walks, not to stare into the cages. The peacock steps among them, darting at tossed crumbs and pistachio nuts. The earth is becoming ripe and the wind is still cool but has a sweet touch.

She is waiting by the lions' enclosure, wearing dark glasses and a discreet bandanna, with her hands in the pockets of her camel-hair coat, watching the lions. He cannot see his own breath but the lions' mouths are steaming fiercely. He comes up, shoulder glancing hers, and watches the beasts. The lioness is twisting and rubbing her head against the lion's neck. The woman is staring through them: she has been in that lioness's body or one like it a score of times, perhaps her husband prefers her as a lioness.

"Which one?" she whispers.

"I want to try the lion." He wants, but is uneasy, his first time.

Her mouth quirks. "I've done that with him already. Too many times. Out in the wild all they get to do is hunt food for the males and bring up the kids."

"Still ..." Perhaps that's why he wants it.

In the depths of the old Observatory there are three rooms in use: the first where men and women wait for their turns to live in the beasts of their choice; the second where they lie in tiers of bunks while patient white-coated assistants cup electrodes to their heads. In the third room the lewd old inventor and his assistant, a woman whose face is thick with hair-sprouting moles, carefully connect the wires. Twenty minutes they will give you, by Visa, Mastercard, Amex; you pay dear for a taste, a spice of that hot kingdom. If lovers come and couple as animals it is not yet a legal infraction of the marriage vows. It is a ritual; perhaps it is their pornography.

Without a glance at her lover, the lioness/woman strolls down the path toward the ape house. He follows.

Monkeys and apes are more expensive to get into, they have hands after all, but now they are sluggish from having been kept shut away from the cold weather all winter; their house is hot and reeking, they squat dimly on their shelves. In back of the ape house there is an aquarium where dolphins clown and whales whack the glass walls with their flukes. In the bottom of their tank the sharks are circling, flickering their tails. He stares and wonders if they are occupied, then follows her steps to the ancient domed Observatory.

He works to adjust his reduced consciousness to this alien body and wonders if her husband has ever tried this lion. He shakes the great mane and his neck aches; the topaz eyes focus strangely and his hearing is dim. The beast hates the cold weather, has a toothache, and has lost his fierce dreams of the veld. He draws in a lungful of the deep scents that would satisfy him if he were truly a lion. He feels awkward and hot, cannot master the natural rhythms of breathing and walking, and he senses the lion's resentment at the touch of his mind.

The lioness observes him, does not quite recognize him, whisks her tail and turns away toward an older and bigger lion he has never noticed before, one that snarls at him and plants a splayed paw on the lioness's hip.

What is this? He opens his jaws and the roar crackles out of his chest. The old lion's claw is reaching for his eye in a savage moment, the moment freezes while he tries to cry "No!" and the sound emerges a choked squeal in a puff of steaming breath, the spectators are screaming – this can not possibly be happening, it can't! – being trapped here between the lion's body and the man lying cupped with electrodes, the claw tears –

No. The lion's instinct has turned his head away and the claw has scratched him beside the eye. The scratch stings sharply, he swerves away retreating to a corner where he can spit on his paw and rub the blood away.

When they walk down the steps of the Observatory the air is already cooling toward evening.

"What did you think of being a lion?"

He resists the impulse to rub the area on his temple that still seems to be stinging, though the experience is fading, he is astonished how quickly. "I didn't much like that one. I still wouldn't mind making love to a lioness."

"I won't go into a lioness again."

"What would you rather be?"

"A vixen, a wolf, a shark. A cobra." She walks away. Beyond the wrought-iron gate and across from the park where the nannies wheel the babies and the cruisers walk their dogs, there is a small hotel, old as the Observatory, with a palm-lined coffee shop. Its rooms have old brass beds with flowered knobs, it is a place where they make mild love on sprung mattresses.

She is headed there and diminishes with distance, but he realizes that she is also diminishing in his mind, as he might be in hers, fading toward her husband, the mild vegetarian botanist with magnifiers and tweezers, the old and too possessive lion under the skin. He thinks of looking for other women, other lionesses

He glances back once. The old lion approaches the bars suddenly and widens eyes to stare at him with pupils like black stars, raises and splays a huge paw, shoots claws and roars. The peacock spreads wings, squawks hideously and dashes away half-flying, its droppings spatter behind it.

The lover pulls back quickly though two ranks of bars protect him, and hurries away. The lion yawns hugely, crouches and falls asleep; the lioness rubs her jaw along his shoulder, rests her head on it and leaves one eye half open.

1988

THE NEWEST PROFESSION

Melba took her walks Upstreet in the bluing part of the evening during the few moments before the lights came on, and turned back downward before they had reached their peak. In her mind her hair was a long ripple, and her neck, wrists, fingers waited for jewels to add facets to the rising brilliance.

The streets were nearly bare now, shops idle. She got the occasional mildly curious, mildly contemptuous glance; she was hardly visible in the dark uniform cape, empty hands hidden behind its slits; she was a big girl in good proportion, but her face, without make-up, faded in the dimness, and her fair hair was cut mercilessly straight around at earlobe length. The long, strong legs in flat-heeled shoes paced evenly: their only ornament was a small pedometer on a fine chain about one ankle.

When she crossed the road and turned downward there was a shadowland to pass before safety. The keepers of the shops and the servants of the rich who bought from them lived in narrow streets; they did not trouble her, but their children absorbed and vented the attitudes they did not express. When the wind howled up the street from the west and folded back her cape on the expanse of her belly, children young enough for tag and hopscotch yelled names they had likely not thought of by themselves. "Bitch", "cow", "brood mare" were mild enough; tripping and stone-throwing were not.

The stone that hit this evening landed on her temple and made her lose balance. She did not fall this time but turned her ankle and knocked her shoulder against a lamppost. The policeman who came from shadow – they always turned up afterward, never before – reached an unnecessary hand to steady her and said, "You all right, miss?"

"Yeah."

"There's a cut on your forehead and I –"

"I'm late already and I can walk. You want to give me a ticket or somethin'?"

The hand pulled away, and she went on, limping slightly. Maybe the damn pedometer had gone bust.

Children, back of her, being called to supper, yelled:

Monster, monster, suck my tit!
Dunno if you're him, her, it!

Himmerit! Himmerit! The words slurred. She knew. It was *her* and it would never suck.

She looked outward at the bloody Sun splayed on the horizon, gross as her belly. Way out beyond Downstreet the spaceport blasts sparked, then warehouses, repair shops, hostels climbed.

Out of shadowland into near darkness. Retired Astronauts' Home and Hospice – safe enough, window lit here and there, harmonica whispering of cramped quarters in rusty scows that crossed the voids, words no cruder than the children's song. Safe enough for her to give in to the pressure pains and bend over, straighten up.

Next door, NeoGenics Labs, Inc. Home.

"Three minutes late," said the Ox in the Box, not looking up.

"Yeah. Tripped over my feet." Stiffly she bent to un-hook the pedometer, not broken, and showed it at the wicket. "Two KM."

The Ox looked up. Her name was Dorothy, and she and Melba were not at odds, merely untalkative. A stout woman in her forties, greying black hair chopped short and brushed flat back. Sterile or sterilized, sometimes she flushed in heats that no chemical seemed to cure. "You didn't get that thing on your head from tripping over your feet." She rang for a doctor.

When Melba reached the dining room with a patch on her head and a tensor round her ankle everyone else was half through. She picked up her numbered tray and the white-capped jock dished out a rewarmed supper from under the infrareds. "Bump into a door?"

"What else?"

She took her seat beside Vivian. There were no rivals for it. She was Number 33, Table 5, and there were never more than fifty eaters. Alice, Pam, and Del glanced up and went on shovelling in. Vivian said, "Up-street again."

I like the lights, Viv."

"Second time this month. What was it this time?"

"Kids."

"Whoever made up that shit about sticks and stones will break my bones knew at least half of what he was talking about. What did the Ox say?"

"Nothing. Just got the doctor. She's okay." Melba pulled herself as close to the table as her belly would al-low and stared at the little card on the tray: *Meat 200 grams, starchy vegetable 150 grams, green vegetable ...*

Pam said, "She knows you could knock her here to hell and gone with your belly."

Melba shrugged. That was what passed for wit here,

and she had little of it herself.

Vivian laughed, but she was a nervous laugher and Melba not easily offended. Viv was the smallest and liveliest of the lot, and Melba liked her for making up what she herself lacked. Her hair was black and curly, with the barest hint of premature grey at the temples; her eyes were Wedgwood blue and her lips a natural red envied by a company of women forbidden cosmetics for the risk of dangerous components.

Melba always ate quickly and finished first, in contrast – as they were contrasting friends in every way – to Viv, who was picky. Her tray was empty by the time the jock came to replace it with the pill cup.

Viv's nostrils flared: She was not among the few who were allowed three cigarettes a day and flaunted their smoke after supper. There was more harmless dried herb in it than tobacco, but it smelled like something she loved. However, she was one of the favoured allowed a cup of tea to wash down her pills.

Melba drank a lot of milk fortified with yet another drug or vitamin. She turned the medicine cup into her hand and stared at the palmful of coloured pills. "Ruby, pearl, emerald – and what's the yellow one again?"

"Topaz – or vitamin D. Only a semi-precious stone. Still think you'll get to wear them?"

Melba smiled her long, slow smile. "I hope."

Viv shook her head. A room with fifty women in cone-shaped denim dresses. Metal chairs; metal tables with artificial-wood tops; institutional-cram wall. "Maybe you will. Maybe."

Because the money, after all was tremendous. What did not get put into surroundings went to equipment, technical expertise, and the bodies of the women.

It was Melba who waited for Viv, after all, while she lingered over her tea. Pam and Del left to play euchre;

Alice, yawning, deflated her cushion ring and went to bed: she was only two weeks post-partum. One of two of the jocks hung around, mildly resentful of the still cluttered table. They were men chosen for low sex drive and lack of aggressiveness. There was no sexual activity allowed the gravid women, except in their dreams, and none on the premises among inbetweeners. Whatever there was had been made difficult enough by propaganda harping on dozens of forms of VD, major and minor.

"Goddamn nunnery," said Viv.

Melba didn't mind. She liked the money. She was big, healthy, slow-thinking, and did not have much trouble pushing back her feelings. Others put up and shut up with resentment. They all knew none was considered very intelligent. No one within their hearing had ever called them cows or sows, but the essence of the words hung like a cloud, drifted like fog. The women turned their backs on the jocks, the Psychs, the Ox, and told each other the stories of their lives.

Melba said softly, "You didn't take your water pill again."

Viv gave her a look of mingled guilt and reproach. "How'd you know?"

"Saw you palming it."

"They make me feel sick."

"I don't like that rotten milk either. You get high blood pressure and you're out."

Viv had a tight water balance. Her belly specialized in dry-worlders; Melba, who bred underwater life, drank all the time, thirsty or not.

"I don't care. This one's my last."

"Not if you don't watch out. I'll be in emeralds and you'll be lying sick somewhere."

Viv, cyclonic, turned bright red and stood up quickly.

Melba grabbed her by the arm. "I'm sorry, Viv, I'm sorry! Please! Take the pill."

Vivian sat down slowly. Melba's eyes were full of tears. "I'm sorry, Viv. I don't mean to be so dumb."

"Oh, for Chrissake, don't call yourself dumb. You've got a mind like one of those mills you read about that grinds slow but fine."

"Yeah, and they rot to pieces and everybody says what beautiful scenery. Don't forget the pill, Viv."

"And you never give up, do you?" Viv sighed, fished the pill from her pocket, and swallowed it with the dregs of her tea. "Four male, three female." Her belly was a small polite bulge with the third. "In a thousand years they might fill a planet. In the meantime, I'm tired."

Melba had never asked if Vivian went down to the crèche, nor often what she did with her spare time besides visiting library and bookstore. Most women here were of a class to whom steady high unemployment and the debilitation of the nuclear family gave little choice. Men in this stratum had even fewer opportunities. The Y chromosome could be found in any healthy man

But few women went down to the crèche, though none failed to promise herself to do it. Not many boasted of affairs, either with men or other women, or discussed what they did with their time, even when they visited their families, so that they were in the peculiar situation where few knew what others were doing, but all knew what everyone had done before she came to NeoGenics. Loose talk was discouraged by the Company, to preserve, they said, anonymity. Nevertheless, Melba, though she did not know if Viv had seen those children, down in the huge rooms of tanks and enclosures, knew that the age limit was thirty, Viv was twenty-eight, and that both she and NeoGenics agreed that seven would fulfil her contract.

"You're lucky you've only got a couple of weeks." Viv slowed her walk to match Melba's, careless of the grateful clatter of table-clearing back of them.

"Yeah, but I still need the two males, and they're not the kind of little mousy thing you grow."

"Hey, don't insult my kids!"

"I'm not, Viv. I hope they look something like you."

"Then go down and see!"

Melba shuddered. "I'm scared. I'm scared to think what mine look like."

"Being scared is like calling yourself dumb. Working at being a cow."

Difference. They got on each other's nerves, but they got on. Viv wanted to go to a good school and learn everything she could absorb and then go out and teach anyone who would listen.

"Well. I kind of want to be a cow," Melba said mildly. "I want a nice place with a lot of good stuff in it, and I don't care if I don't spend the money usefully."

"And be a fine lady? Oh, Melba, I'm so tired of hearing that!" She leaned against the dirty cream-coloured wall of the corridor and looked up at tall Melba. Her eyes were not quite like the Wedgewood in the store windows: that did not have the fine glaze. "I bet you think men will come along and load you with diamonds – if you can get a plastic job on your belly that makes you look like a virgin!"

"But I can't learn things in school like you."

"Will I really be able to sit in school after seven births, when my metabolism's shot and my patience is gone – and I'm hyper enough already, not just from blood pressure? It's a dream, Mel, like everybody else has. Did anybody who's been here ever come back or call or write to tell how she's done?"

208

"They want to forget the place. You can't blame them for that."

"It's also because they go out and find there's no other place. They're dead at thirty, with the guts eaten out of them; they run through the money; the plastic job bags out on them; they're ruined for having kids of their own." She looked away. "I have met one or two ... not too keen on remembering or recognizing. They're cheap whores, or if they're lucky they get a job selling second-hand in a basement. What the hell. You aren't listening."

"But I am, Viv. I won't let it happen to me." She added, "And don't be scared I'll end up some junked-up whore either."

Vivian laughed. "I admit I can't see any pimp beating up on you."

Melba thwacked her watermelon-belly with thumb and finger and laughed with her.

Melba lay in bed and reread the letter.

Now the plant got retooled your father went back to work so we hired on Karl Olesson to get in the vegetables. With what we use and what we pay him there's not much left from what gets sold. Wesley has run off with that Sherri in the drug store that I always said was cheap. He left in the middle of the night or your father would of slammed him. He left a note which I wont repeat what he said about your father. He didn't even say Love. Half the radishes got cracked on account of the wet. Noreen is pregnant again and won't say who but I woun't let your father touch her on account of the one that died. Even though it was a blessing God forgive me. They dont dare

give us a crosseyed look in town because I know
all about THEM. She could have an abortion but
she says she wants something to love. I don't
know where she got that idea at seventeen. Her
having something to love means I get to take care
of it while she runs with dirty bikers. I just cant
stand it. Its a good thing your father is working
again he just sat and moped and all I got from
Wesley and Noreen was a lot of mouth. You dont
say much in your letters but I guess you cant help
it if its Govt work. It's hard enough writing to a
PO number you don't even know what city its in
and I dont know what your doing. I wish you
would just get married. I dont see why not.
Everybody used to say Noreen was beautiful and
look where it got her so beauty isn't everything. I
hope what your doing is respectable. It is enough
to drive you crazy around here. I guess that is all
for now. Write soon.

    Your loving Mother. Your father says him too.
ps I'm glad you could spare the money because
we needed it.

She folded the letter away with all the others and
reached to turn off the light. The intercom buzzer
sounded, and she switched on.

"Mel —" The voice was Vivian's but so slurred it
sounded dead drunk. Viv did not even like whiskey.

"Viv? What's the matter, Viv?"

"Mel?... Come, Mel...."

She pulled her awkward terrible shape out of bed and
knotted the rough terry robe. Viv's room was three
away. In the few seconds it took to reach it a terror
seized her, and she slid the door with shaking hands.

The lights were on. Vivian, still dressed, was lying

diagonally on the bed. Her eyes were open and glazed. The left one turned out slightly, and from its corner tears were running in a thin stream; the side of her mouth dragged down so far her face was distorted almost beyond recognition.

Melba knew a stroke when she saw one. She did not ask whether Vivian had called the doctor but slammed the buzzer and yelled.

Viv raised her working hand a little. "Be all ri ..."

"Oh God, Viv, why didn't you take those goddamn –"

But the one comprehending eye Vivian turned on her was terrible. "Never meant –"

Melba grabbed at the hand. "Oh, Viv –"

"So sorry...."

"Don't talk. Please don't talk."

"Stay, Mel."

"I'm here. You'll have help soon."

The hand was moist and twitching. It wanted to say something the mouth could not speak.

"Now ... who ... will love ..."

"Everyone loves you, Viv. I and everyone."

"Don't mean ... mean, the children, Mel ... the chil ..."

Stretcher wheels squealed around the doorway and attendants lifted Vivian in her blanket. Her hand pulled away from Melba's and her eyes closed.

"Stroke," one of the men muttered.

"I know." She had seen her grandmother taking pills by the handful, and dying too. But her grandmother had been seventy-five.

"Good thing you found her when you did."

"Yeah."

The room was empty. Very empty. The pot of russet chrysanthemums sat on the window-sill like setting suns between the muddy blue drapes. The coloured spines

on the orderly bookshelves blurred into meaningless-
ness. Melba pulled herself up and shuffled back to her
room.

Two or three heads popped out of doorways. "Viv
took sick," she muttered. "I dunno if it's serious."

She lay on her bed and turned the light dim. The sea
beast swam in her belly. She had become so used to its
movement, the fact that she noticed it now surprised her.

Big, slow thing, like me.

Vivian, all tight wires and springs, had broken.

She'll be through here. Maybe crippled – and oh, I
said –

Floors below there was a white room where doctors
worked on that frail pulse. Deep below that there were
tanks where monstrous children turned in sleep so that
terrible worlds could be reaped and mined. For *them.*
They would not care. They had the four females and two
males they would breed to build their stone gardens. She
beat her fist once on the unresounding drum of her
belly.

Buzz.

Her hand, still clenched, punched the button.

"Melba?" The Ox's rasp voice, expressionless.

"Yeah."

"Wake you?"

"No. What –" Her throat went dry.

"She's dead, Mel. Thought I'd tell you first."

"I – thanks, Dorothy."

"For goddamn bloody what!" the Ox snarled and
slammed off.

She sat like stone. She had expected it. What else with
her luck could happen, that she could find a friend, one
friend worthy of respect, and have that good fortune
taken away? She was ashamed of her selfishness, and yet
the fact of *death* was too painful to go near.

She lost track of time, mind blanked out, until her diaphragm buckled sharply, and she fell back on the bed, choking. Then, as if a dam had burst, the waters rushed out of her, and her throat opened in an uncontrollable and unending howl.

First there was the tube in her nose. Then the cone over her mouth, oxygen tasting like dead air already breathed by everyone in the world. Tubes in the wrist and belly. Shots in the buttocks.

Tubes ... and pain ... in the belly?

She opened her eyes. Nurse pulling off EKG cups, pop-pop. Scraggy-beard face of A.J. Yates. Her doctor. Old Ayjay.

"We had to do a Caesarean," he said. "She was a damn big walloper."

She closed her eyes and dreamed of walking Upstreet with her long hair blowing in the wind. Jewels on neck and wrist, wings on her heels, bells on her toes.

You know that's silly Mel, said Vivian.

"What?"

Ayjay: "I said you know we can't let you go through more than one other now you've had the cut. It'll have to be the male, and it'll have to be good."

Yes. They guaranteed their product: They had tried a male once before, and aborted because it was malformed.

"But the males are a lot smaller, so it shouldn't be too much strain. Maybe we can try for twins. Um-hum. It's an idea. Hum-hum. We'll think about it later. In the meantime, you're in pretty good shape. When you graduate after the plastic job you'll be in fine shape." He stood.

"Viv. Isn't."

"Um, well ... oh, I'm glad you reminded me. The inquiry's in four days, and we'll have to get you up a bit for that, as a witness, but we'll take care not to tire you."

Bye-bye, Ayjay. Her eyes closed.

That's a damn dumb idea, said Viv.

"What?"

"Drink this," said the nurse.

She drank and ran her hand over the bandaged hump, the still huge and swollen womb that slid and shifted as if another foetus were waiting there to be born.

Wings on heels, bells on toes. Twins! *Dumb.* Her eyes closed.

Four days of hell. The walls were sickly green.

"Why do I have to go to the inquiry?" she asked the nurse.

"You were her closest friend, weren't you? They'll want to know anything you can tell them about her behaviour. If she ate or drank anything out of the way, like that. After all, she's only the second death we've had here, and the way we take care of them nobody should die."

In hell it is life everlasting. *You didn't take your water pill again.*

"Will I have to go under the scanner?"

"Of course. You aborted just after I came, didn't you? And you went under when you were questioned at the tissue conference. It's in your contract. Didn't you ever read it?"

Melba said, "I only asked a polite question, Nurse."

The nurse gave her a look. She gave the nurse a look.

"I'm sorry. I have other patients to care for." Whirl away of white skirt.

On the third day, a reprieve. The Ox tippy-toed in, bearing a painted china mug filled with delicate flowers.

The Ox, a friend. The friend.

"Oh, that's lovely, it smells so good. Dottie – did you think of watering Viv's flowers?"

The Ox looked down. "I took the pot to my room. You can have it when you get out, if you like."

"Oh no, you keep it, please. She'd have been happy ..."

"Melba, don't cry now. Wait till after tomorrow."

"Dottie, I'm scared shitless. I'll have to go under the scanner, and I don't know what to say!"

"Tell the truth, whatever it is.," the Ox said grimly.

"I'm afraid they'll twist everything around."

"They won't twist you," said the Ox.

But she did not believe that when the jock came for her with the wheelchair. At the tissue conference they had had her almost believing she was some kind of criminal. Viv had pulled her out of that, but there was no ...

"It's only one o'clock. I thought the conference was at two."

"Yeah, but I'm available and so's the chair. What's it to you?"

"I've got a damned sore belly and I feel like a gutted fish. I'm not sitting around in a wheelchair doing nothing for an hour." She needed the hour to think in, but she had been thinking for four days.

"Okay, okay, I'll come back when your ladyship is ready."

A thought ripened. "No. Wait."

"What now?"

"As long as we've got this time I want you to take me down into the crèche."

"Aw, come on! First you're too sick and weak to sit in a wheelchair, an' now I'll end up bringing you up in no condition to testify al all an' I'll have *my* ass in a sling for it. I haven't even any authorization for that."

"You don't need authorization. I *have* read my contract and it says I have the right to see the whatsits."

"Conceptees."

"Yeah. So let's get going."

It was shamefully easy to bully a jock. "Listen, if there's any trouble I'll swear under the scanner that I insisted and I'm to blame."

But it was he who insisted on phoning the crèche first, and was not happy to be invited to come down.

Nor was she, in truth. It was hard sitting in the wheelchair, even through her body did not look the way it had done after previous births, as if a volcano had erupted from it. The pain, in a different place, hurt as much. But she was doing something, besides having babies, that pushed at her from inside.

The white-coated woman, surprisingly, had a kind face.

"You are feeling better now, my dear?" She had sharp foreign features and some kind of accent; her hair was tightly curled blond, dark at the roots.

"Not much. I just thought ... I'd like to see ..."

"Your friend came here often, and looked at many of the children. Yours too. Down this way."

A cold knot in the chest.

Her youngest, twice the size of a normal newborn, slept in a small tank of its own, but the others, chasing through the cool and weed-grown water, seemed far too big even to have been born of a woman.

These were not freaks. Freaks were warped and ugly caricatures, and these were a different species. Very dark red, hairless, their lidless eyes had no discernible expression, and no glance rested on her. The noses and chins were flattened back; the creatures had no fins, webs, or scales, but long, firm rudder-tails like those of tadpoles, and their limbs fitted close to their bodies for streamlining. She felt no pity or horror. They were purely alien. She wondered if they could see beyond the glass and water.

"Can they live outside the tanks?"

"Only for a moment or two."

Upstreet. Downstreet. Undersea. Another direction. Another dimension.

"They don't look much like me."

"Only about the forehead and cheekbones. A good model."

"Oh yeah. What will happen to them?"

"They will mature in a few years, and if they breed well they will make up a little colony and be sent to supervise underwater installations on a world where the seas are suitable for them."

Servants – or slaves?

"When you get a male."

"A viable one. Those are more difficult. But by the time these mature we will probably have developed modified sperms to fertilize them with, so they can breed their own males."

"Oh," said Melba. So much for twins. "Are you allowed to tell me your name?"

"Of course. Natalya Skobelev. So you will know whom to ask for when you come down again."

Again.

"You got twenty-five minutes," said the jock.

"I want to see – to see Vivian's...."

There were hours to crying time.

"Oh, my God. Monkeys!"

"No, no! Arboreal hominids, with one more step to reach humanity!"

That would be some step. But she looked closer. They peered back at her, taut wiry bodies dancing on the branches of the desert tree in the enclosure. Vivian!

These were tailless; they had tiny capable hands and prehensile big toes. Their bodies were covered with light down, but there was dark curly hair on their heads, and they had small sharp noses and neat red mouths. Vivian looked from their blue eyes.

They blinked. Melba scratched at the glass, and they giggled as if they had been tickled and sucked their little thumbs.

"They look much more like her," she whispered.

"We used more of her genetic material."

"And what kind of work will they do?" she asked dully.

"Feed on and harvest medicinal herbs, at first. Then, like yours, they will find other things to do, as they choose, I hope. Build civilization in seas and deserts."

Was this woman here to tell fairy tales? A publicity hack? But her sincerity seemed not only genuine but passionate. NeoGenics was a business that grew servants and slaves. Yet ... slaves had become free.

"Maybe they will. Maybe."

"Time's up," said the jock.

"I know. Thank you for showing me around, miss."

"Remember: Natalya Skobelev, my dear. It is not an easy name."

"I won't forget it."

She felt shrunk and distorted, but the scanner did not register that.

There was no broadcasting of any sort in the auditorium, and no public audience except for the carefully picked jury of six unbiased civilians. Plus the coroner, a group of company officials, and two lawyers.

She let the preliminaries run over her head. A great deal of explication. What NeoGenics had wrought, for the benefit of the jury. Circumstances leading up to, unknown. What medical staff had done for the stricken patient. Useless. All evidence given under the scanner. No one else looked frightened or sickly.

Finally she was helped to the stand and fastened to the scanner.

"Note pseudonym: Ms Burns."

Melba Burns. Toast.

"Ms Burns, do you swear to answer truthfully according to your knowledge?"

"Yeah. Excuse me, yes."

"You have been employed by NeoGenics for four years and three months, during which time you blahblahblah?"

"Yes."

"Control; set," said the woman at the scanner console. The Ox slipped in and sat in the back row, a patient block of stone in her good dress, flowered navy, incongruous out of the grey uniform. No reassurance there.

Melba could not see the console screen, nor the one that was projected in back of her; the framework about her head prevented that. There was no chance of conscious attempt to control the lines of blips. She did not believe she could do it, and would not try. She was here to betray and that was the end of it.

The lawyers were a Mutt-and-Jeff pair: the big one to protect the Company's interests, the little one acting for Vivian's relatives, to make sure the Company could not prove she had reneged on her contract, and refuse to pay out the money owing her.

Lawyer Number 1 said, "Ms Burns, to our knowledge the deceased, Vivian Marsden, considered you her closest friend here."

"I hope so. She was mine."

"I know the Company does not encourage confidences among their employees in order to protect their anonymity in the community, but –" syrup mouth, "I am sure there must have been some confidences exchanged –"

Number 2: "That is an improper question."

Mutt raised an ingratiating hand. "I am not asking the witness for gossip about personal details confided by deceased or gathered from others. I also wish to keep this questioning period brief because of the personal suffering of the witness –"

Number 2: "Very sound and thoughtful."

Melba did not care. The *arboreal hominids* leaped from branch to branch, giggling.

"But the basic question rests on the physical condition of the deceased, Vivian Marsden. Not what has been reported on by medical staff, but what may have been observed by the witness, or told her by Ms Marsden. Whether she looked ill or complained of feeling ill. Whether ... she might have been harming herself, unknowingly or not, by taking unprescribed drugs, alcohol, tobacco, or ignoring dietary regulation?"

Number 2: "Mr Coroner, my friend is asking the witness to condemn the deceased out of hand!"

"But that does seem to be the point that must be addressed," said the coroner. "Ms Burns, will you try to answer the question as simply as possible, even thought it is a complicated one?"

"Again, was Vivian Marsden taking unprescribed drugs, or alcohol, or tobacco, or not eating properly?"

Melba wet her lips. "She didn't when I was with her, and she never talked about it. She hated alcohol. I know she missed cigarettes, but she didn't smoke." Her heart was in her gut. She glanced at the Ox. The woman's face was flushed, and her eyes full of pity.

The little lawyer said dryly, "I think it has been established by general inquiry that no one has more exact information."

"There is another direction to travel," said the Company man, just as dry. "Ms Burns, is there anything necessary to the state of her health that Ms Marsden *neglected* to do?"

Melba stared ahead and breathed hard.

"You must answer, you know," the coroner said gently. "It concerns the health of all the other employees of the Company."

Melba did not need the screen to know that her heartline blipped like mad. "Sometimes she put her water pill in her pocket after meals. She said she didn't like taking it because it made her feel sick." *Forgive, forgive!*

"Ah. You mean the diuretic."

"Whatever took away the extra water she wasn't supposed to have."

Number 2 said quickly, "That is no proof of the cause of an aneurysm. She may have taken the pill later."

"Or not at all. It is suggestive. How often did this happen, Ms Burns?"

Melba found herself grinding her teeth. "No more than twice a week that I know. I kept an eye on her to see what she did with it, and when I noticed her hiding it I made her get it out and take it while I was watching her."

"She could have found ways to avoid ingesting it if she were determined. Hidden it under her tongue, vomited it up –"

Melba snarled, "Oh, for God's sake!"

"Please restrain yourself, Ms Burns, and strike those last two remarks. What deceased did *not* do cannot be accurately inferred from what she was observed to have *done* by an untrained witness."

But the lawyers, ignoring witness and coroner, were

engrossed in each other, doing some kind of mating dance.

"I suggest that we ask permission to recall the pathologist to enlarge on his report."

"I agree. Absolutely. Mr Coroner, may we call the pathologist to witness?"

"You may," said the coroner. "Is Dr Twelvetrees present? Ms Burns, would you please stand down now?"

The millstones ground. "No!" Melba cried. "It's not right!"

"Ms Burns, I know you are distraught –"

"If that means I'm upset, I'm damned upset. And maybe everybody thinks I'm stupid. But I'm not crazy. Sir – please let me speak for one minute!"

The coroner sighed. "If you have a contribution to evidence, Ms Burns, go ahead. But please keep your remarks brief and to the point, as the lawyers are supposed to do."

There was a mild snicker. Melba despised and ignored it. "Maybe I can help bring out evidence." She took breath. "I thought we were here to find out just why Vivian died – but this fella here acts like she fell in a ditch when she wasn't looking, and this other one is trying to put her on trial for murdering herself. I've answered all the long questions as well as I could, and now I'd like to ask two short questions." She pointed. "This guy."

"You wish to address the Company lawyer?" He scratched his head. "This is an inquiry not a trial. Go ahead, but –"

"I *will* keep it short. I want to ask, Mr Lawyer: Did Vivian Marsden have high blood pressure before she came to work for you – when she was nineteen? And would she have been cured of it after she left?"

Silence fell with a dark grey thud. A man slipped out

of the room, and no one blinked. The lawyer opened his mouth and shut it again. Then, "After all, Ms Burns, everyone knows there is some risk —"

"Yeah. I guess that's all. Only ... the last words she ever said to me were: *Now who will love the children, Melba?* – and I didn't even know what she was talking about. I'm sorry I took up your time and I'll stand down now. Please ask that lady in the corner if she'll take me back to my room. I don't feel well."

"You did good," said the Ox.

"Yeah. And a lot of good it'll do. Everybody will be mad at me for telling about the pills."

"Between you and me, I think a lot of people knew she was trying to hide them, but nobody else made sure she took them, the way you did – so they can be as mad as they like."

She dreamed, a layered and complex dream of creatures in tanks, and children screaming dirty words in the streets, and worlds where the children of NeoGenics stared with empty eyes and died sterile. And her sister Noreen giving birth to a –

The door chimed.

"Come in," she said in her dream. Noreen's child was –

"It's over," said the Ox. "Death by misadventure. Nobody to blame, officially. Vivian's heirs will get their money."

She rubbed her eyes. "I hope they don't throw it around."

"No use being so bitter."

"I have no friend."

"You can count me as kind of half of a friend. I wouldn't mind."

"I'm sorry, Dottie. I'm behaving like a crud. You are

a friend." And Skobelev. She would be useful if old Ayjay got twins on the brain again.

"There were some jury recommendations. You interested?"

She said drowsily, "I guess so."

"About giving the public greater access to information about our beloved Company. Knock off some of the name calling and stone-throwing. Not fast and not much, but some. And letting government health organizations have a hand in the choice of breeders. The shit hit the fan when they found Twelvetrees. He'd run out to dig up Viv's county health records – which he should have done in the first place – and found cases of blood pressure in the family history."

"Huh. I was trying to say they'd given her the high blood pressure."

"They brought it out by accepting her without investigating enough. And there were one or two things you said that they needed to hear. Well, I guess I better get back to work – but like you, I have one more question. Now you got your brains working – the way Viv always said you ought – what are you going to do with them?"

Melba smiled. And she had not even cried yet. "Gimme a chance, Dottie. They're still awful creaky."

I did pretty clumsy, Viv, but it was the best I could. You never belonged here. You should have had a man who could give you proper kids, and I'll never know why not. I don't know why I didn't either, except the home I came from isn't the kind I'd want to have. Maybe I never thought I was good enough to make a better one, but I dunno. The old man's a bastard, but he's proud of working, and Ma won't let herself be shamed. There's nothing wrong with that, is there? But kids can't find enough work to be proud of now, and we're not ashamed of the same things. Poor Noreen. She really is stupid, God forgive me.

One thing I can do with the money is get her out of there. Maybe in some kind of shelter, Dorothy'd know, but not around this place. So her baby could at least have a chance to be a person.

Viv? We had all those, and what will they do? They should have had worlds that could grow them by themselves to make their own dumb mistakes, not the ones we make for them ... but I can do something for Noreen....

And if I'm very good and very lucky there'll still be some money to throw around. Aw, Viv, you know there's nothing much wrong with that either. Better than wait until.... Emerald, ruby, diamond ... and the yellowish one. Topaz. Long hair for fingers to tangle in and kind of go shivering down my back ... ah ...

Where'd I find a fella like that, Ma? Well, I'm not preg all the time, and I've seen other eyes on me besides yours. Looking for different things. And maybe ...

She slept without a dream.

1982

BLUE APES

A man sat on a rock outcropping in a valley, weeping. His clothes were torn, his body bruised. His hands trembled on his knees; tears watered the blood of cuts on his face and neck, stinging.

The sun shone brightly, the air was fresh and crisp. Wind ruffled the green and yellow trees, blowing down yellow leaves even as green buds sprang on the branches. Blue-furred animals giggled and chattered among them; once in a while one would pause and stare with pink eyes down at the seated figure, sometimes break off a twig and throw it at him. They were not hostile; mildly, they discouraged intruders.

The man plucked a twig from his hair and let it fall. He did not listen to the blue apes. The wind was singing him a song.

König moved quietly from the hypnoformed shuttle. It blended with the bedding of yellow leaves in the dip of the forest floor. The air was cold. He stood for a moment. There was no moon in the dark sky, the stars were unfamiliar. The wind rustled the leaves of the great-branched trees, whistled thinly among conifers. He pulled up the hood of his robe and tied the string. The rough brown hopsacking did not keep out the wind but his hair and beard were thick, close-curled, and he was wearing a quilted suit underneath. He took one tentative

226

step, crunching the leaves, and heard a chirr in the branch above his head. His hand slipped into the knapsack and found the stunner between the knife and the bread crust. He went on slowly without looking up; the branch shook, a few dead leaves fell on his shoulders. He stopped rigid: his imagination, like an ancient memory, felt the weight of the animal on his neck, the bite, his own scream, the vomiting bowel-loosening death.

The animal jeered. The leaves fell. He shuffled gently through the leaf-layer, away from the tree, between two blue-black conifers. Another animal woke, whistling, the two muttered for a moment, became quiet, slept. Some flying creature in the conifers whooped, swept up and sheared by him with long wings, found another tree. The forest slept again.

Beyond the conifers the woods ended in a low thicket and the land fell in a short steep cliff toward a stream that frothed over stones. König pushed through the scrub; it tore at his robe and scratched his hand. The wind quickened, smoothing away his leaf-spoor. The cliff-side was covered with woody vines. He dropped the stunner in his pocket and climbed down, pausing at each creak of a stem.

He stood on the stony bank, unseen by the forest, and licked at his hand. Dipped into the pack again and pulled out a film bag, rummaged until he found a vial with capsules and took one: it was a powerful antibiotic, but it did not protect against the bite of the blue ape. He returned the vial, took out and unwrapped a bundle of three rod-shaped instruments. With the first, an infrared scanner, he found no significant heat-source in any direction. The second was a pen-light, and he hunkered against the cliff, spread the wrapping on his knees and studied it: it was a survey map. Presently he rose, dropped the light, map and scanner into bag and pack,

pulled out the knob on the end of the third piece, un-
coiling a length of fine wire, and set the knob in his ear.
The illuminated dial on his wrist gave him two hours to
dawn. He felt his way along the cliff; his thick rawhide
boots hardly crunched the stones. Fifty metres of cliff-
side told him nothing until the earpiece began to hum,
and the pointing rod, a metal detector, gave him destination. He backed one step, pushed a button on his wrist
chronometer, and a section of the cliff-side rose, wrenching away roots where a few vine-ends had taken hold.
He did not like the shriek of rusty metal, and allowed the
hidden door to rise only enough to let him roll under
into the cavern; with the pen-light he found the switch.

The light inside was very dim, and he was glad of
that. He could see clearly enough the skeleton of a
shuttle, and the skeleton of a Solthree human.

The shuttle had been gouged by rough hands; there
were no electronic equipment, clothing, utensils, flight
recorder. The shell had withstood attempts to tear it
apart; the place was dry, and there were only a few rust
spots in its dents. He did not touch it. The registry number on its side showed clearly through dust and
scratches. It was half-a-century old.

He threw back his hood and reached into the neck of
the robe to unbutton the high collar of the suit, dragged
at a chain around his neck until he was holding the silver
locket. He pushed the manual release button in its centre.

"König recording." His voice was quiet but clear.
"Shuttle found and corresponding. Equipment removed. No GalFed ship in orbit, probably long captured
by scavenger." He turned unwillingly to the skeleton of
bone. It was sitting on the dusty floor up against the wall,
bending forward slightly and saved from collapse by the
propping of a pitchfork whose black-stained tines
pierced its ribs. It had been stripped by theft and decay

of everything but a few shreds of cloth and several swirling locks of faded hair hanging from patches of dry scalp on its skull. Though the body seemed longer than his own, he thought by the bone shapes it might have been female. "Also in hangar skeleton of body stabbed with pitchfork staining tines and breaking ribs, presume caused death. By body size not a native of Colony Vervlen." Perhaps he should have brought the camera; but he doubted it would have made a difference. Especially to the bones. "Long narrow structure. Strands of fair hair probably faded, long and straight. Pelvis shape suggests female. Almost certain this is the ... the body of Signe Halvorsen."

Why the quivering lip, König? If she'd lived she'd be dead by now.

Pitchfork....

König, lots of people in the Department think you're a bastard. I'm not sure. Others work on tiptoe, and you take a bunch of grumbling colonists and con and bully and kick them out of danger farside or offplanet. I'm not sure, because you've always saved them, no matter how much they've wanted to kill you. This thing that's come up — you might say it was made for you — and maybe you'd like to leave this one to rot....

But he was here, and he wondered if it was the colonists who were in danger. His feelings shifted, his plans changed every minute....

He switched the lights off, rolled under the door and shut it. There was the subtlest of pale shading on the eastern horizon and the diurnal creatures were beginning to whicker and grunt. He rearranged the vines as well as possible, and felt his way back to a place near his original descent. Studied the forest, the stream, the vines. Then he rewrapped his instruments in the map, laid them on a flat stone, hesitated, added the stunner, pulled the chronometer with its remotes from his wrist, the recorder from round his neck. He dropped the heap of objects into the film bag, rolled it until the air was squeezed out, sealed it with the pressure of his fingers. He lifted the rock aside and scratched a hole with his knife, an implement suitable only for cutting bread and cheese; packed down the parcel, replaced the rock. Now he had nothing to defend himself with, nothing of his that could be used against him.

Pitchforks.

He pulled off his robe, rolled it into a pillow and sat down at the cliff's base. During the next half hour while light swelled and birds began to caw he used the knife to scrape the annealed metallic GalFed symbols from the breast of his suit.

His fingernails grew purple with cold. A drift of cloud let down a few snowflakes and the sky cleared again. König's teeth were clacking like a shaken skeleton's. He pulled on the robe and a pair of knit mittens and climbed up to the forest. An animal dancing on the lax arm of a conifer stared at him. At first he could see only the pink bouncing eyes, for the fur was the blue of the brightening sky. The creature was ape-like, not anthropoid but prosimian, a big lemur with a long plume tail and sharp claws. A group converged and threw pods at him; he went very slowly over the fallen leaves, barely glancing up to notice that some gripped shadow-coloured infants to their breasts. None dropped to take its bite of death. The forest cleared at last into open farmland, and he reached the mud track that served for a road.

Nearly three hundred years earlier an ultra-orthodox sect who lived by farming had tired of Sol III. As the world pushed up against their fences the very air smelled of spiritual as well as industrial contamination.

They had decided to leave the planet in their physical bodies.

They had religious stockades to breach: they must travel by starship using the technology they repudiated; accept a world terraformed to their requirements; allow the modification of their children's genetic components to fit them for the isolated place they chose. A planet without seasons whose axis lay perpendicular to its orbit, where the equator was barely temperate.

They studied the Holy Books, argued long and loud, and in marathons of study and discussion found justification in the eye of their God.

Terraforming was a matter of land-clearing and terracing to prevent water run-off; the Vervlin knew nothing of their travels because they had been put into deep-sleep before loading; their gene-pool was modified by engrafting the stock of Ainu, Inuit and other cold-land peoples who lived by hunting, herding and small-farming. Founding population was 750. By second generation census they numbered 982, a fair increase in a hard land. But some had become disenchanted; the Ninety and Nine demanded and got repatriation. Ten years later they changed heart and asked for return but were repudiated by their brethren.

Colony Vervlen lived on. At fifth generation census they had increased only to near 1200; GalFed worried at their low growth rate and slow pubertal development and prescribed dietary changes, since Vervlin would not take drugs.

Tenth generation census, in the person of Signe Halvorsen, would have been GalFed's last uninvited landfall on Vervlen, but she did not return. By last spacelight relay she was in orbit on the way to landing, and after that, nothing. There were no calls to send or receive: Vervlin would not use radio. The search team, sent a year later, had been shot out of the sky in a war between two other planets of the world's sun, and the whole system, which supported no other GalFed colonies, had been twice quarantined, for a total of fifty years....

Between forest and road, König paused. He did not know how to approach a people capable of murdering a Galactic emissary, even though it was half a century ago. Many colonists would have liked to kill him; none had tried. A couple had flattened his already snub nose a little further.

He squatted among the bushes, half turned to keep an eye on the blue enemies among the trees. No great antlered beasts shouldered them now: they had been hunted out or added to domestic stock. No saplings had been planted in many years. All that grew had risen from seed-droppings, in disorder. Spiralling down in darkness he had seen no roads, lights, steeples, meeting halls. Only twenty or so clumps of thatched-roof houses huddled together, perhaps a hundred buildings in all.

From the ground he could see that they were small, with parchment windows lit from within by stoked fires; wisps of smoke rose from old stone chimneys. Out of the centre of each clump a taller chimney protruded like a raised finger among knuckles. East and west, Vervlen covered no more than half a kilometre.

Without birth control.

Shadows began to slip from houses and move in the grain fields –

And sharp points jabbed the base of his spine. He had left one quadrant unguarded, and rustling leaves had covered footsteps. He scrabbled round with a yelp, for he was too locked in his crouch to rise quickly. And yelped again, gawking up at the gnome.

He did not even care that pitchfork tines pierced the

cloth at his breast.

"What you want?" the gnome growled in the old rough language. "Where you come, you stranger?"

König was a short stocky man with brown hair and beard, grey eyes and flat-saddled nose. The strong contour of his body was smoothed down with a light layer of fat and covered with a great deal of hair. The fatty thickening of his eyelids made them almost oriental. With darker colouring he would have looked like an Ainu, or with less hair an Inuit, for he was a descendant of Vervlin – of the Ninety and Nine.

"Where you come, say!" The pitchfork jabbed. The gnome had König's eyes, nose, hair, breadth, and was wearing the rough leather and homespun of his people. But it was as if a hand had shaped him in clay and thumped him down. Eye-slits between thick brows and knob cheekbones, lips thickened till they curled to nostril, chin vanished in beard, neckless, waistless, bandy-legged. An ancient without a grey hair.

König fell to his knees and clasped hands, begging; whined, spilled words without thinking. "Hungry, master, 'm hungry!" He had been uneasy about the dialect for fear of change and development, but there had been no change here but shrinkage and reversion. The sense of it filled him with irrational terror. He pleaded in good earnest. And doubly, because he had fasted several days. "Ha' not to eat, ha' come many day from town east – master, see!" He showed the gaping bag with its one gnarled crust. He could not keep from babbling at the terrible dull-eyed gnome, "Name of König, and a' come many days from east!"

The eyes lit briefly, the pitchfork moved down slowly. "Here's many Königs and many hungry, but a' know no man east."

"Oh, ay, master, is many men east, truly."

The tines sank to earth, the Vervlin leaned on the worn handle. His arms were thick and strong, though the fingers were knobbed like tubers from arthritis. "Will y' workn to eat?"

König dared pull himself up. "Gladly, lord."

"Lord, hah!" The slit eyes took his measure. König was nearly a head taller than the Vervlin but this did not seem to impress him. He was looking for the breadth of a hardy labourer, and where his eyes lingered was at the heavy boots. König cursed himself. His foot-gear was not fine, but far better than the farmer's, cut like moccasins from single pieces and laced with thongs. How was he to have foreseen that? But the shrunk man's eyes were dull. "Come with." König was careful to stay abreast of the pitchfork on the path to the nearest house.

Inside was firelit, and would not grow much brighter through parchment windows during the light of the day. König had to stoop to go through the door, and as he stepped in the gnome bellowed, "Aase!" and turned to him with what might have been a glint of humour. "Name of Rulf, König man, 'm no lord."

Aase, the female of the species, appeared round the fireplace in homespun skirts and shawl, noted without surprise that there was one extra for breakfast, and disappeared to yell an order to someone unseen.

König himself was a result of genetic engineering, and he had seen many others, but none so grotesque, so terribly wrong. Inbreeding? Isolation? He simply let his mind go out of gear and ate the porridge with its milk and butter at the table before the fire.

The interior of the house surprised him: it was neat and clean, and seemed to mock the bodies that lived in it. The furniture was well joined and sanded, softened with knit cushions; the old chimney was freshly tuck-pointed, the plank floor smooth as if it had been varnished. He heard slight noises underneath, and wondered if there were a cellar with mice. One glance into a corner showed him a trapdoor latched with a wooden bar and an iron loop; in his state of mind it would not have surprised him if a monster lived in the cellar.

But the porridge bowl emptied quickly, and the hard hand on his arm invited him to labour; he dared not look more.

And he laboured. The barn was filthy and ramshackle, a big rough shelter patched together and used in common with the community of dwarfs in the housegroup. Whatever explanation Rulf gave his fellows he did not hear: there were five or six of them, slightly bluer or greyer in eye, darker or lighter in hair, shorter or taller by a few centimetres – cousins or brothers. None questioned him and he did not speak. Where stupidity reigned he obeyed. Forked hay, yoked oxen, shovelled dung. At noon women brought baskets of hot cakes; he ate, standing in mud, and worked on. Once when a plough stuck in a furrow there was a yell of "König!" and he started and looked up quickly. But a stunted man dropped his spade and shambled out to help. Cousins.

The day clouded over and promised rain. The forest turned pale under the cloud-lid and rustled, but no animal ventured from it. Men raked and hoed and ploughed and stacked. They did not joke or curse or discuss or quarrel, and left their work only to relieve themselves in an open pit outside the corner of the barn. When he was forced to use this, König, whose sense of privacy was acute, suffered bladder spasms. They were the day's only stimulation; he began to wonder if stupidity was contagious.

Toward sundown he pulled his mind back into operation.

Men work outside, women indoors. No children in sight. Why? Why filthy barns and spotless houses? Implements old and uncared for. No metal work done now. No poultry. Too hard to run after? There are a dead calf and two dead piglets in the stalls. No one has noticed them yet. The woman who brought the midday meal hasn't washed in a thirtyday. By rights they should be buried in their own dirt. But the clothes are well-made. The cakes were wrapped in a clean cloth. Maybe elves are doing the work for them. Why would they bother? The food is good, but no one says grace. Where are the churches?

He leaned on his rake handle and watched Rulf leading in the oxen to unyoke. The wizened man stopped at the entrance, eyes glazed, mouth open. After a few moments he blinked, closed his mouth, and moved on.

Epilepsy? No, they're all like that. Degeneration. Worse than we could have expected. I wonder how old they are....

When a bell rang among the complex of houses to signal the evening meal the rest of the men came in from the fields, dumped their rakes and hoes in a corner and left without a backward look. Rulf finished unyoking the oxen. König untangled the rakes, spades, forks, hoes and hung them on rusty hooks set in the barn wall. He wanted to provoke a little reaction, but only a little. Rulf's beetling brows rose and settled. When König plucked up a handful of straw to wipe the mud off his boots he found the eyes on him and met them with an ingenuous stare. Boots you may need, Rulf, but why did your grandfathers strip the electronics from Halvorsen's shuttle? "Eh, master?"

Rulf grunted. "Y' want eatn?"

"Oh ay, thank y'"

In darkness the hearth-fire burned brightly, and within
the limit of movement he dared allow himself, König
tried to examine the place. The massive fireplace projected into the room and to either side was an inglenook.
One was filled by a standing wardrobe and a wooden
bedstead with an oil lamp above it, but the other was in
shadow and he could not see where it ended. Since there
were no stairs or any other door visible he presumed it
led to a kitchen; Aase had gone there to call for and
bring the food. Elves' cooking.

Supper was meat stew with barley and root vegetables, a few raw greens like cress on the side. Rulf and
Aase gobbled. So did König. He was hungry.

The mice/elves under the floor were busy tonight. Almost, his imagination gave them voices. Perhaps they
would come up at midnight and lick the plates clean
with small pink tongues. Rulf stood and dumped the
bones into the fire: König followed, and Aase took the
rough-glazed bowls back into the shadow.

Rulf stared at König during the slow turn of his cogs
of thought and said, "Y' work morgn?"

"Oh ay, master."

Grunt. "Here y' slep." He opened the wardrobe and a
jumble of odd ragged things bulged; he heaved and
tugged at an old bundled mattress of rough cloth with
straws sticking out of its holes and unrolled it on the
table, disregarding food scraps and gravy puddles.
König moved the table slightly, away from the fire's
heat, not too near the cold of the walls. He looked up to
make sure he had not offended Rulf by this rearrange-
ment, and his glance was held at the mantel-piece. There
was a big clay bowl on it, half filled with ashes, and,
perching on the rim, back resting against the bricks, a
wooden figurine. He squinted against the glare of the
flames and saw its shape was that of a forest ape, just

over half life-size and roughly stained blue, lower part blackened with smoke.

Where the churches had gone.

The sight of the idol crystallized a decision he had been slowly approaching all day. At midnight, when the trolls were asleep, and no matter what the elves or mice might do, he was leaving.

There was no kindness he could do these people and no harm he would be willing to commit upon them even if their ancestors had been the bugbears of his childhood. Leave questions unanswered, let failure smudge his record. *Maybe you'd like to leave this one to rot.* No, Director. You decide.

Rulf knocked the logs down with a poker and the flames lowered. He blew out the lamp above the bed and yelled, "Aase!"

She came shambling. "Still y', still y'." She dropped on the bed and pulled up her skirts. Rulf flipped the lacing of his breeches and fell on her.

König hastily climbed his table and lay with knees drawn up and back turned, still wearing the robe, suit and boots he had sweated in all day. It was the style here. Folded his arms against the cold, tried not to hear the grunts and whimpers from the bed. Rain beat against the walls. His back was warm, there was still heat in his full belly. He was weary, his eyes closed.

He did not want sleep, but sleep was coming – not as sweet release from labour but as a dark imprisoning lid.

Drugs. He could not move.

He thought he heard steps from afar, and the scrape of wood on iron. The lid fell closer, blacker, hands grasped his ankles and pulled him straight.

Boots.

His arms were unlocked from his chest. Unconsciously his mouth opened for the last cry of the pierced man.

König, you bloody fool, murdered for a pair of boots!

Voices: he was not dead. Possibly.

Speaking in *lingua*: "He can't be one of us."

"But he's like them. Even hairier."

Fingers moving in the hair on his belly. Damned cold fingers. His robe must be off, he was unbuttoned to the navel.

"Must be thirty good year anyway."

"Thirty-five!" König snarled, simultaneously opened his eyes and sat up. "What the hell do you think you're doing?"

His sight went black and starry; he blinked darkness away with the force of anger, hands pulled back, voices stilled. On a table again. He swivelled and hooked legs over the edge.

An underground room, a vault supported by beams, opening almost endlessly into the flickering lights and shadows of wall-sconces. Around him were children, children, twenty-five to thirty of them. Real Solthree children. Dressed like the gnomes above, in clothes rough-cut but carefully sewn.

A child began to weep.

"Shut up!"

A firm-voiced girl slapped the table. "Don't be rough! You will wake *them* up and you are scaring him!"

"What are you trying to do to me?" He zipped thermal underwear, buttoned furiously, fingers half-numb and all thumbs.

Children ... as he had been? The ones he should have? Curly-haired small and medium Königs with blue, grey, blue-grey eyes, sharp bright ones here under the eyelid fold. Smooth faces, sweet mouths. Girls rough-breeched like the boys, hair scarcely longer because it was so curly.

"Why do you have buttons?" They spoke *lingua* in the rough cadences of the Vervlin tongue. He studied the speaker. First beard-hairs showing. Not so sharp, this one. On the way to changeover. But not stupid either. He knew a foreigner when he saw one.

König felt even duller. "I come to where buttons are used." He looked for the robe, saw it crumpled on the floor and left it. The air was warmer here. Far among the beams stood a huge complex of fireplaces hung with pots and ladles, source of the big outside stack.

"Your buttons are riveted," said the girl, as if she were joining a game with infants. Fifteen, perhaps? She might be the leader, for a while.

"Technology," said König. "You don't do badly at it. Do you drug people often?"

"Sometimes to make them sleep longer when we want freedom."

"Where did you learn *lingua*?" She was as pretty as a Vervlin girl might become. Her hair was a little darker and straighter, she had pulled back the strands over her ears and tied them with twine.

"We always had it as a second language. Starwoman taught us more."

"Taught you?"

"The ones of us here when she was."

"Signe Halvorsen?"

"Starwoman. You with the riveted buttons and the thirty-five years, you are Starman, who lied to the Elders about far towns in the east. Why are you not surprised, Starman? The other one was."

"That you are children? I knew there had to be children somewhere. I didn't think of here. I thought there were mice in the cellar."

Giggles all around. A shiver went down his back. They were so normal, so innocent, Halvorsen stabbed with a pitchfork.

"You answer no question, Starman." Cool voice of a boy farther back. "Why no surprise that we are not as the Elders?"

His mind was too foggy to explore a dangerous question. He answered with the simplest truth. "I have already been surprised by the Elders. I knew something of what was happening, but not that it had gone so far. And my name is König."

"So is mine – and ten others here."

"I know: many Königs and many hungry. But I am tired – and drugged, thanks to your cleverness. Let me go back upstairs now."

"No," the girl said. "By morning they forget everything. You stay down here, Starman. You have much to tell."

He let it go. He could not fight even one of them now. "What is your name, Younger?" A little touch to the word.

She reddened a bit. "Ehrle."

"And mine is König. Why are you kept down here?"

"We do all the work that needs cleverness, and they are afraid we order them about. It is all the same to us. We have ways out, when we choose to use them, and we have not to work in the stinking barns."

Nor would she, as an Elder. Aase lay above, gibbering under pounding Rulf.

"And why are you here, Starman König?"

"To find out what became of Signe Halvorsen – and my people." He yawned, fought dizziness once more to retrieve his robe and roll it into a pillow.

"But you must tell us –"

"Later. I am asleep."

And he was, folded on the table, knees pulled up, robe under his head, asleep.

"Wake up, Star-König, we want to use the table."

He got up very stiffly, even though some of them had been thoughtful enough to slide folded blankets under him. His first thought was: they don't have a spare bunk; you'd think they'd prepare one if they expected company. But when he looked up he saw groups of them gathering bedrolls from the tables as well as from the tiers of shelves on the walls, and realized he had been given the spare bunk.

He had a headache but was not nauseated; there was no brightness to hurt his eyes here either, only the firelight he had seen so much of already, and small squares of dusky sky where the ceiling joined the walls. Openings screened with fibre meshes, presumably to keep out small animals, they were not quite big enough to let out small humans. They also had wooden louvers to shield from rain and snow.

He wanted to see more of these surroundings, but there were children, children, children who wanted to see him. Some, he was sure, from the groups of houses beyond this one; they wove and cut their cloth a little differently, sometimes with a stripe or a twilled weave. Did they come overland, or were there rabbit-warrens of tunnels with lookouts, codes, sentries? Why not? They knew all he had done and said above. And had children killed Halvorsen? Not these.

He looked at them. There was a harelip, a few cases of cross-eye and a few with buck teeth. Some scars from cuts and scratches, but no boils or impetigo that he could see. Halvorsen had been a doctor. Probably those who were badly crippled and could not be cured were kept somewhere together, not to be hidden but to be cared for efficiently. From what he could tell of these children, they were efficient. "Don't smother me," he said quietly; the table was digging into his back from their pressure.

"I'm like you, only bigger, is all."

"You are not like *them*," said Ehrle.

Three or four bells chimed at once, from all the houses this cellar must run under. Half the children ran away, and to the others Ehrle said sharply, "Get the pots stirring, Willi, and you, move away before you spill something hot."

The lightly bearded boy who was a bit dull went to supervise the porridge-making, others to different tasks, some, reluctantly, to sit on benches by the tables. All eyes on him. Their candle-power was nerve-wracking; compared to it the stupidity of the Elders was soothing.

Troops of servitors worked without bumping or slopping: one to send bowls of food upstairs on dumb-waiters, another to man their ropes, a third to serve the seated ones.

"Don't spit, Mooksi, you need not be a slob." Ehrle was a super-martinet.

König said, "Will you rap my knuckles if I ask for a little more milk?"

There was a ripple of laughter around the table. König locked eyes with Ehrle and wished he had not spoken. He understood what was happening.

The children were clean, cleaner than he was, and more disciplined than an armed force. They were, after all, fathers to the men, and would play later in as much filth as they chose. A clumsy Gulliver might upset an inverted social structure that was the only basis here for existence and continuity: a structure balanced on a very sharp knife-edge.

No one knew just how much time there was, for Ehrle or anyone else, but she seemed determined to extend it by the pure force of her personality. Uselessly.

He took a drop of the milk he was offered and said, "Yesterday I saw a dead calf and two shoats in the stalls."

A boy said, "I know. I got rid of them last night."

"I wasn't sure you'd noticed them."

"We know about everything here."

"Yes, of course. You knew of me."

(But not where he had left the ship and controls. He hoped to God not.)

He was reaching for equality – to be neither overbearing nor overborne. Sophisticated Gulliver. For König there was far too much intelligence and organization here. He must leave before he was overborne.

As the bowls emptied he was quick to rise and stack them. Ehrle said, "You need not serve, Star-König."

"A' mus workn for to eat, not?" He laughed. "If I break things you may put me to scrubbing floors." He joined a line of children waiting to put crockery in a tub of soapy water. Eyes on him, always. Questions to come.

The floors were worn brick, neatly grouted and well scrubbed. Probably torn from old houses. Population did not quite replace itself and as it shrank, living-space compacted for warmth and ubiquitous efficiency. The children surely lived better than their elders. Building bigger houses to their standards would require greater strength, and more knowledge and equipment, than they had.

The eyes, pair by pair, moved away from him and turned their attention to scrubbing, spinning, weaving. Bone needles, bits of metal to pierce leather. Sacking and woollen cloth grew on the unwieldy looms; some yarns tinted, probably from dyes scraped out of the soil. Water boiled and food simmered by the fires; dough was rising.

"You don't do tanning here, surely?"

A voice at his elbow laughed. "Would raise a mighty stink if we did. Shed's outside with the kiln and smokehouse."

"I think you're spoiling them."

"Ehrle doesn't let them push us too far."

A voice at his shoulder said, very quietly, "That one, there, thinks she'll never change. All them do."

"Which them, Willi?"

The boy was standing awkwardly, looking into the top bowl of his pile with its milk puddle and cereal lumps, broad thumbs hooked carefully over the edge. He raised his eyes.

"Leaders, like." He was a burnt-out lantern compared with the others, but his features had coarsened very little. "I was one. It's like I did wrong, growing. But I want to go upthere," he made it one word. "I want a woman. 'M not right, here." He spoke without lust or anger, facts.

A voice hissed, "Shut up, Willi!"

"I'll get there." Willi set his nest of bowls into the water and turned away.

And she would follow. And perhaps be his woman and bear his children....

König gave them a day of work, as he had done with the Elders, but for more complicated motives — aside from discouraging questions before he thought of the answers. He did not care for idleness, nor wish to set himself above them, and he did not want to become indispensable, like Halvorsen. He was trying to bond himself to them just enough so that they would think twice before taking extreme action. He felt this might be possible because he himself was a Vervlin. On the other hand, for the same reason, they might expect more from him....

He knew from long experience how to be helpful without getting in the way. He wiped up, swept up, changed diapers in a roomful of babies, and stayed away from those with organized serious tasks. One or another of the children was always with him, usually the boy with his own name, who was near Ehrle's age and probably the next contender for leadership. In all, they were the most solemn group of children he had ever seen. They never smiled, and rarely laughed except when he provoked them purposely. A few of the babies chuckled when he nuzzled their faces; several were wasting with dysentery, but most seemed quite healthy.

"Are these fed on cows' milk?"

"Only when they can drink from cups. It is too hard to make bottles. When we find a good milker upthere we keep two or three babies on her until weaning. She never knows the difference."

"Do you know your mother?"

"No. How can I?"

None of them had parents, except for their siblings, the busy ones who, humane as they might be, did not know how to be kind or joyful. The babies had a few stuffed toys, but there was no other sign of game or toy, no tag or rough-house. He picked up a fretful child; it fitted the curve of his arm quite properly, and fell silent pulling at the fine chain around his neck.

"What is that on your neck, Star-König?" Puzzling at the square centimetre of filigree.

"A Galactic Federation emblem. Do you grow sugar beets?"

"A small crop. Why?"

"And put a little sugar in the cereal you give the children – or let them suck on a piece?"

"Sometimes."

"Keep it away from the ones with loose bowels."

"You have children of your own?"

"No."

Serious face close to his again. "What are you, König?"

König put the baby down; it whimpered for a moment, and slept. "A person who travels to new communities on strange worlds and tells them to move or leave because of dangerous conditions."

"What kind of conditions?"

"Disease, poisonous land or water, approaching war." Genetic instability, he did not add.

"And you come to ask us to move?"

"No. To find out how you are getting on, because we could not come earlier on account of wars on the planets near here. To help you stay healthy and live –" he caught himself before saying, longer "– more easily." He watched the babies playing with their toes. A short youth and a stern one. He added, "I was chosen because I am descended from Vervlin."

"Yes," the boy said contemptuously, "The Ninety-nine who ran away."

"They tried to come back and were not allowed by the others here."

"I didn't know that."

"Now you know, it doesn't make much difference."

"Yes it does, Starman. You are a normal adult, and we want to know why."

He was becoming tired of crowding and pressure, of attention, nudging bodies, endless murmur of voices. The focus. The wrong choice. What was the right one? An armed fleet, against despairing children? He took it head on.

"Galactic Federation made a mistake when they formed your bodies in the shape you have. There was a flaw in the seed, and because everyone had it, and had children with someone else who had it, it stayed. It took a while to show itself, so nobody was warned soon enough, and it stayed in the generations. Most of the flaws of that kind are weak and wash out in descendants, but this was not that kind. Many of the Ninety-nine married stranger-peoples before the flaw had time to affect them so badly, and if they thought they might be affected they had no children." Before young König had time to react he asked, "Didn't Starwoman talk of this?"

"I believe so, but no one understood. This we can understand." König shut up and let him think. "Galactic Federation must owe us something, not? Our fathers sold rich lands on Sol Three and paid to come here."

"They owe you something," König said grimly. Try to collect.

Out of mercy the bells ran for lunch.

"Today we have light lunch and early supper," Ehrle said.

"Is something special happening?" König roasted on spit.

She smiled without humour. "Tonight they have their Sabbath celebration and we get out and watch them behaving like fools."

"They are not all such fools," said Willi.

König said quickly, "Do they know you get out?"

"Likely."

"They're not afraid you will run away?"

"No." The word cut like a knife. Of course not. The runaway would turn into the enemy.

König asked for and got the favour of a tub of hot water. While it heated he squatted in an empty niche, to be alone, unregarded for the moment. He did not want to see how the Elders would celebrate; the prospect repelled him. But for the children it was probably some kind of object lesson in superiority; actually, in futility. In spite of the regimentation, the industry, the cleverness, the almost purposive lack of differentiation between the sexes. *I want a woman.*

The niche was not bare: it was lined with shelves piled full of worn things for which uses would be found. He ran his hand down them idly. Old leather, sacking, wool. And something hard. He pulled apart two folds of blanket and found it: a heap of the fragmented pieces of Halvorsen's radio and electronics. He smoothed down the blankets and got out of there in a hurry. There were not many pieces, nowhere near enough to account for all of the instrumentation. Perhaps every house-group had its little heap. Perhaps it was the equivalent of the carved blue god of the Elders.

He found a shadowed corner for this bath and took it in a worn wooden tub which appeared to be the community bathtub. The lye soap did not smell pleasant but it washed well, and, watching his toes curled over the tub's edge he allowed himself to relax to the point of mild relief that these colonists at least did not apologize for the primitive conditions that for him were merely a commonplace of the many outworld communities he had visited.

The moment he was aware of relaxing the trapdoor grated and opened, and Aase came downstairs. The children whispered and muttered, and began deploying themselves to keep her turned away from König. König came out of his lull into the sense of a loose situation with an open door: he sat up and reached for his clothes, ready to call out. A hand snatched the clothes away; another grabbed a fistful of his wet hair and pushed his head back: "Keep down, Starman. Do you think she will fight for you?"

He clapped his mouth shut in a fury and watched her between bodies, peering into the steaming pots, poking about like a supervisory witch. Once, when she found one of the little ones in front of her, the one Ehrle had called Mooksi, she stopped and put her hand on his head. He turned his face up, they looked at each other, but neither knew what to search for, and she went on, and finally up the stairs again, and the trapdoor slammed.

König, left to himself once more, dried himself with his underwear, put on his suit and washed the underwear in the used water; he wrung it out with the anger he would have liked to use on a couple of necks, and hung it on a wooden rack by the fire along with diapers and other clothes. The sight of this garment, with its long sleeves and legs, gave rise to the first spontaneous burst of laughter he had heard on Vervlen, but it did not temper his mood. A few of the older boys, and perhaps girls, for all he knew, whispered and giggled a bit on the possibilities of physical strength and sexual prowess in a person big enough to wear such clothing; much as the Lilliputians had done with Gulliver. König was wondering how much strength was necessary to knock aside all those hard young bodies. But Gulliver had been a prisoner too.

He went into the room where the babies lay, stood with arms folded and watched them, because he knew he could not be angry with them.

He did not speak at supper, though his face was calm. The whole area seemed subdued: no one was willing to break his silence.

At the end of the meal, Ehrle whispered with some of the others, and said, "Please, König, don't be angry with us. We need help."

König said, "You cannot get help from a prisoner."

She was no longer imperious. "We are prisoners – of – of ourselves and them. Give us a little time, tell us what can be done. Then we will let you go. You have a ship and a radio, and can bring help."

"We don't know he has a ship and a radio," said

young König. "Might be he was dropped here."

König said, "I have a ship and a radio, and you have a strategy." He stood and began to gather empty dishes. "You are playing hard against soft, and that is a very old game. It is no longer clever. It is against Galactic Federation's rules for me to tell you where my ship is, because there is no one to guard it, and if you try to force me to tell my conditioning will break my mind and you will be left with a real drooling idiot. I will tell you where it is not: it is not in the hangar with Halvorsen's bones and the remains of her ship. Nothing else is."

"Hangar! Bones!" Surprise and horror swept the vault.

"You didn't know! I see, I'm glad to see that." And he was, for no lie could be so well orchestrated. "And yet you have pieces of her equipment in your stores."

Ehrle's arms went out involuntarily. "You –" it began as a yell and she brought her voice down, "you think we, us down here, killed her!"

The movement had pulled the collar of her shirt apart and he saw the silver glint on her neck. The last thing. He sat down. "None of you killed her. She stayed quite a while – perhaps more than a thirtyday – and then what became of her?"

"One morning she was gone."

"As you had been told ... and the ones here, did they think she had gone in her ship?"

It was someone else who muttered, "Until the broken pieces were found on a midden heap."

"The Youngers would have used the radio to call for help, but the Elders smashed it," König said. "Vervlin never did care for radio ... and I suppose the young ones thought she had run away, and eventually died somewhere on this world." Slow nods. He was giving an out, which both parties needed very badly. "But she was stabbed with a pitchfork. No one knows who killed her, and I don't want to know."

"Someone on Vervlen killed her," a hardy soul ventured, reaping black looks.

"Fifty years ago," König said. "Galactic Federation can punish no one here for that."

"But they will not want to help us," Ehrle said gloomily.

"They will want to help. I can swear that." But, the one last thing. "You are also wearing something on your neck, Ehrle." Halvorsen's recorder. He could not do what he had never done before: find a way to be alone with her and take it by seduction or force. There was no time, no room, and he had no talent for it.

She said nothing, but pulled up the chain slowly, unwillingly, until she had the silver locket in her hand. Then, "This was in the trash, also ... it did not seem to belong there. We thought it was a thing a leader might wear, and the leader in this group has worn it for many years." She looked up. "Swear again that you will help. You lied to the Elders."

"About the men to the east? How many ears you do have! There are many men to the east, Ehrle, all over the universe. But I do swear. That is the recorder from Halvorsen's ship. Would you like to hear what she has to say?"

"Starwoman's voice...." Whispers spread.

"Will she tell who killed her?" young König asked.

"I doubt she would have been recording then. If you let me have that I will show you how it works and give it back to you."

Slowly she drew the heavy chain over her head. "I often thought this was some kind of instrument but I push this button often and nothing happens." She gave it to König; her eyes held a trace of fear.

Young König, leader-in-line, said, "We should call all of the others and let them hear Starwoman too."

"When I hear, everyone will know," said Ehrle, rap-on-the-knuckles. "Go ahead, Star-König."

König took the fine chain from his own neck.

"You said that was a Galactic Federation emblem. Was that a lie?"

"No. It is what I said, but also a key, something that opens things. Each one of these is made a little differently, to fit one recorder." He did not know where the fit was on this one, the light was dim. He moved the side of his key around the edge of the locket until it was retarded by slight magnetic force, and pushed. The filigree slipped in with a click. He pushed the button. Silence. "Reversing." Click. He pushed again. Squeals and whines. "Those are coded records of distances and directions; this piece is connected to the controls when the pilot is aboard." Click.

"Signe Halvorsen recording ..." The voice was dry and matter-of-fact, but breaths drew in. König held his own.

And Starwoman told what they already knew: that Vervlin were degenerating in the pattern already suspected, and accelerating; that the Elders were unintelligent and almost helpless, and the children astonishingly bright, efficient and well-organized, as well as self-sacrificing – the voice wavered and lowered a bit "... and very brave ..." a pause. "Halvorsen recording a new day,..." voice crisp and cool, describing organization and communal practices ... slightly longer pause, and König said, "I think it needs rewinding," pulled the key half out and pushed it in again. Nothing else then, except a faint buzz and crackle. "No ... it's very old, and probably broken." Not really; he had wiped it. Halvorsen was dead and he was alive and he truly did not want to know more about her death.

"Very brave," Ehrle whispered. Leave it at that. "I wonder why she was killed?" Question asked for the first time.

König thought he knew. That cool fact-gatherer would not swear to bring help. König had sworn to try, because he was a Vervlin. And they were brave. He pulled the key out and gave it to Ehrle with the locket. "You can listen to the beginning again."

When the table was cleared he took his dried underwear and went behind the chimney to put it on. He had suppressed evidence and did not care. He doubted the missing parts were of much value and he had already allowed the most explosive information to surface and dissipate. Halvorsen could not describe her own death; he believed he could reconstruct it.

Would the Youngers have used the pitchfork? They had more subtle ways. Perhaps they had manipulated the Elders who must have seen Starwoman as an only too obvious foreign body, with her ship, instruments, authority – all things Vervlin in their right minds avoided and twisted ones hated: they had smashed them.

Children locked in cellars. Halvorsen had more sense than to decry them openly, but her attitudes would speak: *very brave....* But to the young, the leaders among them, her very unwillingness to rebuke their elders and make promises to themselves would speak even more loudly. If he judged it right she had unwittingly fed fears and prejudices until she became to each party the ally of the other: a mutual enemy. And she had not come back, and the youngest had been allowed to build a legend.

A conjecture. Director, you decide.

He came round the chimney to find a group of younger

adolescents choosing straws for baby-sitting and guard duties. The bells began to ring, old church bells struck with broom handles. The hammering of their clappers in confined spaces would have loosened teeth.

"Put your robe on, Star-König. It's cold, the night," young König said.

He did not want to watch the Elders degrading themselves, and he did not think he would be given the opportunity to escape. The young knew the night terrain better than he did without his direction-finder, and he wanted to leave freely with their good will, and keep his promises. He doubted GalFed would expend another search team for dead König. He tied the drawstring of his hood beneath his chin and accepted the loan of a pair of mittens. Except for the very young, all Vervlin had big hands like his; most, like him, were left-handed.

He thought Willi was a certain candidate for guard duty, but he was among the dark bundled figures shifting aside a cupboard at the back wall. There was a niche to get through on hands and knees for a few metres until the ground lowered and allowed standing; the natural cleft had not been dug, though a few heavy uprights and cross-beams warded off collapse. The passage curved down for twenty metres into a shallow puddle, and rose sharply until a cold wind flowed in from the starry opening and the lantern was blown out. The children were quiet, almost solemn, like a tribe preparing for religious rites themselves.

They squatted in the brambles of a hillside looming over a trampled area back of the sheds where the tanning and smoking were done. Beyond them the houses crouched like tame beasts; above, the two bright planets moving among the stars had made the long wars of fifty years ago.

König was relieved to find that the ceremony was no

orgy. In the centre of the trampled area a larger carved ape crouched on the edge of a much wider basin in which something was burning, and around it a circle of fifteen elders was moving slowly in a simple dance, shuffle-hop, shuffle-hop, each dipping a stick with its end wrapped in rags into the basin until all held lit torches. The wind carried an aromatic breath of the burning stuff, perhaps a psychotropic; after some minutes the dance quickened, though not greatly: the bodies were thick and graceless, the legs crook-shanked. The faces only fire-lit blobs.

The children did not giggle or whisper but remained silent, crouching, arms on knees, chins on arms. The jigging torches dropped sparks that shook themselves off clothing almost miraculously without scorching their bearers.

In the distance among branches König could see three more circles of dancing light from far houses. He was squatting among thorns, shouldered by bodies. The area was bordered by sheds, houses, hill-slope and crest, only a thin wedge of forest visible to his left. He thought for a moment that he heard the chirr of one of the blue apes, and the hairs prickled on his neck, but there were no trees for them here.

The dancers started to sing tunelessly, "Ay-yeh!" shuffle-hop, "Ay-yeh!" shuffle-hop. König was wondering how long it lasted, how long he would be forced to last it out, when a figure behind his shoulder sprang up with a yell of "Ay-yeh!", ran down the hill in leaps and grabbed a torch from its bearer, joining the chanting circle.

The children called in low urgent voices, "Willi! Willi!"

Ehrle said hoarsely, "Shut up! Just let him go!"

König realized why Willi had been allowed to come. Ehrle, after all, knew her limits.

The dancer deprived of his torch staggered round outside the circle for a moment and sat down scratching his head in great puzzlement. But Ehrle was already slipping down into the opening of the hill and summoning others after her in silent procession.

No one reproached her aloud; a few hard looks were directed at her. In the cellar each child seemed to want to get as far away from any other as possible.

Ehrle threw off her mittens, hooked legs over a bench, sat, propped elbows on the table and covered her face with her hands.

König dropped his borrowed mittens beside hers and loosened his drawstring to pull back the hood. "They all go that way?" he asked, very quietly, to let her ignore the question if she chose.

She pulled her hands away, down the length of her face; the displaced flesh suggested more age than she had or he had allowed her. Her eyes were a bit reddened. "Everyone chooses ... what seems the best way." Then her eyes lit with anger and she pounded both fists on the table. "König! Star-König! Tell us about the Ninety-nine again, the normal ones!"

There was a little stillness following her change of mood, a stopping of motion by König and everyone else.

He heard the chirr again.

A few more children had come into the room, and one, an older girl, he thought, was wearing what seemed to be a blue fur collar. He watched, he could not turn his eyes away, as the blue fur sat up on her shoulder and began to eat some morsel it held in its claws. He stood very still.

"What are you looking at?"

"What do you call that blue animal?"

"An ape. Why?"

"We also call them apes. Is it dangerous?"

"Only if a bite or scratch becomes dirty, and they don't bite or scratch often. We bring one in sometimes to feed."

They were immune. It seemed it had come with the genes. And they had playfellows.

"Why are you afraid, König?"

"In the beginning –" Dared he give them the weapon? The story would be a lie without it. "In the beginning a bite or scratch would kill."

The girl launched the ape: it leaped from shoulder to table to shoulder toward him. He did not move. "Dead Königs don't help much, not?"

Ehrle snapped, "Helig, take that thing away!"

Someone grabbed it, it chattered wildly, and the girl retrieved it sullenly, muttering disgust to match; it disappeared into the cleft.

König folded his arms. "I don't like that. It is not a joke."

"There is not much joking here."

"That I agree with.... The story is not long or complicated, and it has little to teach. The first settlers were used to cold weather, but not all year round, as here, and they were given a body inheritance of even colder-weather peoples, so they could hunt and fish and work in the woods if crops were bad. They trained with those Solthree peoples to learn the work before they came. They found the land quite good here, and the farm animals grew well, but they took care of the forests as they had been taught in case of hard times. Some grew to enjoy that very much: they cut wood, replanted trees, gathered what they could eat, fished and hunted. They left their land shares to the ones who preferred farming and went on living in the woods. That was a mistake."

"Why, Starman? It seems well-thought."

"Because the Vervlin forgot what they had learned in their histories and holy books. Among many Solthree peoples, and others for all I know, free-living hunters and herdsmen don't get on well with farmers who stay in one place. Not if a hunter chases some great roaring beast out of the woods, breaking fences, trampling crops, galloping through the sheds sending the pigs running squealing their heads off and scaring the milk out of the cows – I'm glad to see you laugh, but where would you be for all your work without the farms?"

"I want to see the roaring beasts," said Mooksi, chin cupped in hands.

"Long gone," König said.

"Were the Ninety and Nine farmers, then?" young König asked. "I thought they were not, but you seem to feel sorry for them."

"They were hunters and woodsmen. But Vervlin have always been respected for their honesty, and these ninety and some wrote down what had happened in their journals as honestly as they could. They had no wish to hurt the farmers. There were no apes here then. Galactic Federation knew about them, but they lived far across the continent and bothered nobody. Then something happened to their forests – disease killed the trees, or earthquakes disrupted them, or they caught fire – or all of these things. The apes moved and settled here. They disturbed the woodsmen, scared the big animals, and whenever they scratched or bit, people and animals died. Their spit was poison – then. Careless children ... dead in a few hours. Men, women, animals. Not so very many; enough to frighten them out of the woods, back to the land. But the farmers were angry and told them – told them it was the wrath of God upon sinners ... and would not let them on the land, even to hire out for their keep –"

"Another mistake," said Ehrle quietly.

"And when the Colonial census people came the woodsmen asked to return, and made still another. They had become very angry. They didn't tell about the poison deaths. A few of them hoped the apes would attack the farmers. I know this because I've read what was written ... and they were ashamed of it later...."

"If they had told? What difference would that have made to us?"

"Very little. GalFed would have moved the colony or destroyed the apes, the woodsmen would have stayed and kept fighting the farmers."

"Why did they want to come back later?"

"I think they enjoyed the free way they had lived here before the trouble. They got over their anger, and thought they might fight the apes, or the farmers, to a standstill, or find other land here. But the colonial Vervlin thought they wanted the original land, and threatened to abandon the whole colony and go before the law and demand reparations –"

"And that was a mistake," said Helig bitterly. "They should have abandoned. Because you were saved and we not."

"There was really only one mistake," said König. "The first one made by Galactic Federation when they believed they could join parts of seed to make people who could live comfortably on this world." He was beginning to droop from lack of a good night's sleep.

"And how can they repay *us*? Your fathers were normal when they left here."

"No. The ones who mated with normal people right away had mostly normal children, but some were not, and those were discouraged from having children." Forbidden. "And a few had abnormal grandchildren. They would have liked to stay together as a group, but could not last without bringing in new blood. The ones who tried to intermarry, about a third of them, had to give up. They were given land and money and whatever else they needed." Like sterilization. "Very few were lucky." When his raw energy was spent he wearied quickly and completely, and he was very tired now.

"But some were, like you," Ehrle insisted. "What can be done for us?"

He took a deep breath. Halvorsen would not have touched this one with a pitchfork. "You would have to stop mating among yourselves and take the seed of normal people, or give it to normal ones. That would not help you at all. It might help a few of your children. Changes in diet with some hormones – the chemicals the body makes to control growth and function – might help you a little, might help your children more." But not untie that unholy knot in the chromosome. "Your children's children's children might be pulled up little by little." The silence tightened like parchment and he let his arms drop. "You are young. It's hard for you to look ahead to the hope that you might have a few normal great-grandchildren ... when I can only ask Galactic Federation for help." He was nearly asleep on his feet.

"How long do *your* Vervlin live, König?"

"To our fifties. It is a short life for Solthrees."

"We die before forty," said Ehrle.

"You are the adults here."

"Yes. We have four or five years of that."

"What shall I tell you?" There was nothing. He was desperate. "GalFed will come here with medicines that will make you three times taller and handsomer than I and you will live to be three times my age!"

"Perhaps it would have been better if you had, Starman," Helig said.

"A child's story? Broken promises and battered hopes

make people sick and cruel and ugly." And how far they had been driven along the road, the brave children. "Youngers, am I on trial, or may I sleep? I got very little sleep last night."

The lamps were guttering, and upstairs the floors were creaking as the Elders stumbled into their beds. König smelled once again a cold drift of aromatic herb washing in through the screened conduits. Thunder whispered far away, rain pattered softly. The youngest children were being put to bed, the oven fires banked down with ashes.

But Ehrle and the other eldest ones surrounded him, heads tilted, eyes far away. Duty had burdened them; as soon as they could walk or grasp they had been made to heed. If they were by some miracle created whole down generations, how many more generations would they need to recognize an instant of happiness? Even he had had to learn his meagre share through outsiders. He said in a low voice, "If I don't go back no one will come here again. No one will help."

The children turned away and began to blow out lamps; a few murmured together. One pulled down the shelf that had been Willi's bed and piled blankets on it, motioning to König.

König lay down on his side, facing inward, and through half-closed eyes watched the shadowed figures moving. It was cooler by the wall, he warmed his hands between his knees and let sleep gather in him. Sentence in suspense. He wondered how long Halvorsen had really endured this place, and how to break the flesh-and-blood prison wall....

"König!" Intense whisper. Ehrle. Hand on his shoulder.

"Let me sleep," he begged.

"König, you!" The hand became a fist that shook and

pounded. He cared little for touching, and surely not like that.

"Oh God, what now?"

"Quietly."

"Mustn't wake them upthere," he muttered and tried to turn away. The grip held.

"Down here you must wake now!"

He pulled himself up on one elbow, his head was sagging. "What then?"

"König, I am eighteen years old, and I have had my bleedings for over a year. Helig is half a year younger than I, and there are two other girls in this house who bleed. You can give us your seed and we can begin the new cycle of children, even if we never know what becomes of them. It's no use to keep you here longer, but you can do that much for us before you go."

König felt his soul shrivelling and the flesh withering on his bones. "Good God, Ehrle! I'm not some kind of – some kind of animal you can use to improve the stock! That's a dangerous idea."

"We don't care about that! No one who comes here will know of it."

He sat up. "I cannot ... I cannot service a bunch of you like –"

"We will wait as long as need be," said Ehrle, every word a bell tolling.

"I'm so tired ... I can't think straight. Please let me sleep and we'll discuss it tomorrow."

"We will discuss it when you have agreed, König. A grown man like you must still have –"

"It's impossible. I can't –"

The hand had never left his shoulder. "Why are you shivering?"

"I told you," said young König. He was dipping a stick into the fire to light a lantern. "A man grown for nearly twenty years and he has no children, when his people are dying out." He came holding the lantern before him, face lit yellow from below. "He knows how to care for children and seems to care about them but he has none. He is telling the truth at least this time. He cannot."

"Maybe he is one who goes with men," Ehrle said.

"He would still have the seed," said Helig.

"This one has none," said young König.

"Goddamn it, if I did such a thing I'd lose my –"

"I think you have already lost," the boy said.

"You cannot have children. Not at all," Ehrle said, and took her hand away at last.

He yelled, "I told you there were those who were not allowed –"

No one woke. He wondered if they had been drugged, if there had been a plan. The faces of Ehrle, König, Helig, others surrounded him. Hard composed faces.

Ehrle said flatly, "Those who were not allowed, you said, were defective ones or had made defective ones. Do you have brothers or sisters, König?"

"No."

"But you are a normal grown man of thirty-five."

His face was beaded with sweat, he wanted sleep as if it had been a drug in his own system. "I made promises, I will keep promises. But I will not make children."

"Why can you not make children?"

No promises were enough for them, for that accumulation of anger and frustration. These would kill, if others had not. The smooth fresh faces. He had no ghost to give up. He had never been quite alive. Hands gripped his shoulders, each finger pitting through the cloth layers.

"Goddamn you, I'd run through the lot of you and the cows too if it would do any good – and don't think I'm joking, you don't have to put on the laugh this time! I am not normal, damn you! I am not a man. I am a clone, a being in the shape of a man, made from a store of cells kept alive for two hundred years. That was the kind of reparation we got! Without internal sexual organs, that means no seed at all, only hormones to make us look like men and women, perform like them, only it doesn't work quite that well and oh God this is the first bloody time I'm glad I never took a clone woman and raised a clone child and my family weren't part of those –"

"There were none! There were none! And you made promises to us!"

"There were a few of them! There were! I told you the truth!"

Helig sneered. "And the truth is, if men come here from your damned filthy Galactic Federation they will not let us have children at all! And we will *all* live as id- iots in filth until we die with Vervlen! And then they will sell it all over again!"

The hands pulled, tore, dragged him from bed. He beat about him with his fists. "I told you –" He did not know if more had gathered or it seemed so; the hard bodies walled him, drove him the length of the vault, into another opening, this uphill, tripping on hard granitic edges; his head knocked against the ceiling, he was dizzy.

And out into the forest trampling moist dead leaves. The rain had stopped, but wind still rustled the trees and the blue apes woke and chittered.

They pushed his back to the trunk of a great conifer, plucked the cord from his hood, dragged his hands around the tree and tied them, ripped down his clothes to bare shoulders and chest, the cold struck him. One of them, he could not see which in the dark or in his terror, shinnied up the tree to grab boughs and shake them, mimicking obscenely the noise of the apes, jumping down and pulling back. All of them in a circle about König and the trunk; and the apes dropped squalling, scratching, biting at his head and shoulders, tangling their claws in his hair, in as great a panic as he; left him clawed and bitten, scampered to find other trees.

There was no mercy to beg for. He had stormed, cajoled, commanded in his life, never begged. Never died. The lantern disappeared and the children were absorbed in darkness. His mind twisted like a worm in contemplation of dying, he sagged against the trunk. He was not a man for contemplation and had never studied the holy books of Vervlen. Had not the farmers driven woodsmen back into the forest to die?

He let himself slip downward until he was sitting, in order to shrug his body into his clothing against the cold. He was still bare about the head and chest and the wind plastered dead leaves on his sweating skin. His nose was running, his breath rattled. He waited for cramps and retching and hoped they would bring death with them quickly. His stomach knotted sooner than he had expected and he twisted grotesquely in order to vomit on the planet rather than himself. So much for revenge. Murdered for a pair of boots. That was simpler. And he had turned his eyes away from Halvorsen and the pitchfork. That had been quicker. Cramping and vomiting drew up his legs and wrenched his arms again and again until his mouth ran with bile. The wind stung the sores on his bared skin, the trees whispered in darkness. He thought he heard laughter, but it was only the barking of blue apes and the hooting of strange birds he had not had time to notice. He had never feared the entity Death but was often afraid of dying. Now it was only a matter of waiting out the pain. He was terribly angry, but not afraid at all. The anger dulled at last and the world turned black.

"Oh ay, Master König, what y' doin' here?"

He knew the voice: Willi.

"Willi," he whispered. His eyelids were cemented shut. He forced them open, blinking away crust and film. His mouth was dry. Alive again? Maybe.

"What y' doin' here?" Willi repeated. He was bending over König, head against black trees and grey sky, one hand holding a string of fish.

König did not say, What the hell you think? but only repeated, "Willi," as if he were as stupid.

But he was unjust. Willi dropped the fish and knelt beside him. The sun was about to rise, the forest blew and flittered and spoke the sounds of its creatures. The boy reached into his tackle bag and pulled out a knife to cut the cord. He dragged the limp hands about until they rested, two hairy purple things, on König's knees, and rubbed them between his own warm ones; then paused a minute in thought as visible as if his skull were transparent, pulled his mittens from his pocket and forced them over König's hands.

"Thank you, Willi." He was alive. He was immune. He was a true citizen of Vervlen, the blind gut of humanity.

Willi flushed with pleasure at thanks from a man half dead and wholly stupefied. "Y'r hurt. Come with me to home and get help."

König shuddered. "No thanks. Just help me up, please."

His legs shook. He clung to the trunk and giggled helplessly because if he had been a fearful man he would have killed himself with the poison of his expectations.

He pulled the clothes about his neck and the hood over his head. His shoulders ached, his hands were turning hot and stinging. "Where was the stream you were fishing in?"

"There," Willi pointed. "It's the only one about."

"Good. Here's your mittens."

"Oh no! Y' keep those." Willi picked up his fish, odd shapes with fins like wings. He drew close to König and said in a loud whisper, "But watch out. They're a bad lot, them, sometime. I know. I was a leader."

"Yes ... good-bye, Willi."

He staggered from tree to tree, working life into his fingers, easing it into his shoulders. He did not touch the crusted cuts on his flesh. On the way there was a little valley, like the dip of the forest floor where he had landed, but not the one. The sun was up.

He sat on an outcropping in the valley's shadow to rest, and though he still felt like giggling he began to weep. He had often cursed himself for whining at his own fate. It was at least permitted to weep for them, the Elders turned useless and the Youngers already warped in every part of their lives, in intelligence, determination, bravery. And cursed both them and those who had created him. The apes threw pods at him and the wind sang an old song his people had found somewhere:

> *Yellow leaves are flying, falling*
> *where the King sits, lonely one*
> *flocking birds are crying, calling:*
> *withered, wasted, dying, done ...*

He pulled himself up the hill and across the wooded land to the cliff-side, slithered down vines and saw the pool Willi had fished in where the half-winged creatures leaped and flopped gracelessly splashing; followed the stream upward until he reached the hangar wall. He did not go near the hangar. He regretted not having taken the pitchfork from Halvorsen so that he might arrange her bones with dignity; likely they would merely have scattered.

He found the flat stone and examined it: one among many, it did not seem to have been moved. He worked his fingers inside the mittens. The stinging and the heat were going with the stiffness. He heard footsteps in the leaves above, looked up and saw Helig, ape on her shoulder. He clenched and stretched his fingers, and stood still. So did she, a few metres away from the cliff's edge. The ape leaped from her shoulder to the fir above, ran cackling to its topmost branch.

König did not take his eyes off her. Squatted and dropped the mittens. She took a step forward. He flung the stone back, grunting. From the corner of his eye he caught a glance of another figure on the cliff, upstream. Young König. No sign of Ehrle. He whipped his head about and back: no one across the stream.

Eyes on Helig he groped for the bag, found it, ripped it open, plunged his left hand in, the stunner seemed to leap into it. Helig took another step forward. Young König took two steps toward her.

The stunner was a little thing, standard issue for colony-shifters. König had practised much and seldom needed it.

Helig stepped nearer. "Can you kill us all, König, before we find your ship?"

König aimed dead on and thumbed the stud.

The tiny nerve-poison capsule burst in the corner of the blue ape's eye. The animal squawked horribly, seemed to try to keep balance for a moment, fell sliding down the eaves of the conifer and landed with a thud at the girl's feet.

She gave a little shocked cry, grabbed up the bruised

and paralysed creature and ran sobbing. König was more shocked than she. "Dear Lord, you can cry for *that!*"

He shifted aim to young König, gloving his gun hand with the other: a gesture; his stance was as hard as a rock. "Which eye do you want it in?"

Let him believe it kills. Let him believe.

Young König stood a moment, empty hands at his sides, and backed away. He would not run.

"– alone!" a voice rode on the wind. "Leave us alone, König!" Deeper in the forest he saw Ehrle, hands resting on the tines of a forked tree. Her cheeks were reddened with wind, a wisp of hair blew across her forehead. She had not come forward, not to lead here.

"Alone," the wind cried.

"You will be left alone." Against his will he saw her in a year, a little more, waiting in line awkwardly with head down, splayed thumbs hooked over the tops of the dishes.

His mouth tasted of bile, of failure. The shadows moved and she was gone.

He put the stunner on the rock, pulled the recorder from the bag and looped the chain over his head, slid the chronometer with the remotes over his wrist, pressed a coloured button for the thin beep of the direction-finder; shoved stunner and bag into his pocket, scrambled up the vines, panting and clumsy. He followed the cliff-edge, gun in one hand and infrared scanner in the other. Its light-strip flickered with the movements of small animals.

When the hypnoformer was reversing he waited listening and scanning for the moment it took the field to dissipate. The shuttle broke like sun through cloud, white dappled with shade, gold numbers burning. He saw no more Vervlin, and when he had climbed in and locked down looked no more on the world. The ship lifted its feral beak to part the sky, pulling after it a whirlwind of yellow leaves that reached the tops of the trees before they drifted in slow circles downward to the forest floor.

1981

Other books by Phyllis Gotlieb (novels unless indicated):

Within the Zodiac (poetry, 1964)

Sunburst (1964)

Ordinary, Moving (poetry, 1969)

Why Should I Have All the Grief (1969)

Doctor Umlaut's Earthly Kingdom (poetry, 1974)

Work of A.M. Klein (essay, 1974)

O Master Caliban! (1976)

A Judgement of Dragons (1980)

Emperor, Swords, Pentacles (1982)

Son of the Morning and Other Stories (collection, 1983)

The Kingdom of the Cats (1985)

Tesseracts² (anthology co-edited with Douglas Barbour, 1987)

Heart of Red Iron (1989)